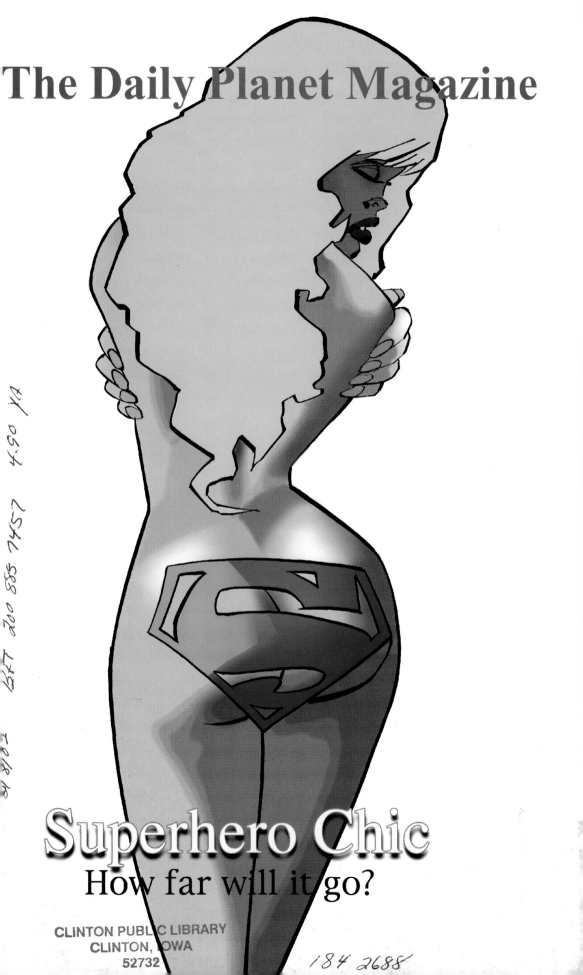

The Daily Planet Magazine

Superhero Chic
How far will it go?

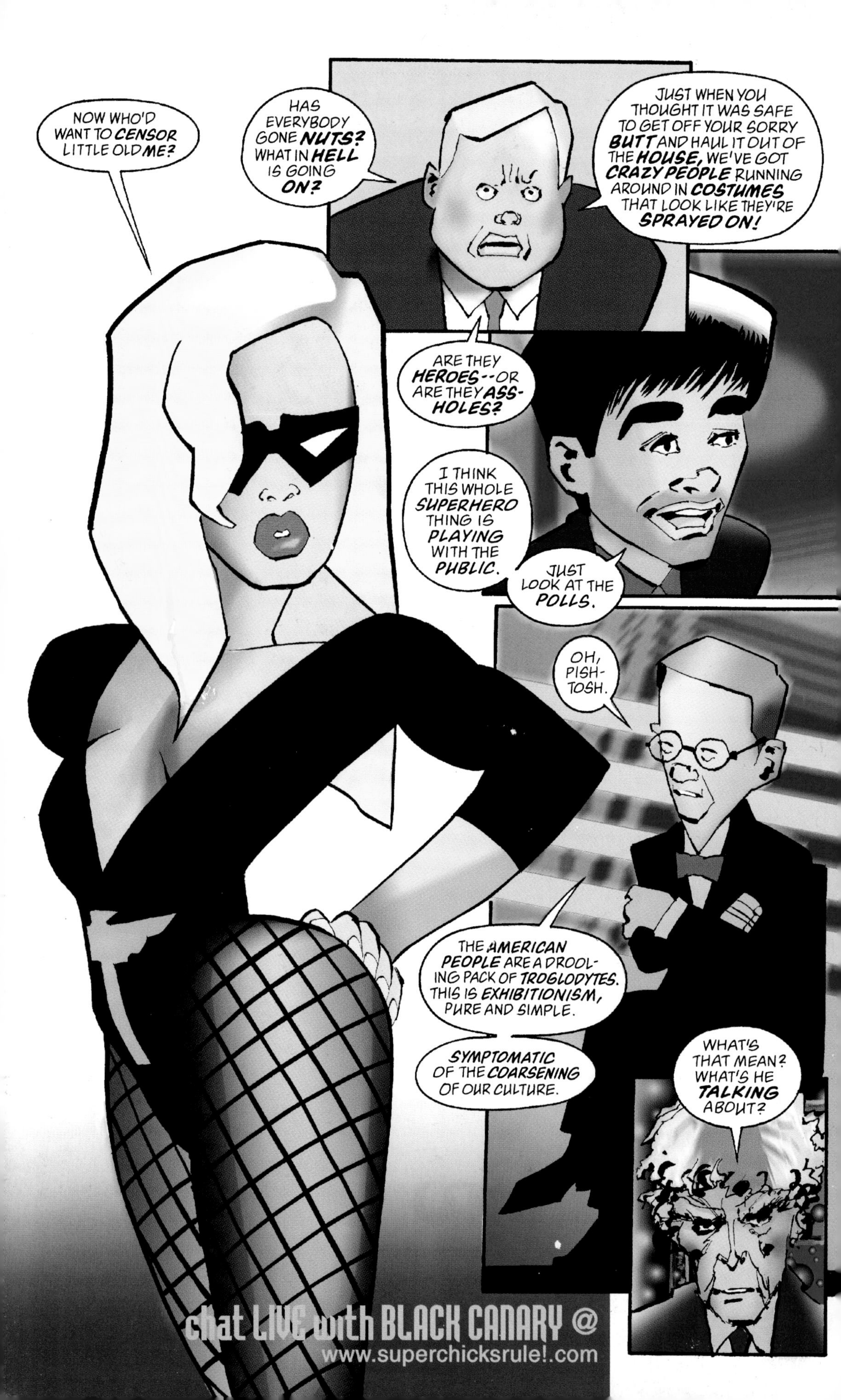
NOW WHO'D WANT TO CENSOR LITTLE OLD ME?
HAS EVERYBODY GONE NUTS? WHAT IN HELL IS GOING ON?
JUST WHEN YOU THOUGHT IT WAS SAFE TO GET OFF YOUR SORRY BUTT AND HAUL IT OUT OF THE HOUSE, WE'VE GOT CRAZY PEOPLE RUNNING AROUND IN COSTUMES THAT LOOK LIKE THEY'RE SPRAYED ON!
ARE THEY HEROES--OR ARE THEY ASS-HOLES?
I THINK THIS WHOLE SUPERHERO THING IS PLAYING WITH THE PUBLIC.
JUST LOOK AT THE POLLS.
OH, PISH-TOSH.
THE AMERICAN PEOPLE ARE A DROOL-ING PACK OF TROGLODYTES. THIS IS EXHIBITIONISM, PURE AND SIMPLE.
SYMPTOMATIC OF THE COARSENING OF OUR CULTURE.
WHAT'S THAT MEAN? WHAT'S HE TALKING ABOUT?
chat LIVE with BLACK CANARY @
www.superchicksrule!.com

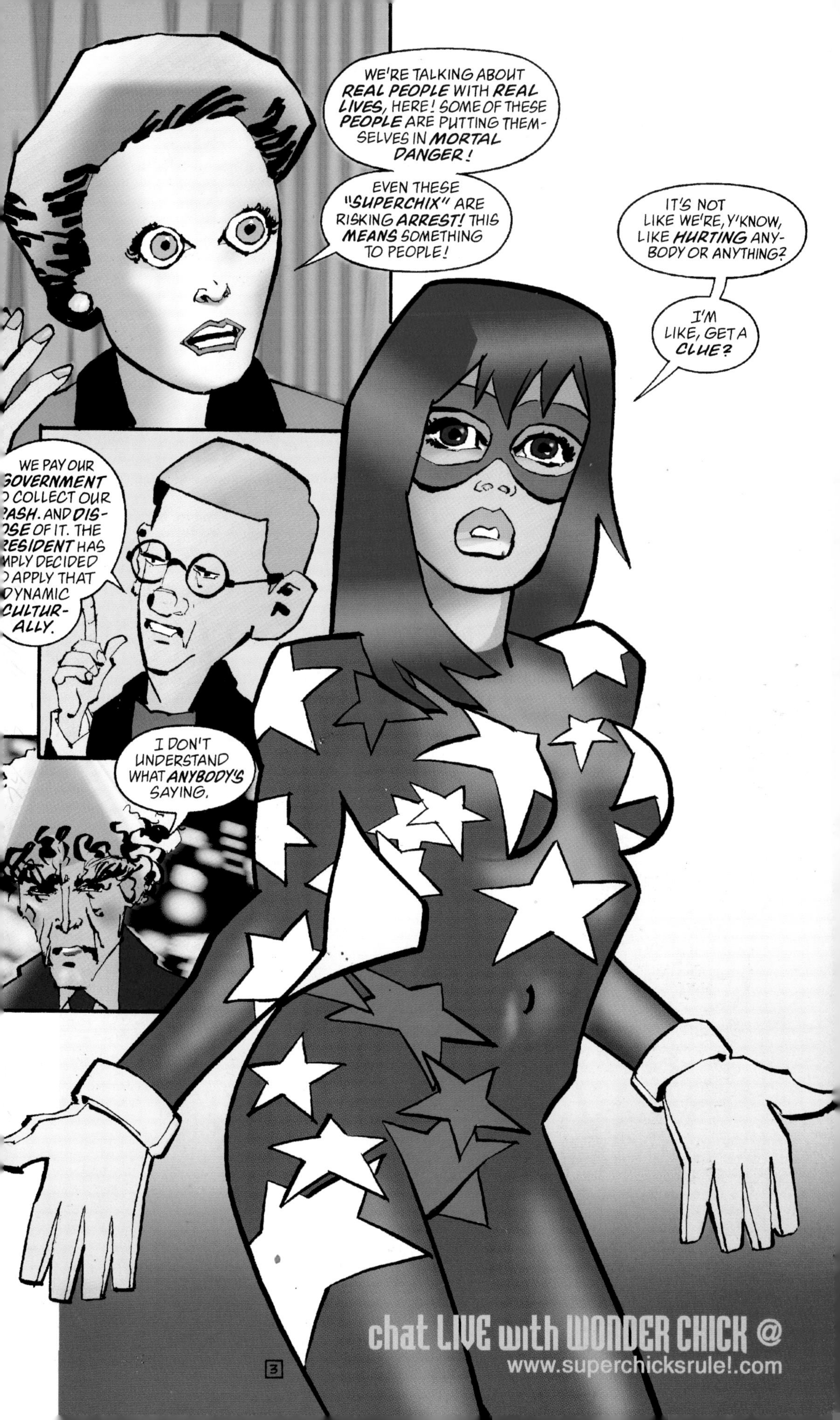
WE'RE TALKING ABOUT REAL PEOPLE WITH REAL LIVES, HERE! SOME OF THESE PEOPLE ARE PUTTING THEM-SELVES IN MORTAL DANGER!
EVEN THESE "SUPERCHIX" ARE RISKING ARREST! THIS MEANS SOMETHING TO PEOPLE!
IT'S NOT LIKE WE'RE, Y'KNOW, LIKE HURTING ANY-BODY OR ANYTHING?
I'M LIKE, GET A CLUE?
WE PAY OUR GOVERNMENT TO COLLECT OUR TRASH. AND DIS-POSE OF IT. THE PRESIDENT HAS SIMPLY DECIDED TO APPLY THAT DYNAMIC CULTUR-ALLY.
I DON'T UNDERSTAND WHAT ANYBODY'S SAYING.
3
chat LIVE with WONDER CHICK @
www.superchicksrule!.com

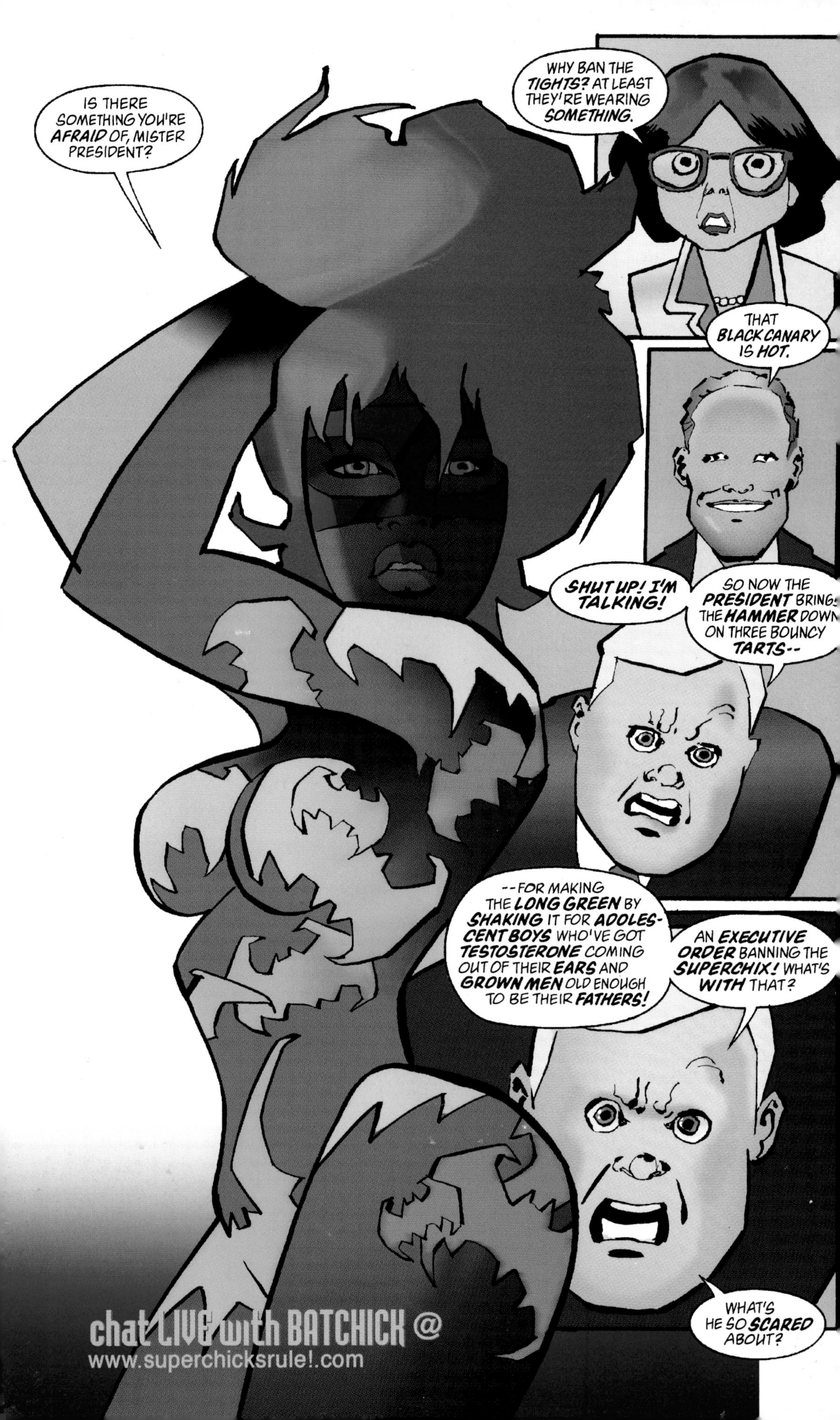
IS THERE SOMETHING YOU'RE AFRAID OF, MISTER PRESIDENT?
WHY BAN THE TIGHTS? AT LEAST THEY'RE WEARING SOMETHING.
THAT BLACK CANARY IS HOT.
SHUT UP! I'M TALKING!
SO NOW THE PRESIDENT BRINGS THE HAMMER DOWN ON THREE BOUNCY TARTS--
--FOR MAKING THE LONG GREEN BY SHAKING IT FOR ADOLESCENT BOYS WHO'VE GOT TESTOSTERONE COMING OUT OF THEIR EARS AND GROWN MEN OLD ENOUGH TO BE THEIR FATHERS!
AN EXECUTIVE ORDER BANNING THE SUPERCHIX! WHAT'S WITH THAT?
WHAT'S HE SO SCARED ABOUT?
chat LIVE with BATCHICK @
www.superchicksrule!.com

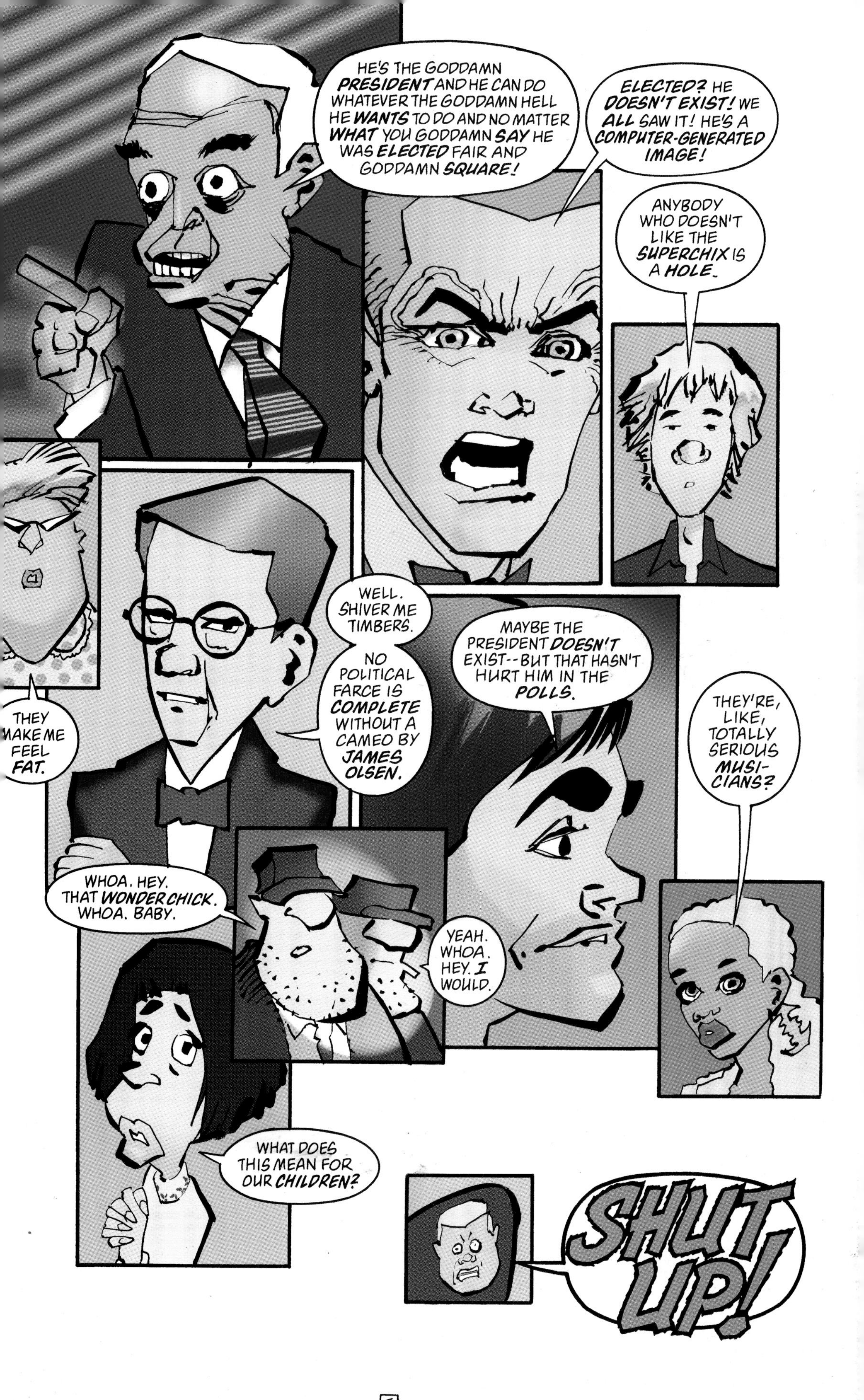
HE'S THE GODDAMN PRESIDENT AND HE CAN DO WHATEVER THE GODDAMN HELL HE WANTS TO DO AND NO MATTER WHAT YOU GODDAMN SAY HE WAS ELECTED FAIR AND GODDAMN SQUARE!
ELECTED? HE DOESN'T EXIST! WE ALL SAW IT! HE'S A COMPUTER-GENERATED IMAGE!
ANYBODY WHO DOESN'T LIKE THE SUPERCHIX IS A HOLE.
THEY MAKE ME FEEL FAT.
WELL. SHIVER ME TIMBERS.
NO POLITICAL FARCE IS COMPLETE WITHOUT A CAMEO BY JAMES OLSEN.
MAYBE THE PRESIDENT DOESN'T EXIST--BUT THAT HASN'T HURT HIM IN THE POLLS.
THEY'RE, LIKE, TOTALLY SERIOUS MUSI-CIANS?
WHOA. HEY. THAT WONDER CHICK. WHOA. BABY.
YEAH. WHOA. HEY. I WOULD.
WHAT DOES THIS MEAN FOR OUR CHILDREN?
SHUT UP!

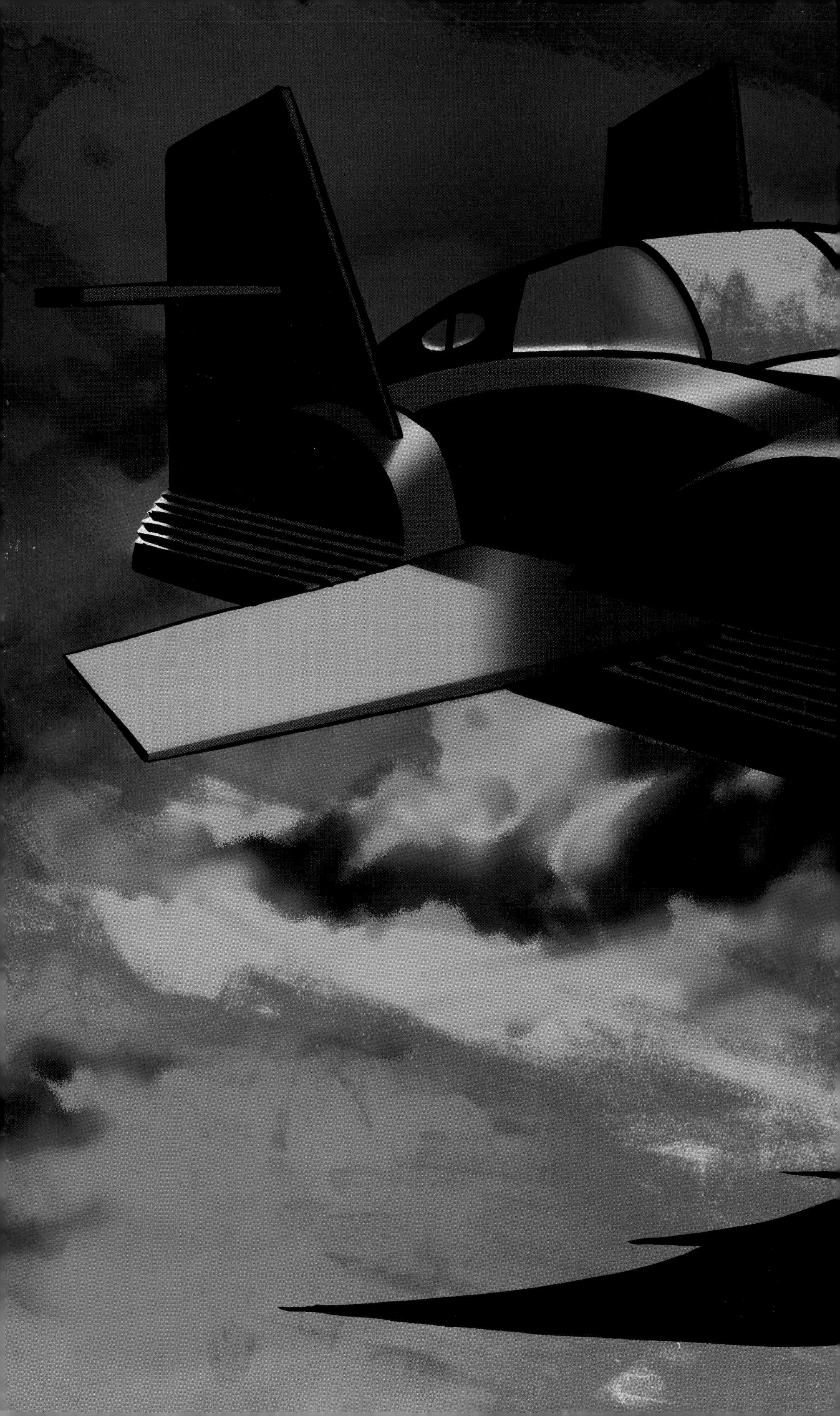

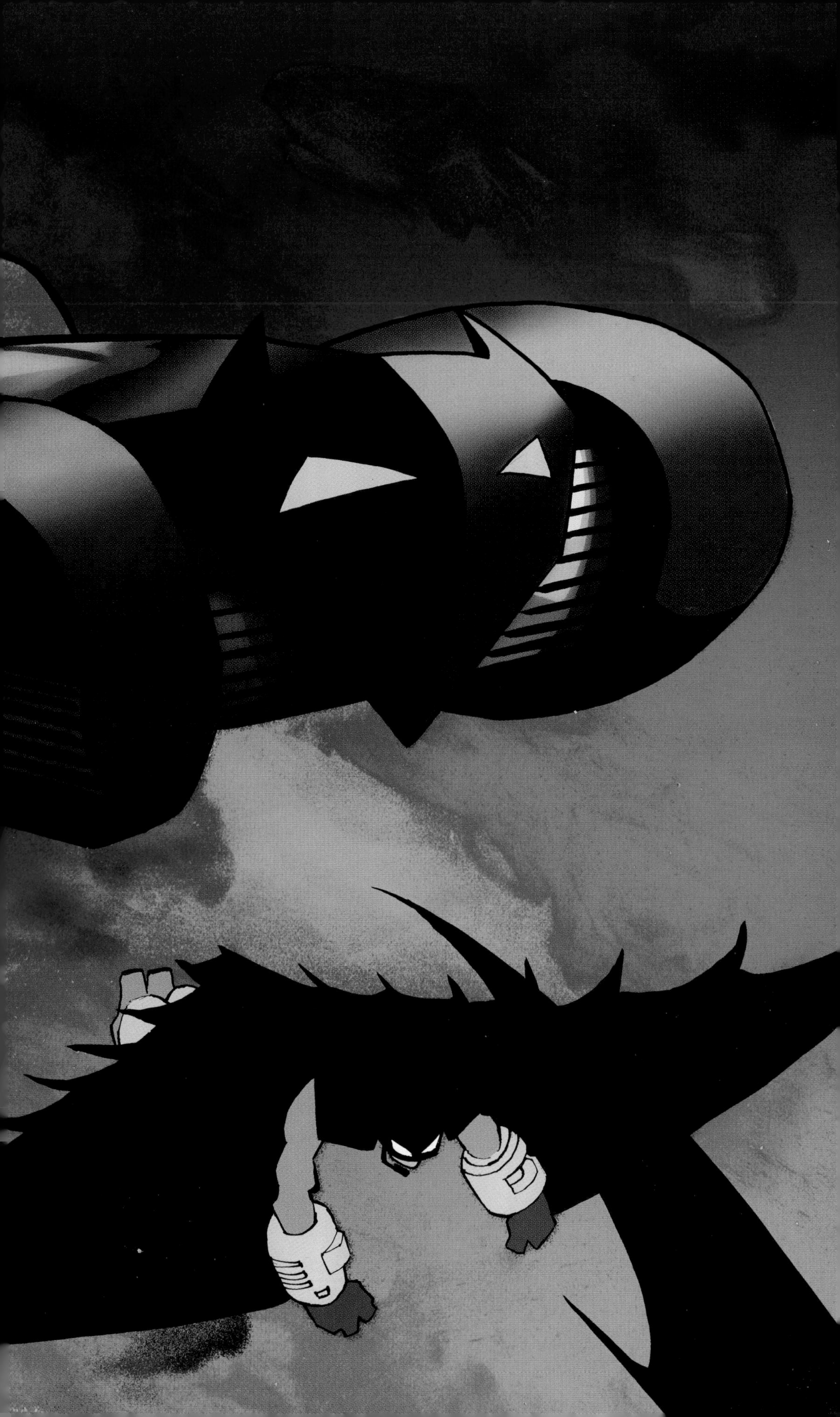

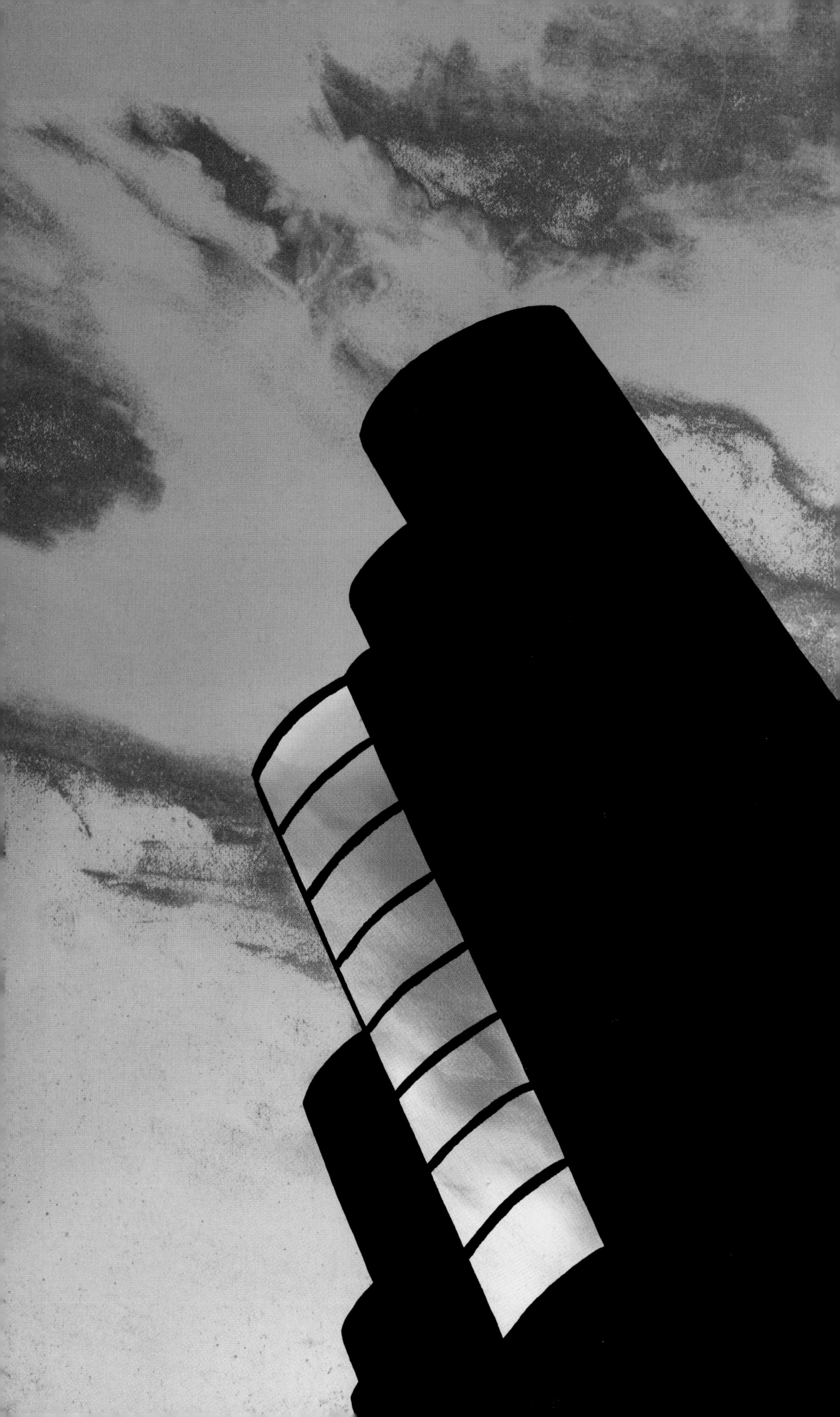

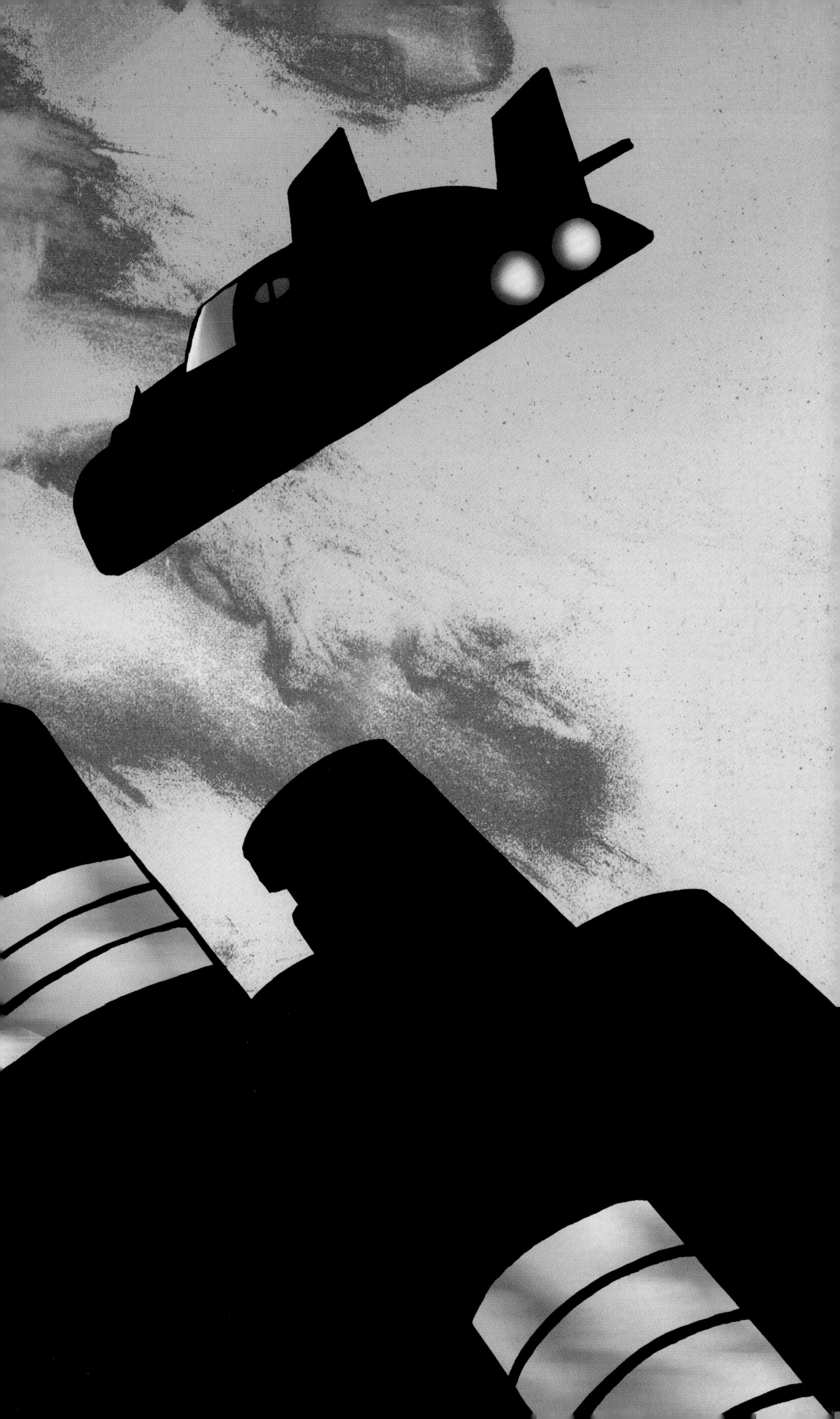

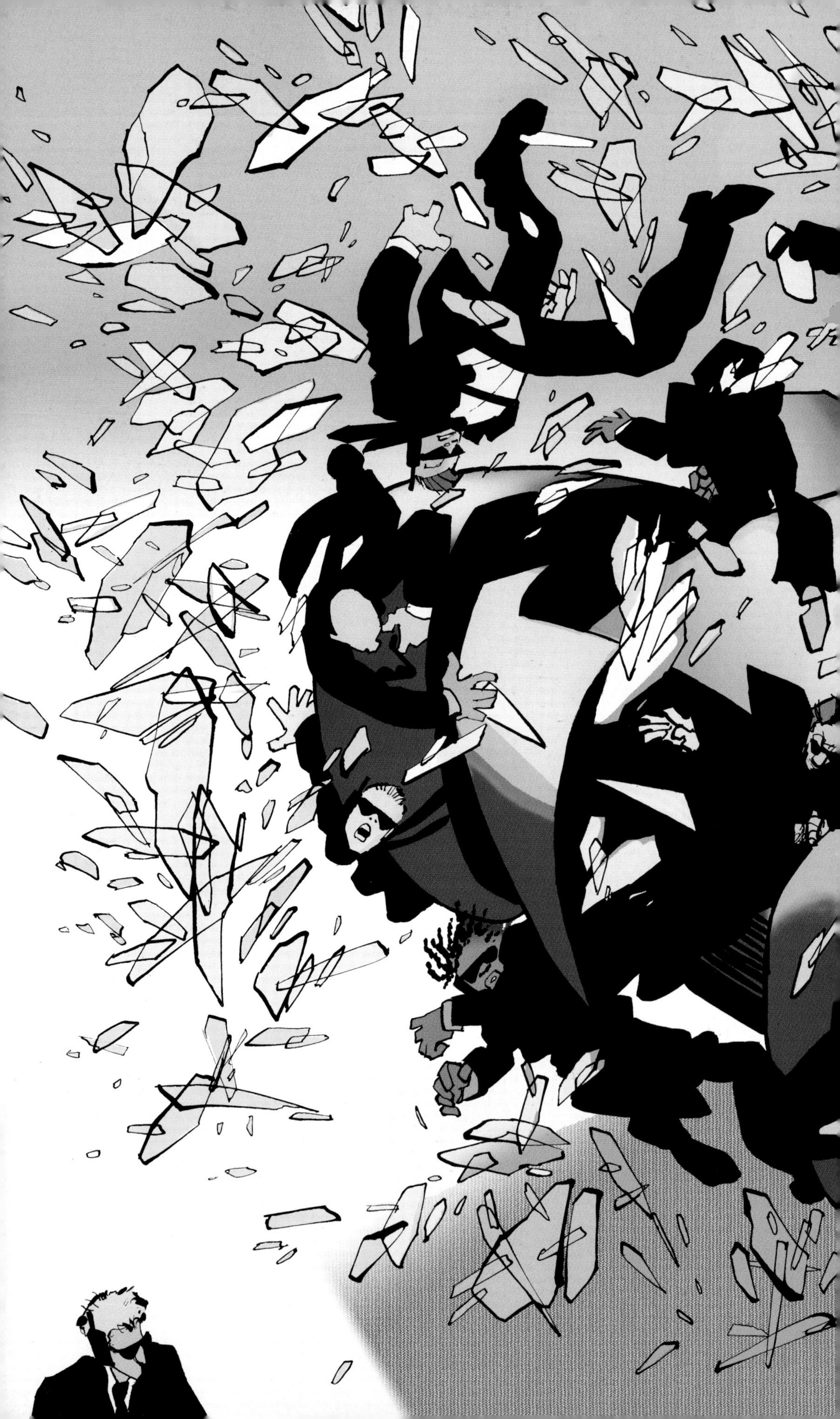

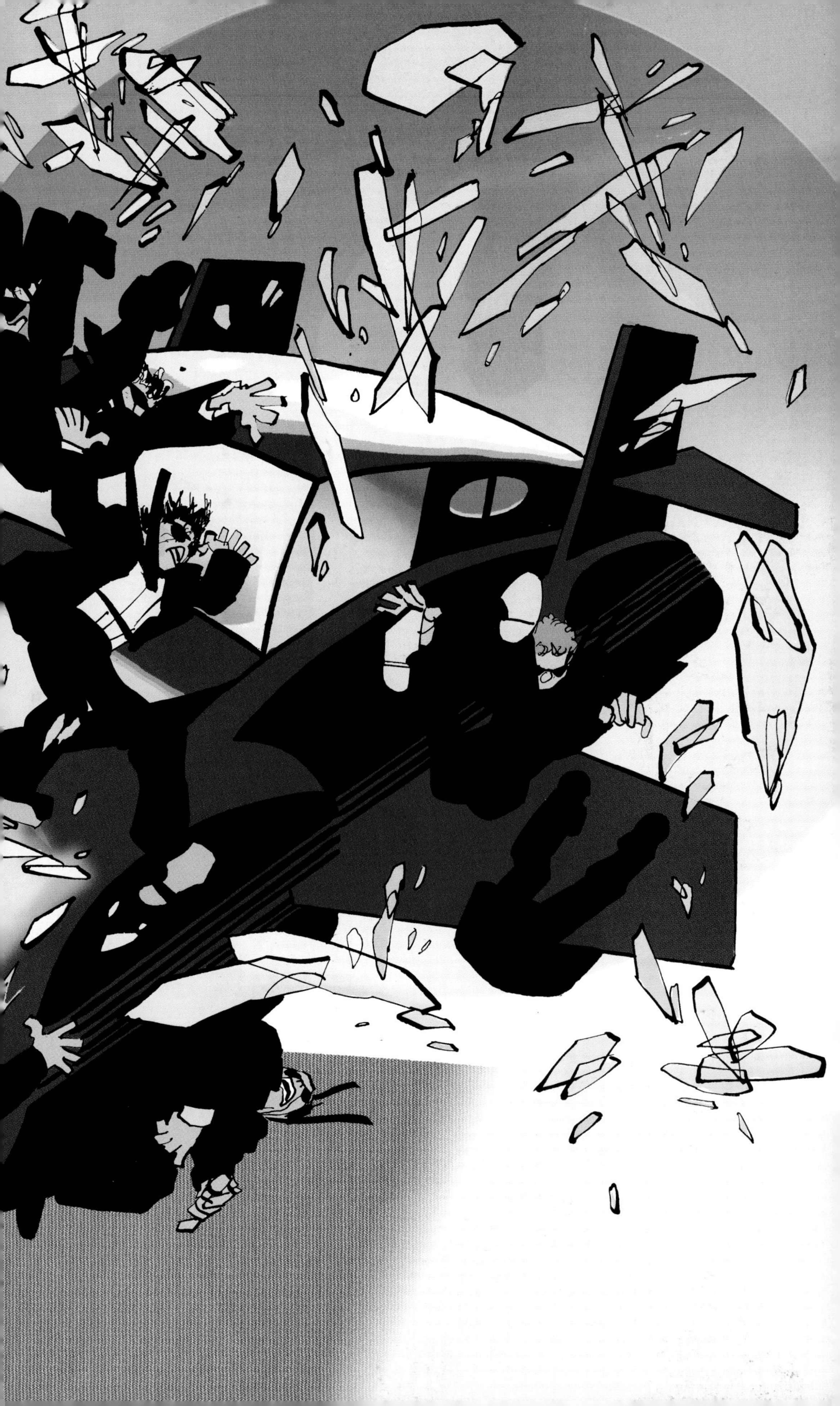

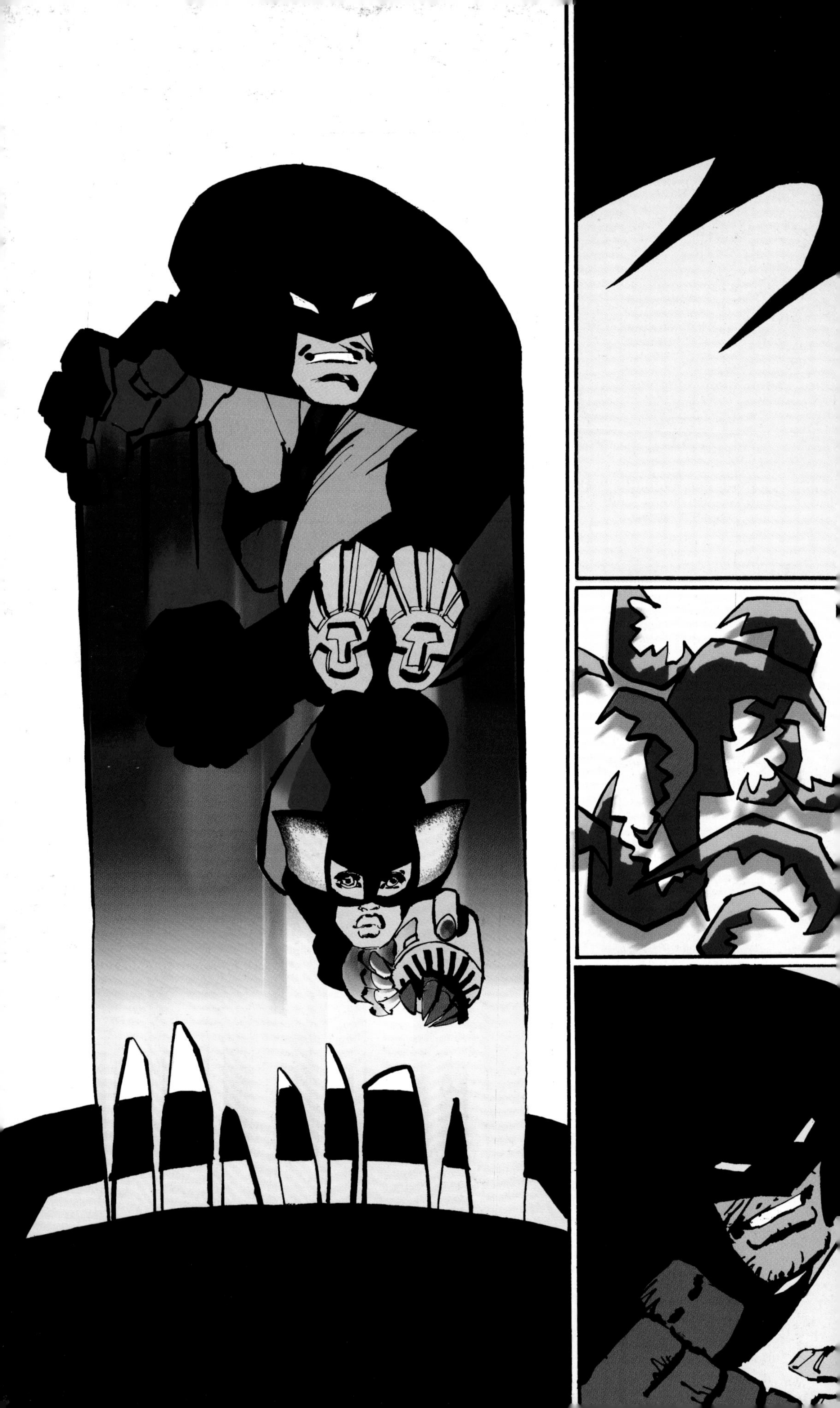

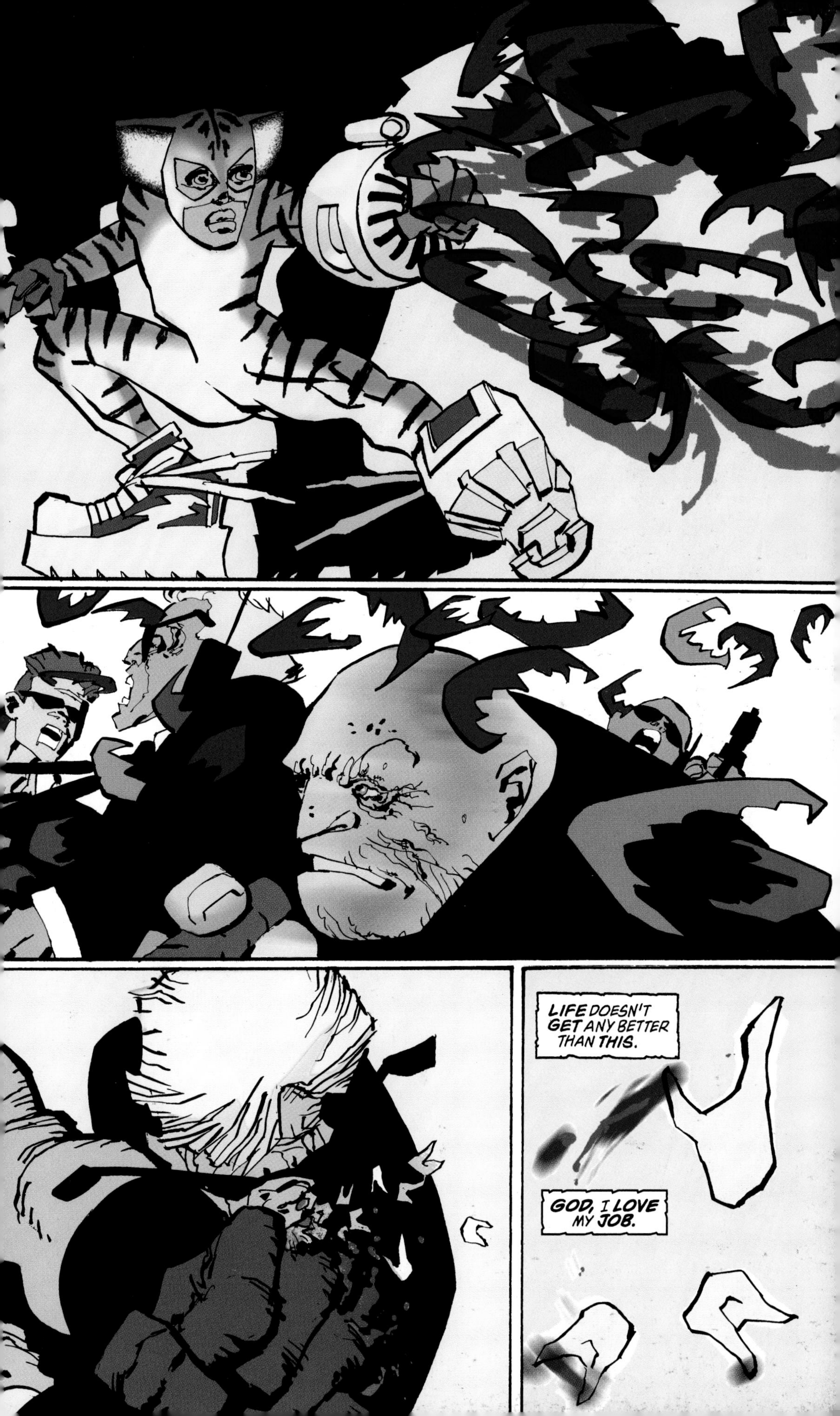
LIFE DOESN'T GET ANY BETTER THAN THIS.
GOD, I LOVE MY JOB.

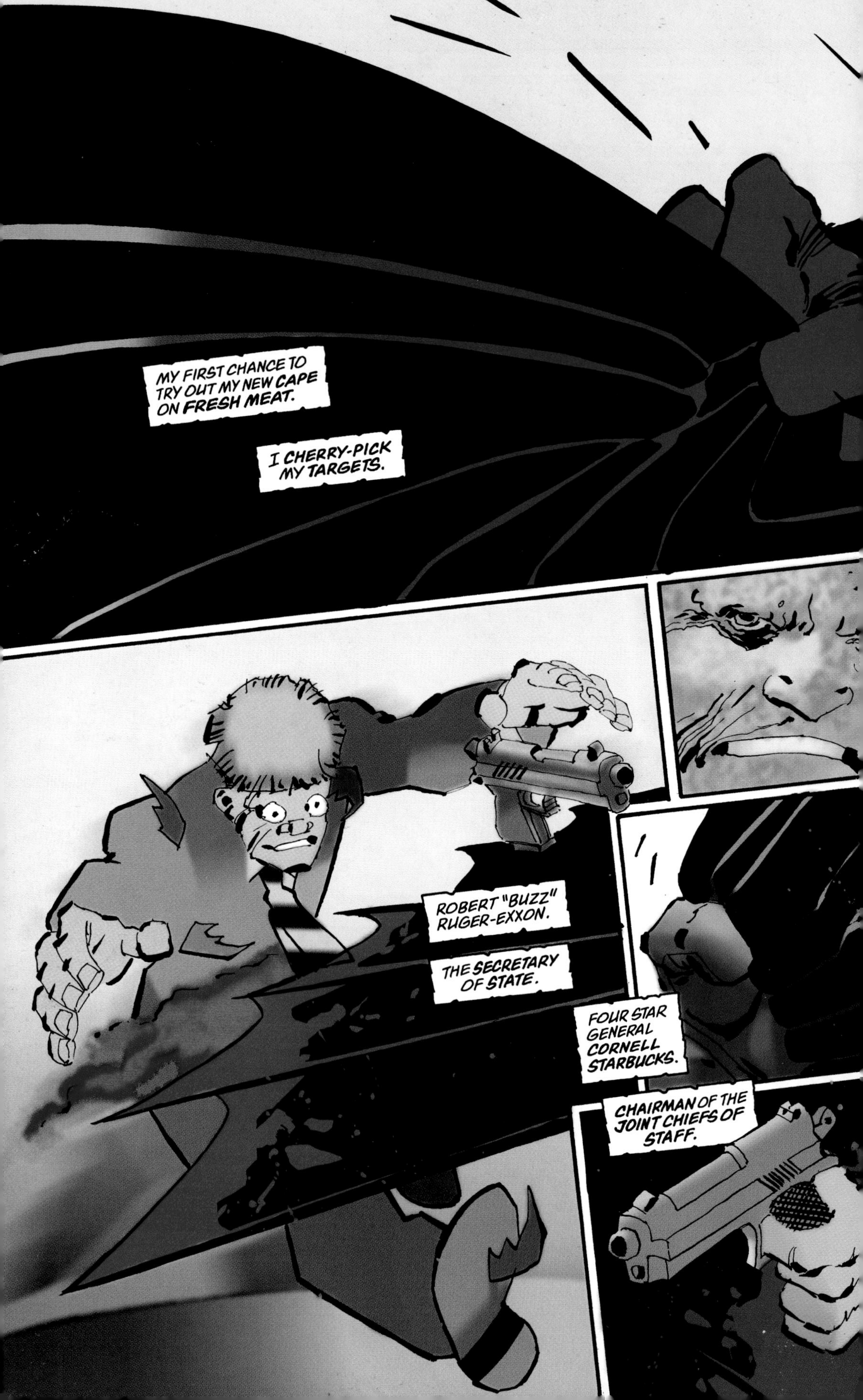
MY FIRST CHANCE TO TRY OUT MY NEW CAPE ON FRESH MEAT.
I CHERRY-PICK MY TARGETS.
ROBERT "BUZZ" RUGER-EXXON.
THE SECRETARY OF STATE.
FOUR STAR GENERAL CORNELL STARBUCKS.
CHAIRMAN OF THE JOINT CHIEFS OF STAFF.

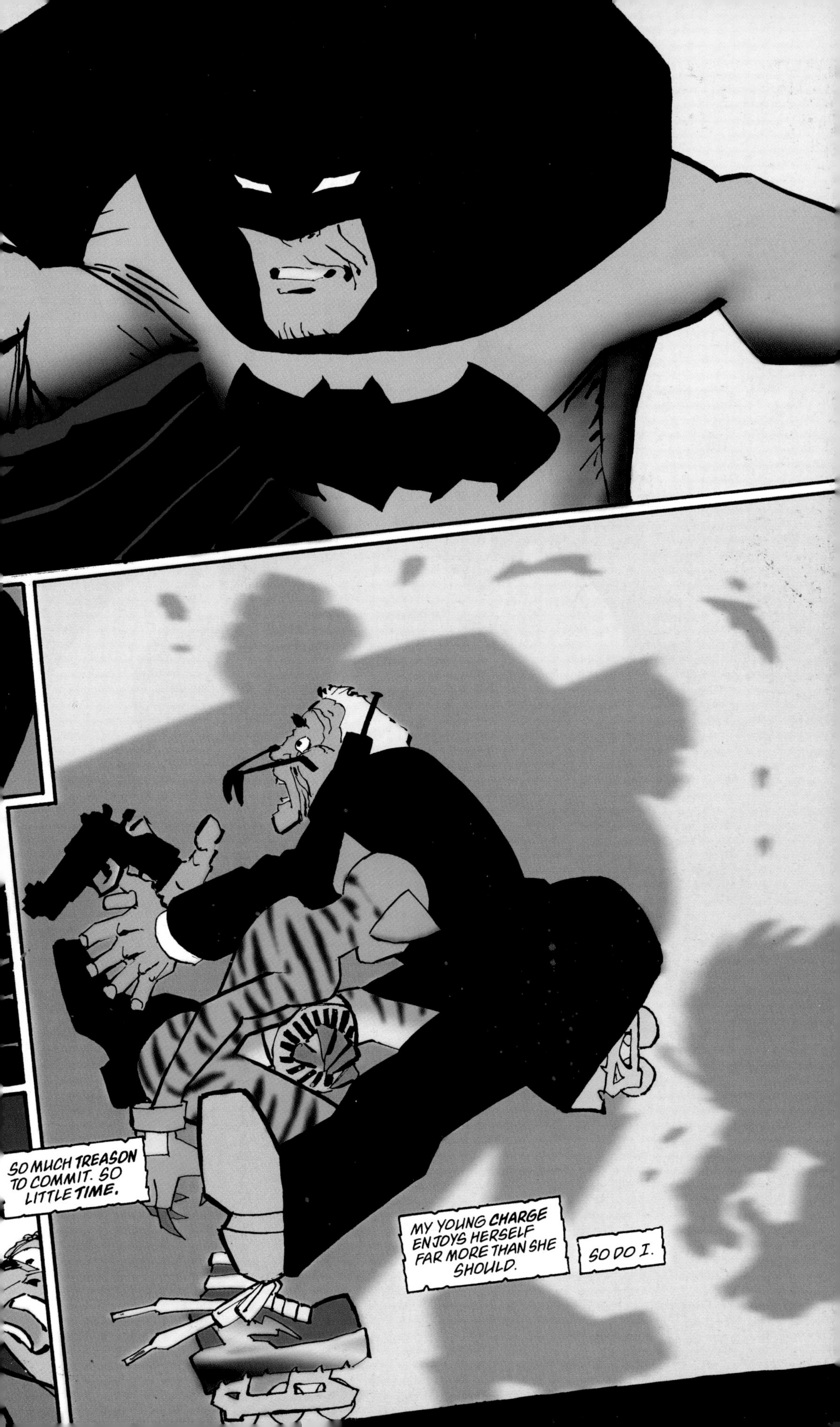
SO MUCH TREASON TO COMMIT. SO LITTLE TIME.
MY YOUNG CHARGE ENJOYS HERSELF FAR MORE THAN SHE SHOULD.
SO DO I.

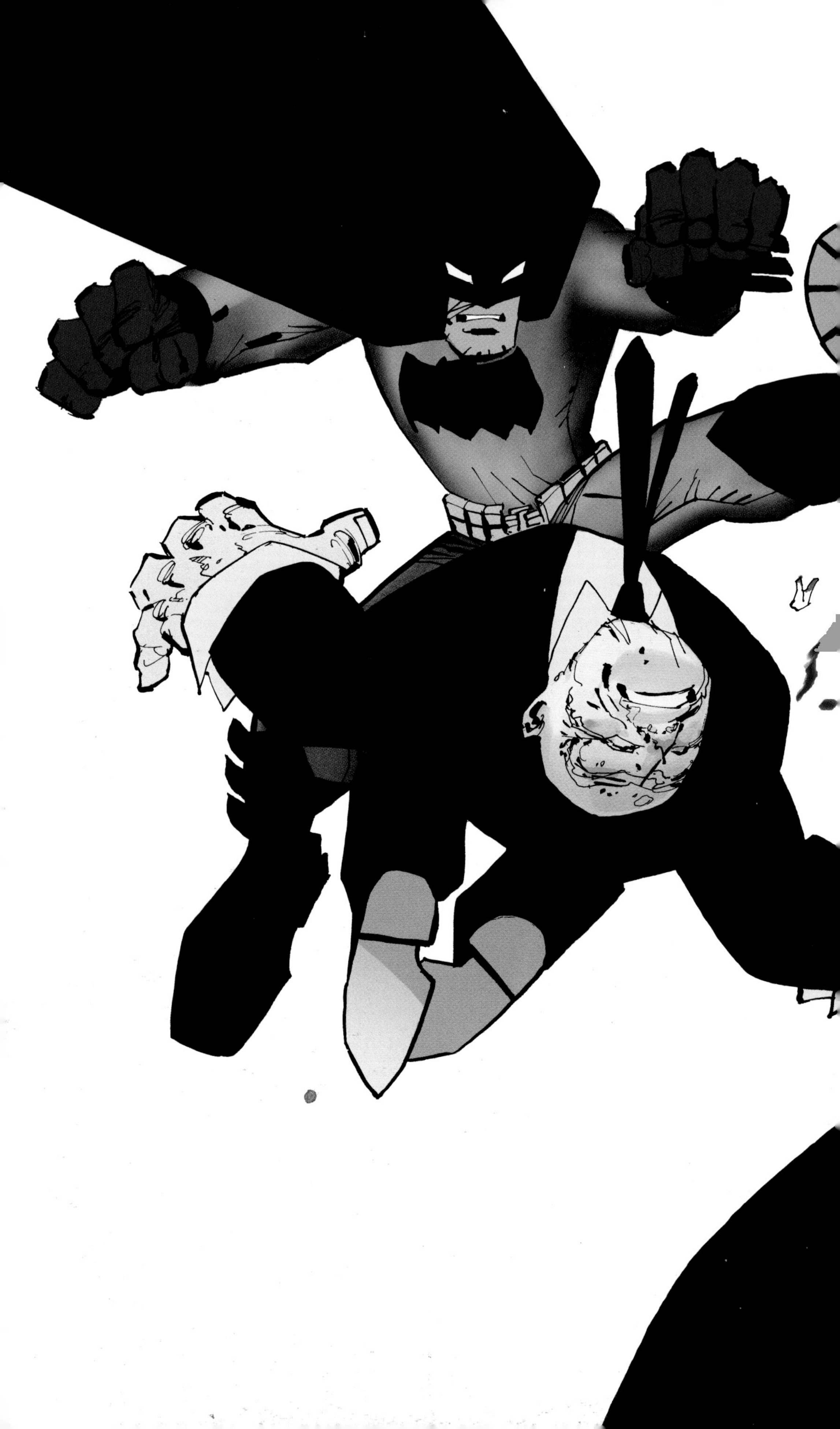

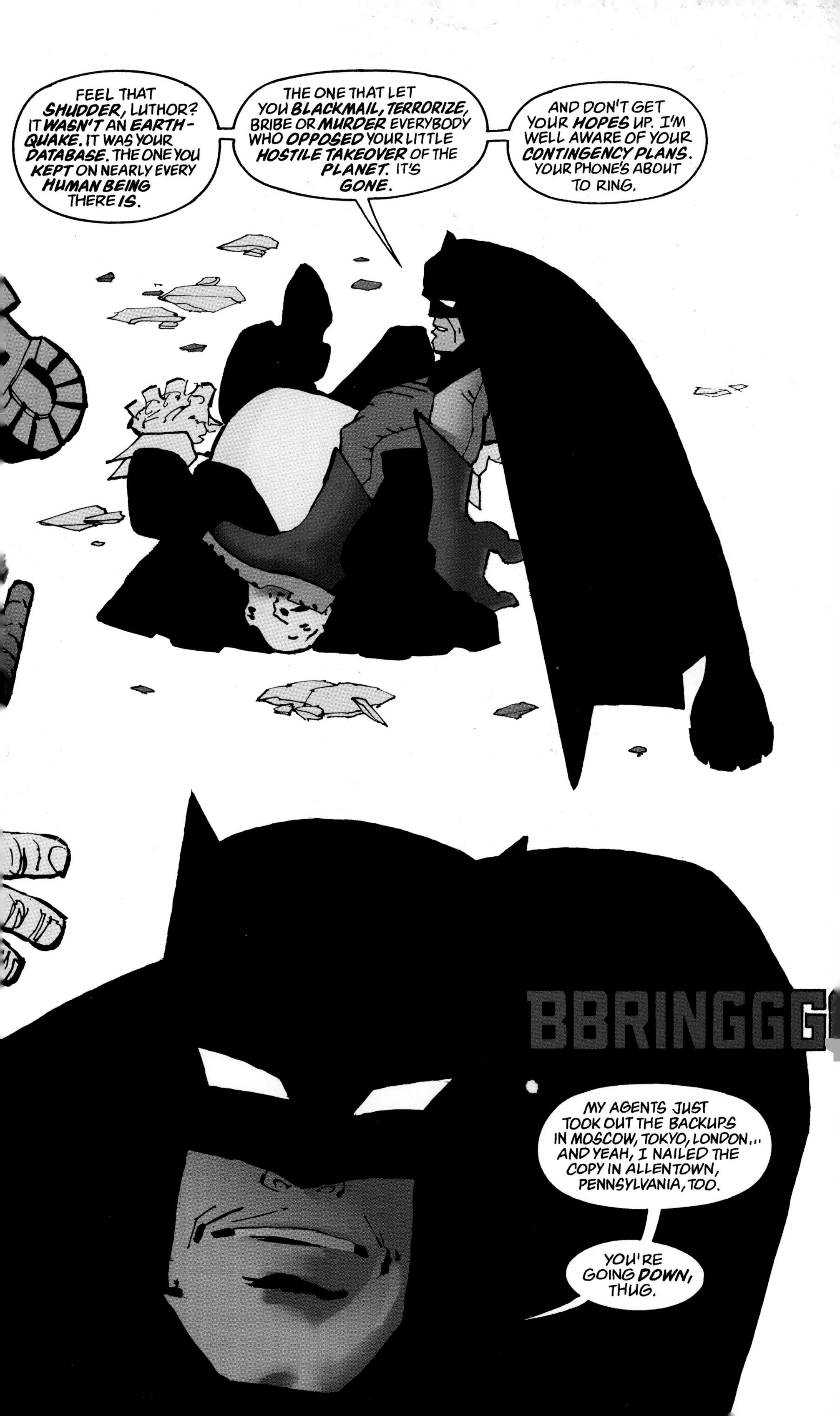
FEEL THAT SHUDDER, LUTHOR? IT WASN'T AN EARTHQUAKE. IT WAS YOUR DATABASE. THE ONE YOU KEPT ON NEARLY EVERY HUMAN BEING THERE IS.
THE ONE THAT LET YOU BLACKMAIL, TERRORIZE, BRIBE OR MURDER EVERYBODY WHO OPPOSED YOUR LITTLE HOSTILE TAKEOVER OF THE PLANET. IT'S GONE.
AND DON'T GET YOUR HOPES UP. I'M WELL AWARE OF YOUR CONTINGENCY PLANS. YOUR PHONE'S ABOUT TO RING.
BBRINGGG
MY AGENTS JUST TOOK OUT THE BACKUPS IN MOSCOW, TOKYO, LONDON... AND YEAH, I NAILED THE COPY IN ALLENTOWN, PENNSYLVANIA, TOO.
YOU'RE GOING DOWN, THUG.

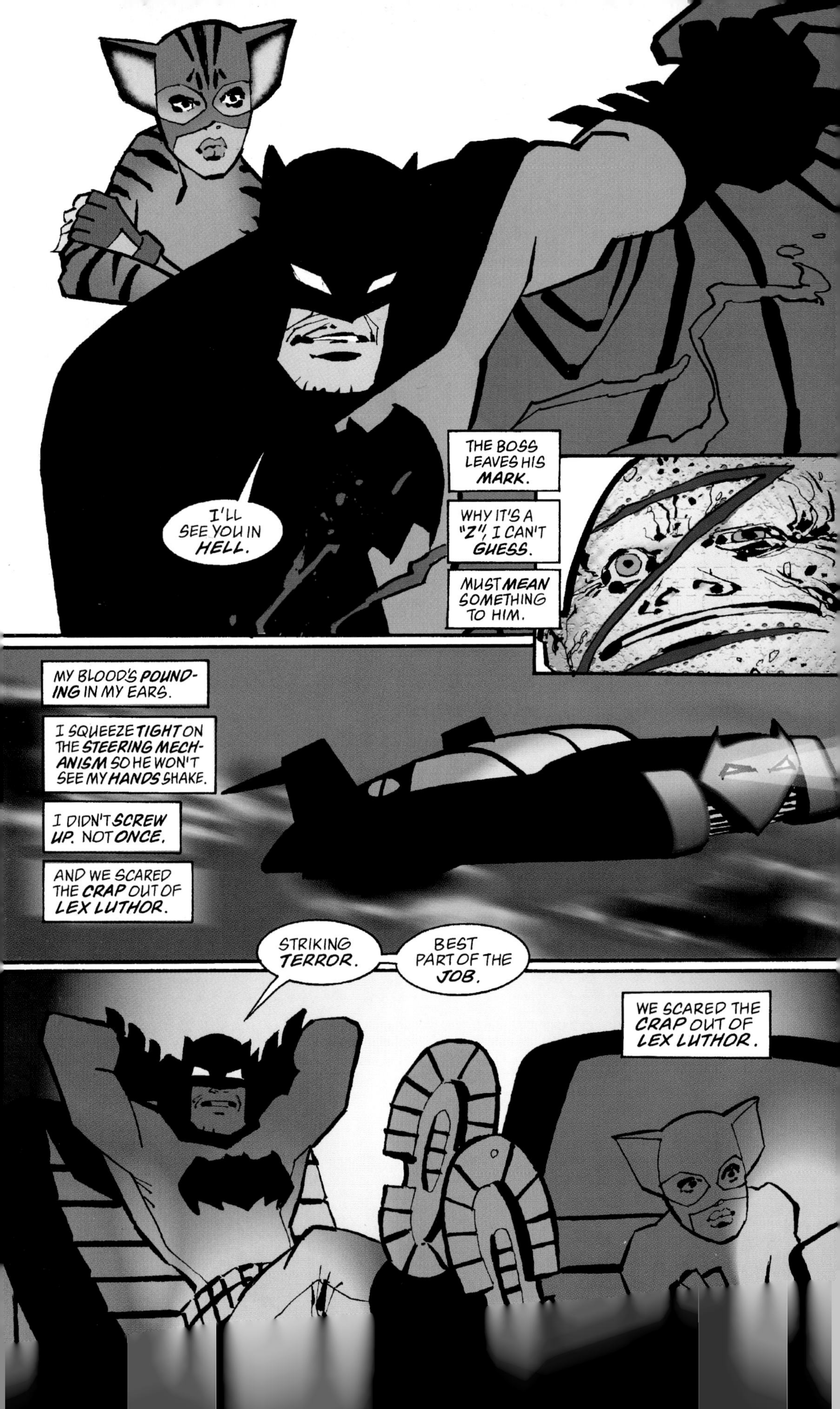

I'LL SEE YOU IN HELL.
THE BOSS LEAVES HIS MARK.
WHY IT'S A "Z", I CAN'T GUESS.
MUST MEAN SOMETHING TO HIM.
MY BLOOD'S POUNDING IN MY EARS.
I SQUEEZE TIGHT ON THE STEERING MECHANISM SO HE WON'T SEE MY HANDS SHAKE.
I DIDN'T SCREW UP. NOT ONCE.
AND WE SCARED THE CRAP OUT OF LEX LUTHOR.
STRIKING TERROR.
BEST PART OF THE JOB.
WE SCARED THE CRAP OUT OF LEX LUTHOR.

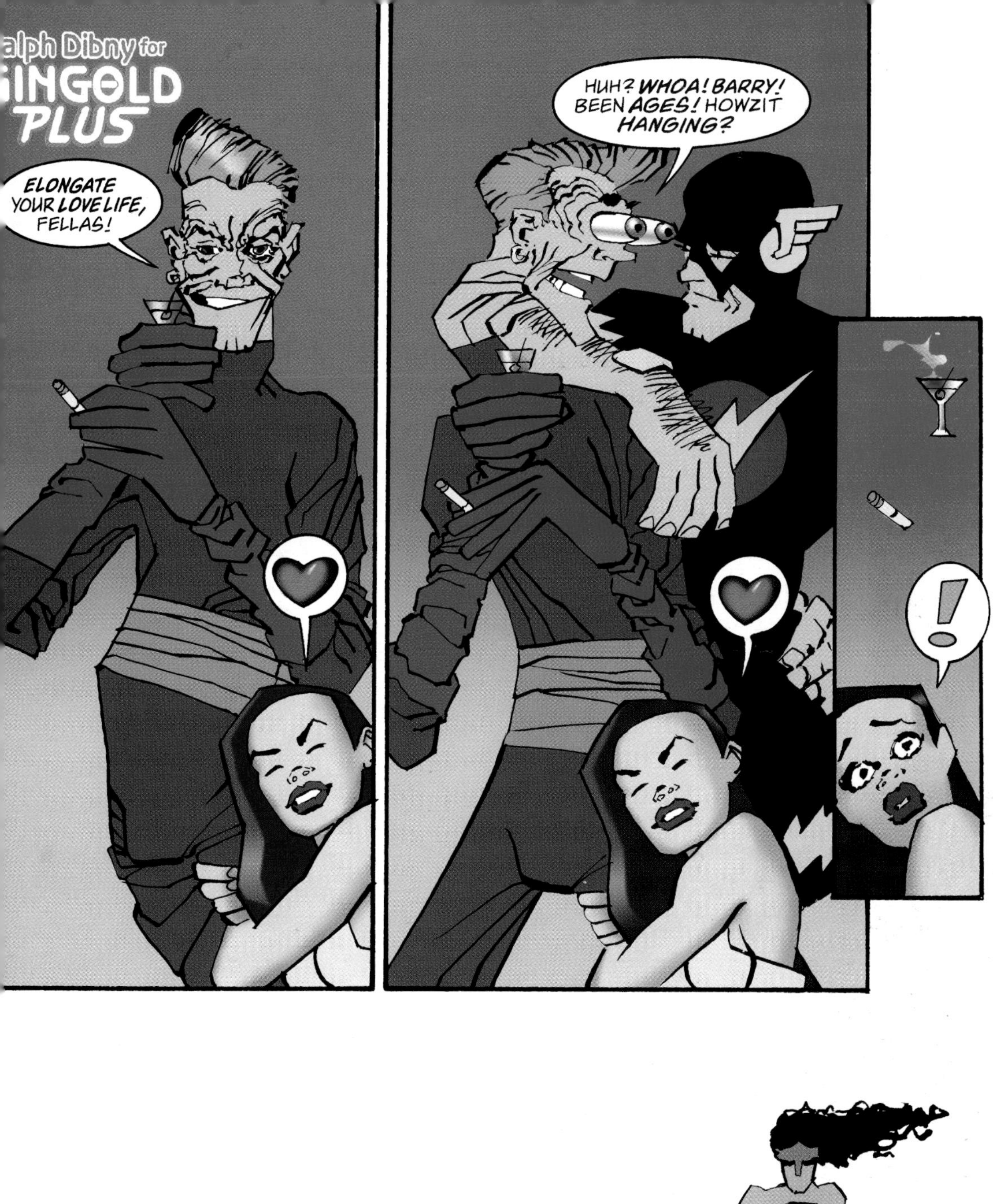
alph Dibny for
INGOLD
PLUS
ELONGATE YOUR LOVE LIFE, FELLAS!
HUH? WHOA! BARRY! BEEN AGES! HOWZIT HANGING?
!

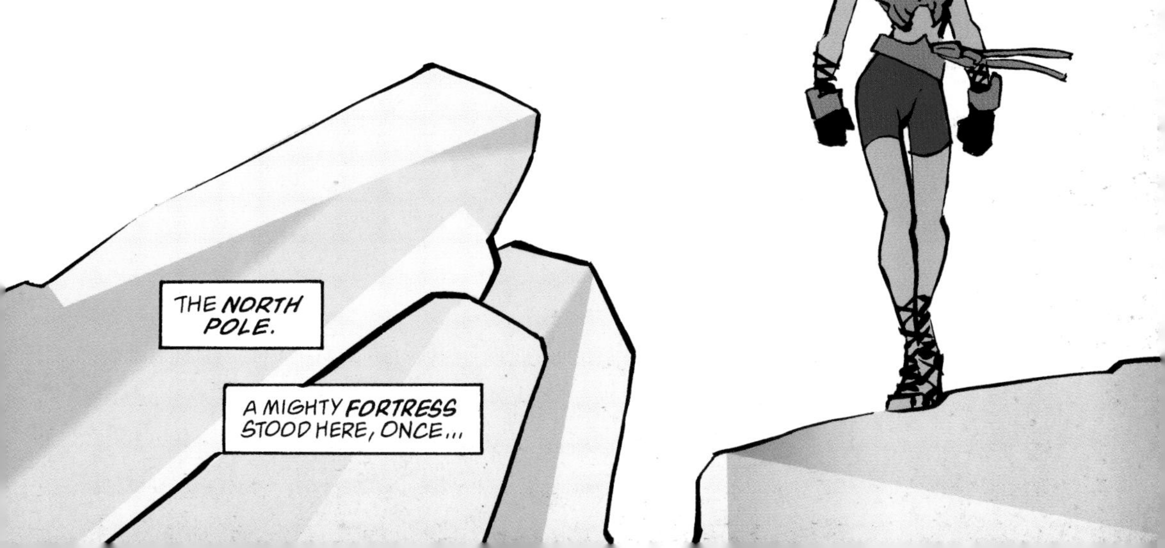
THE NORTH POLE.
A MIGHTY FORTRESS STOOD HERE, ONCE...

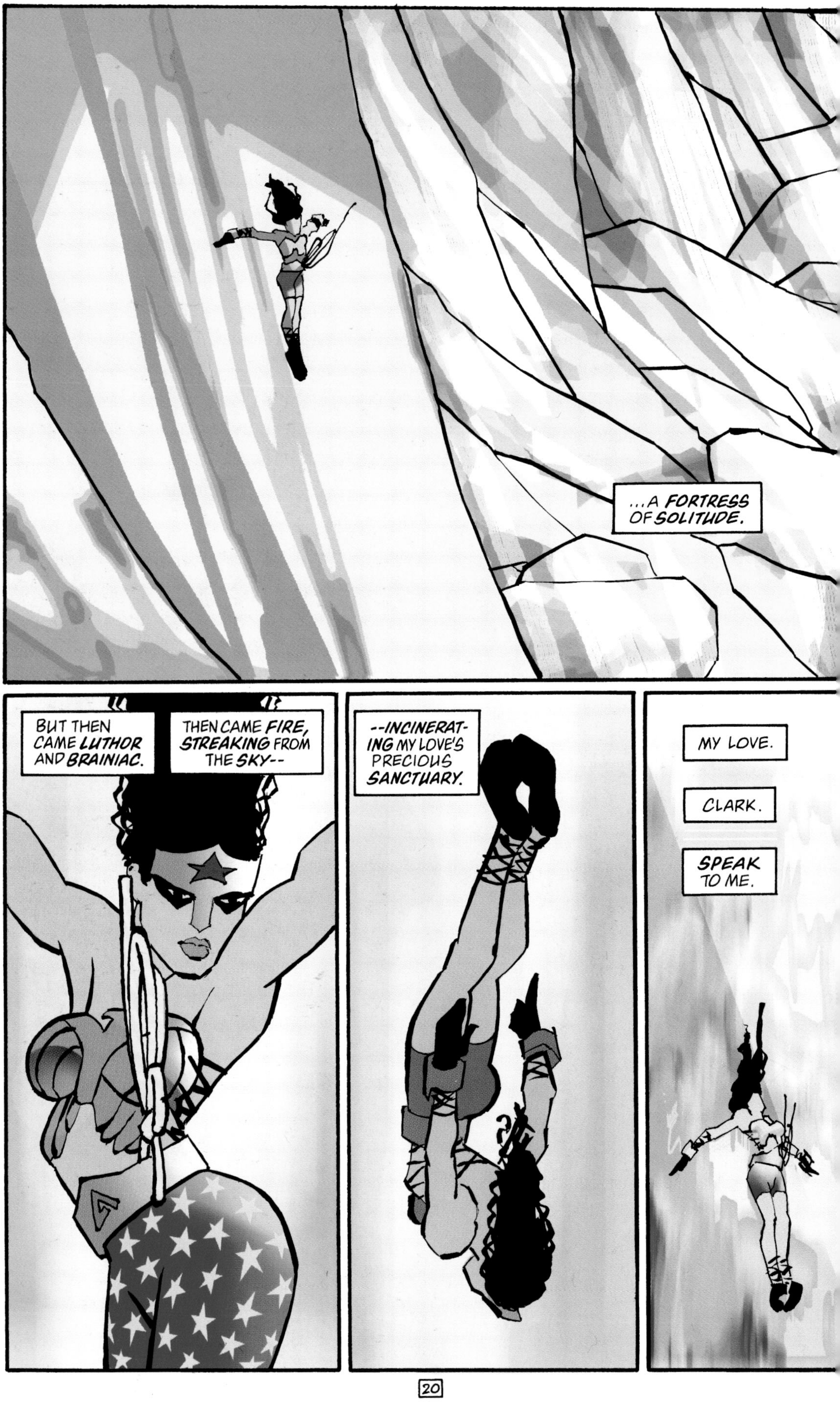
...A FORTRESS OF SOLITUDE.
BUT THEN CAME LUTHOR AND BRAINIAC.
THEN CAME FIRE, STREAKING FROM THE SKY--
--INCINERATING MY LOVE'S PRECIOUS SANCTUARY.
MY LOVE.
CLARK.
SPEAK TO ME.

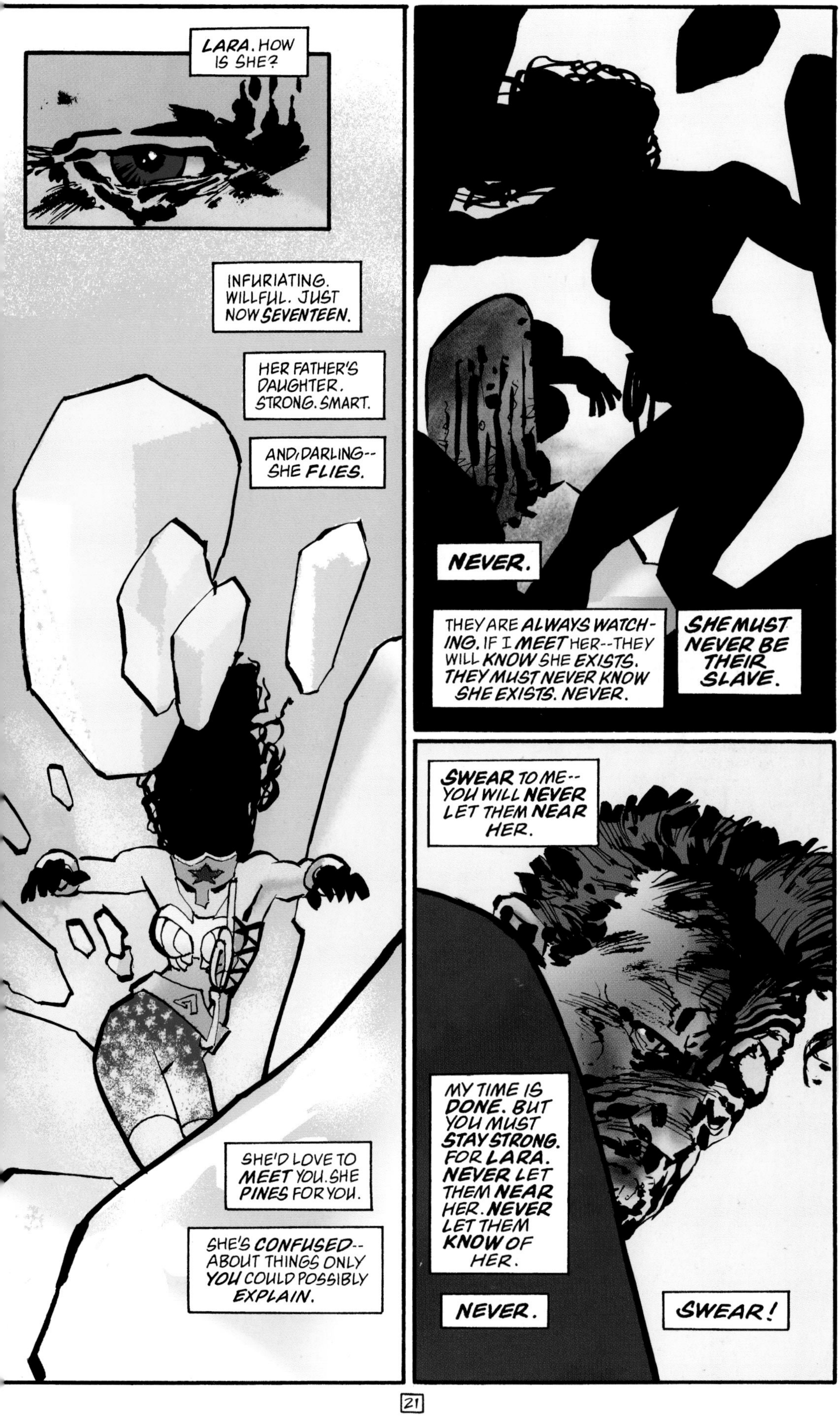

LARA. HOW IS SHE?
INFURIATING. WILLFUL. JUST NOW SEVENTEEN.
HER FATHER'S DAUGHTER. STRONG. SMART.
AND, DARLING-- SHE FLIES.
SHE'D LOVE TO MEET YOU. SHE PINES FOR YOU.
SHE'S CONFUSED-- ABOUT THINGS ONLY YOU COULD POSSIBLY EXPLAIN.
NEVER.
THEY ARE ALWAYS WATCHING. IF I MEET HER--THEY WILL KNOW SHE EXISTS. THEY MUST NEVER KNOW SHE EXISTS. NEVER.
SHE MUST NEVER BE THEIR SLAVE.
SWEAR TO ME-- YOU WILL NEVER LET THEM NEAR HER.
MY TIME IS DONE. BUT YOU MUST STAY STRONG. FOR LARA. NEVER LET THEM NEAR HER. NEVER LET THEM KNOW OF HER.
NEVER.
SWEAR!

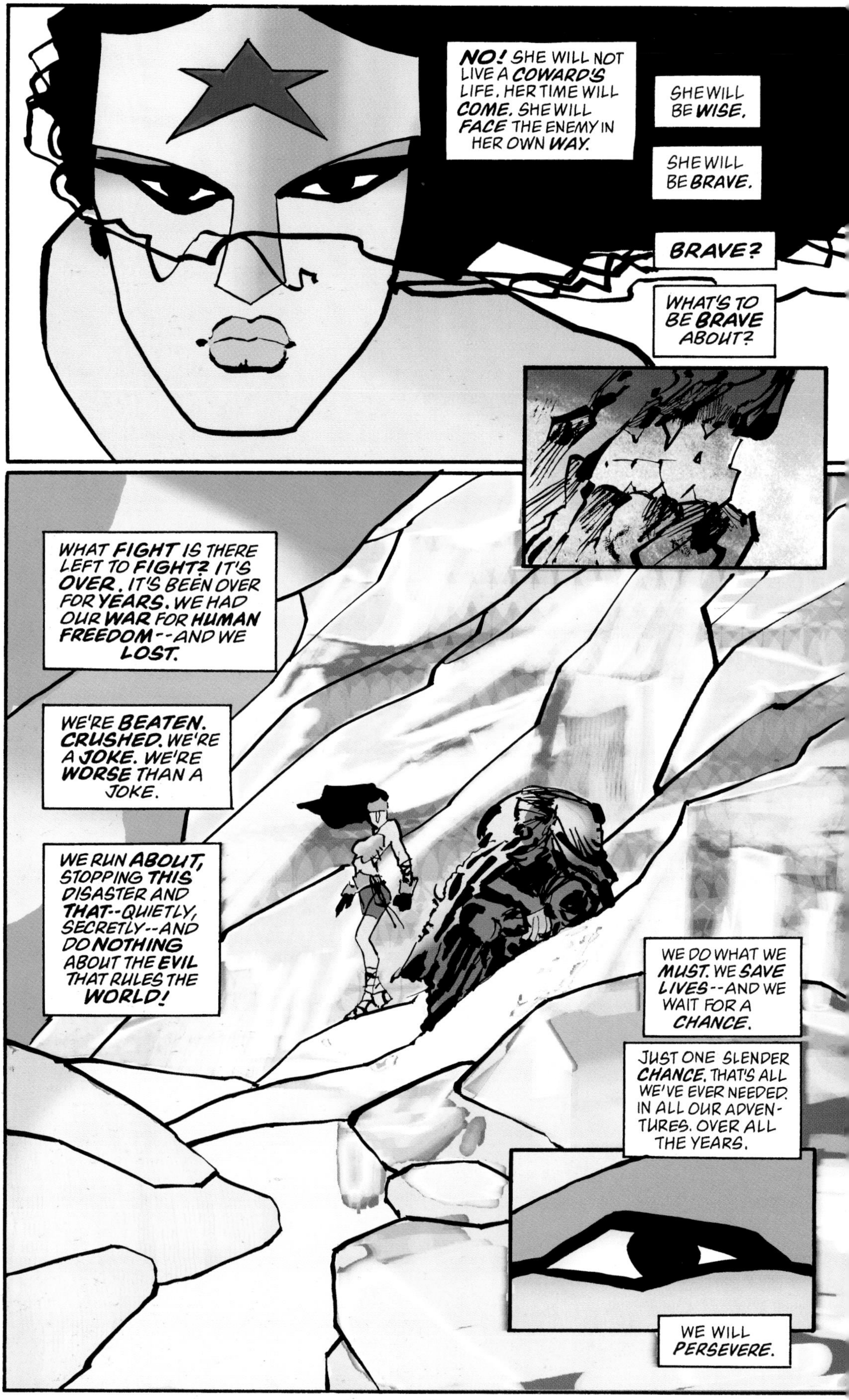
NO! SHE WILL NOT LIVE A COWARD'S LIFE. HER TIME WILL COME. SHE WILL FACE THE ENEMY IN HER OWN WAY.
SHE WILL BE WISE.
SHE WILL BE BRAVE.
BRAVE?
WHAT'S TO BE BRAVE ABOUT?
WHAT FIGHT IS THERE LEFT TO FIGHT? IT'S OVER. IT'S BEEN OVER FOR YEARS. WE HAD OUR WAR FOR HUMAN FREEDOM--AND WE LOST.
WE'RE BEATEN. CRUSHED. WE'RE A JOKE. WE'RE WORSE THAN A JOKE.
WE RUN ABOUT, STOPPING THIS DISASTER AND THAT--QUIETLY, SECRETLY--AND DO NOTHING ABOUT THE EVIL THAT RULES THE WORLD!
WE DO WHAT WE MUST. WE SAVE LIVES--AND WE WAIT FOR A CHANCE.
JUST ONE SLENDER CHANCE. THAT'S ALL WE'VE EVER NEEDED. IN ALL OUR ADVENTURES. OVER ALL THE YEARS.
WE WILL PERSEVERE.

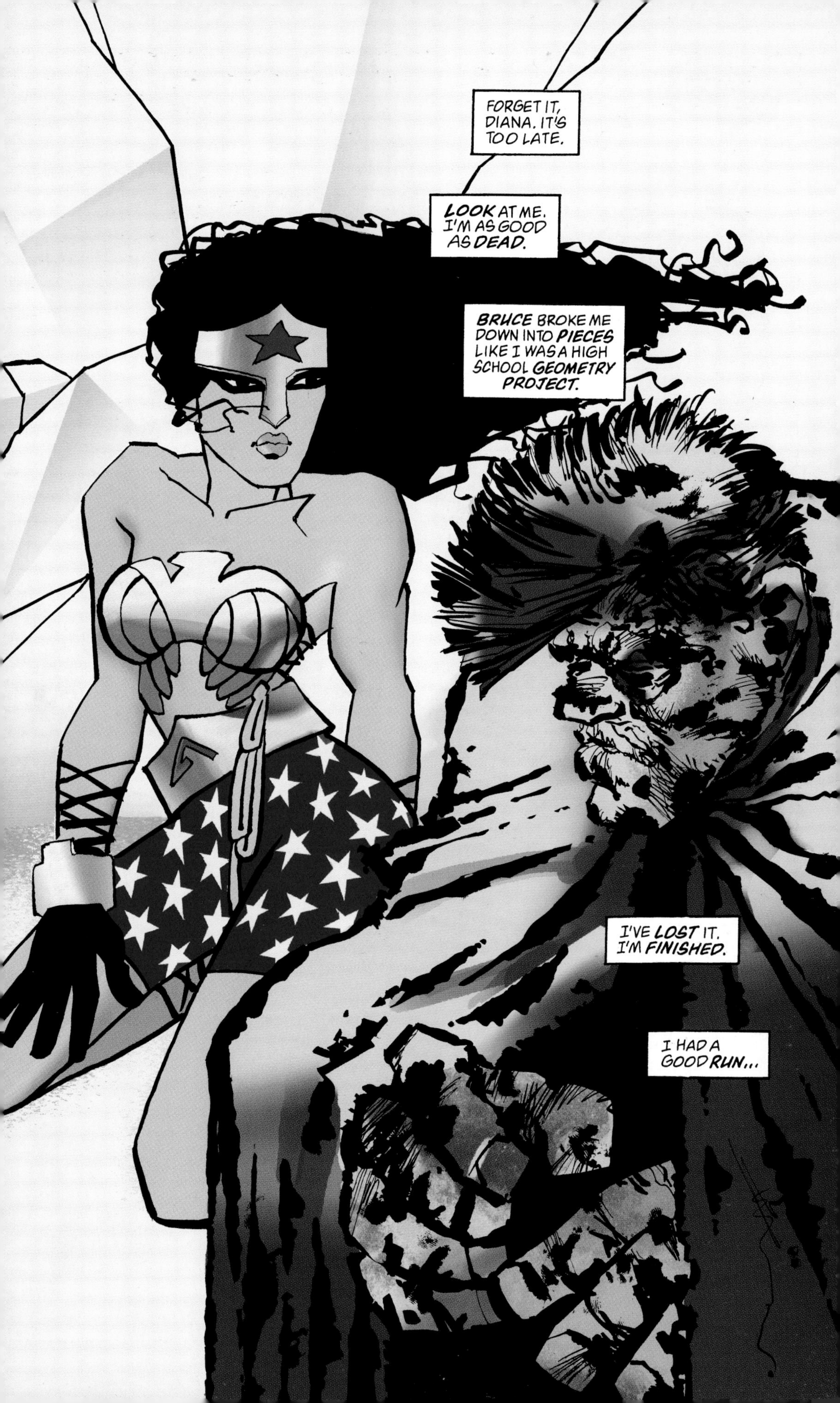
FORGET IT, DIANA. IT'S TOO LATE.
LOOK AT ME. I'M AS GOOD AS DEAD.
BRUCE BROKE ME DOWN INTO PIECES LIKE I WAS A HIGH SCHOOL GEOMETRY PROJECT.
I'VE LOST IT. I'M FINISHED.
I HAD A GOOD RUN...

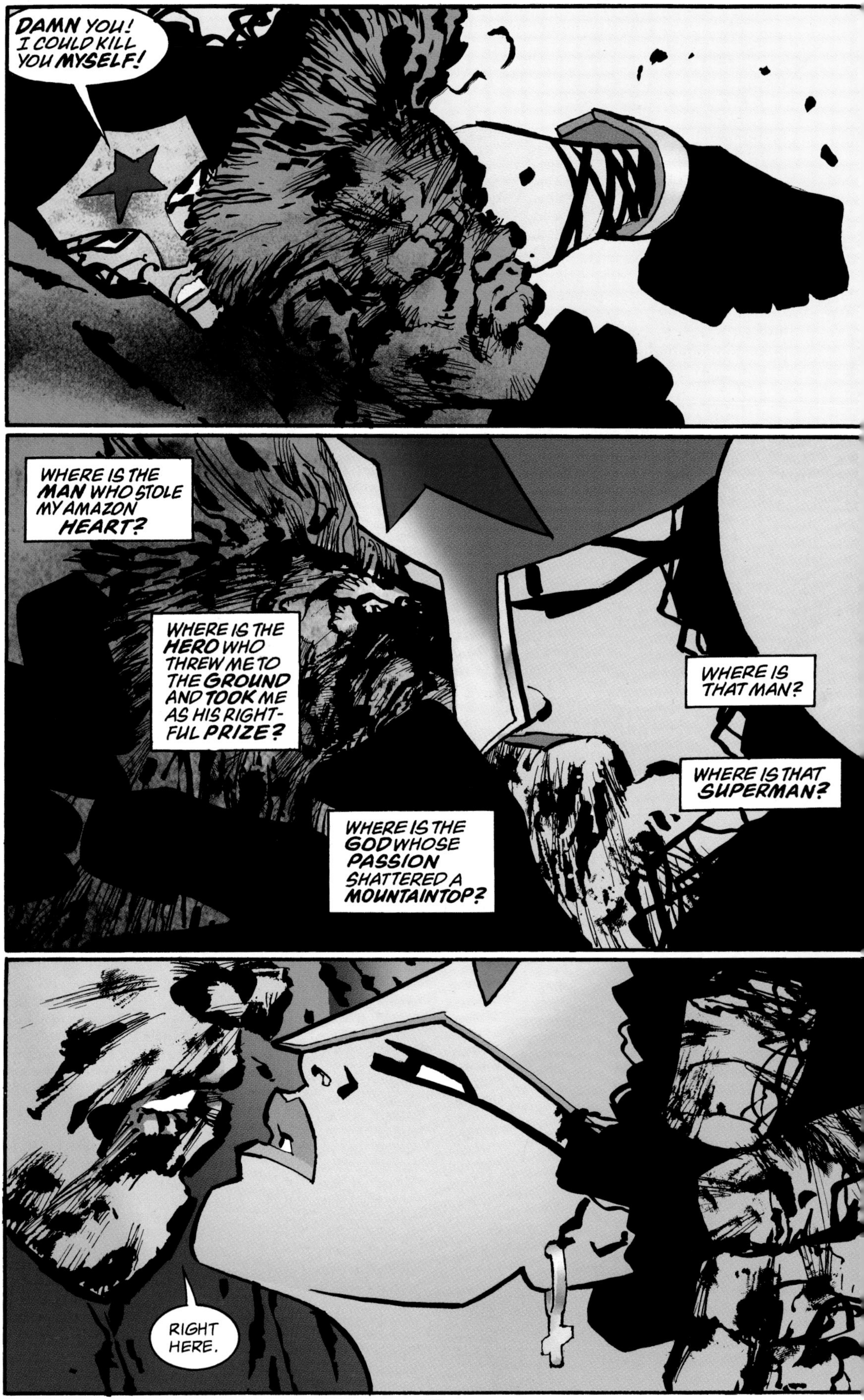
DAMN YOU! I COULD KILL YOU MYSELF!
WHERE IS THE MAN WHO STOLE MY AMAZON HEART?
WHERE IS THE HERO WHO THREW ME TO THE GROUND AND TOOK ME AS HIS RIGHTFUL PRIZE?
WHERE IS THAT MAN?
WHERE IS THAT SUPERMAN?
WHERE IS THE GOD WHOSE PASSION SHATTERED A MOUNTAINTOP?
RIGHT HERE.

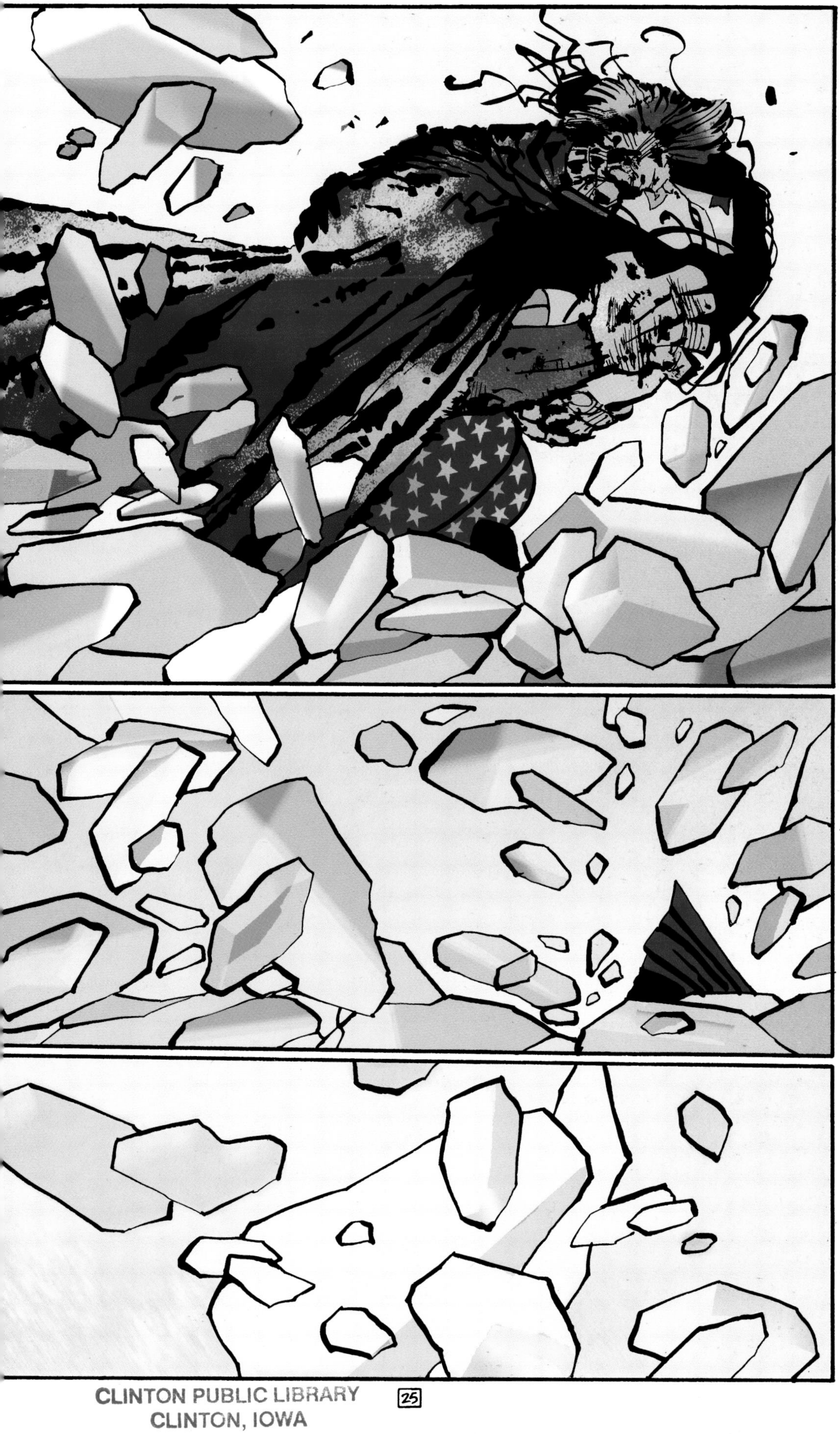

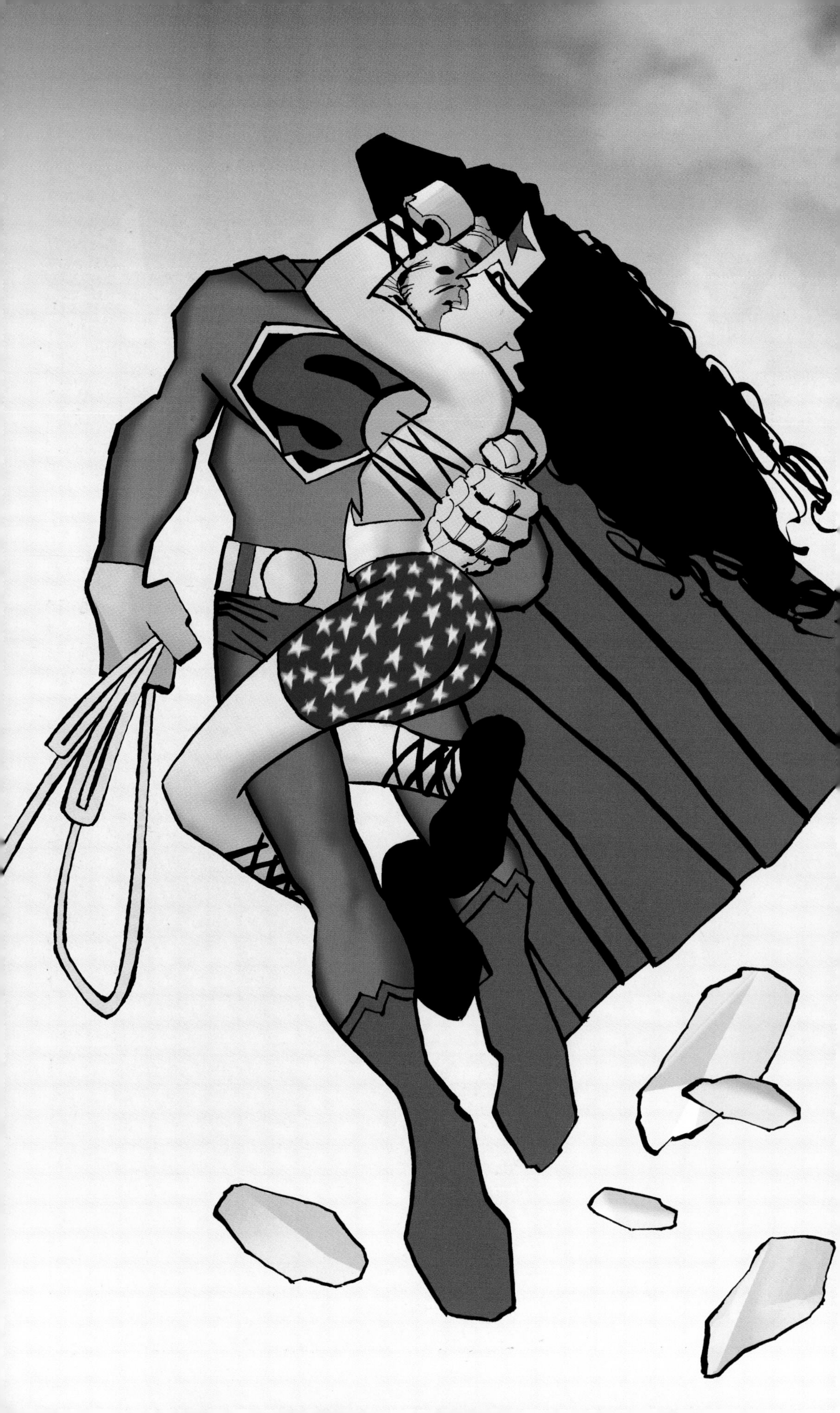

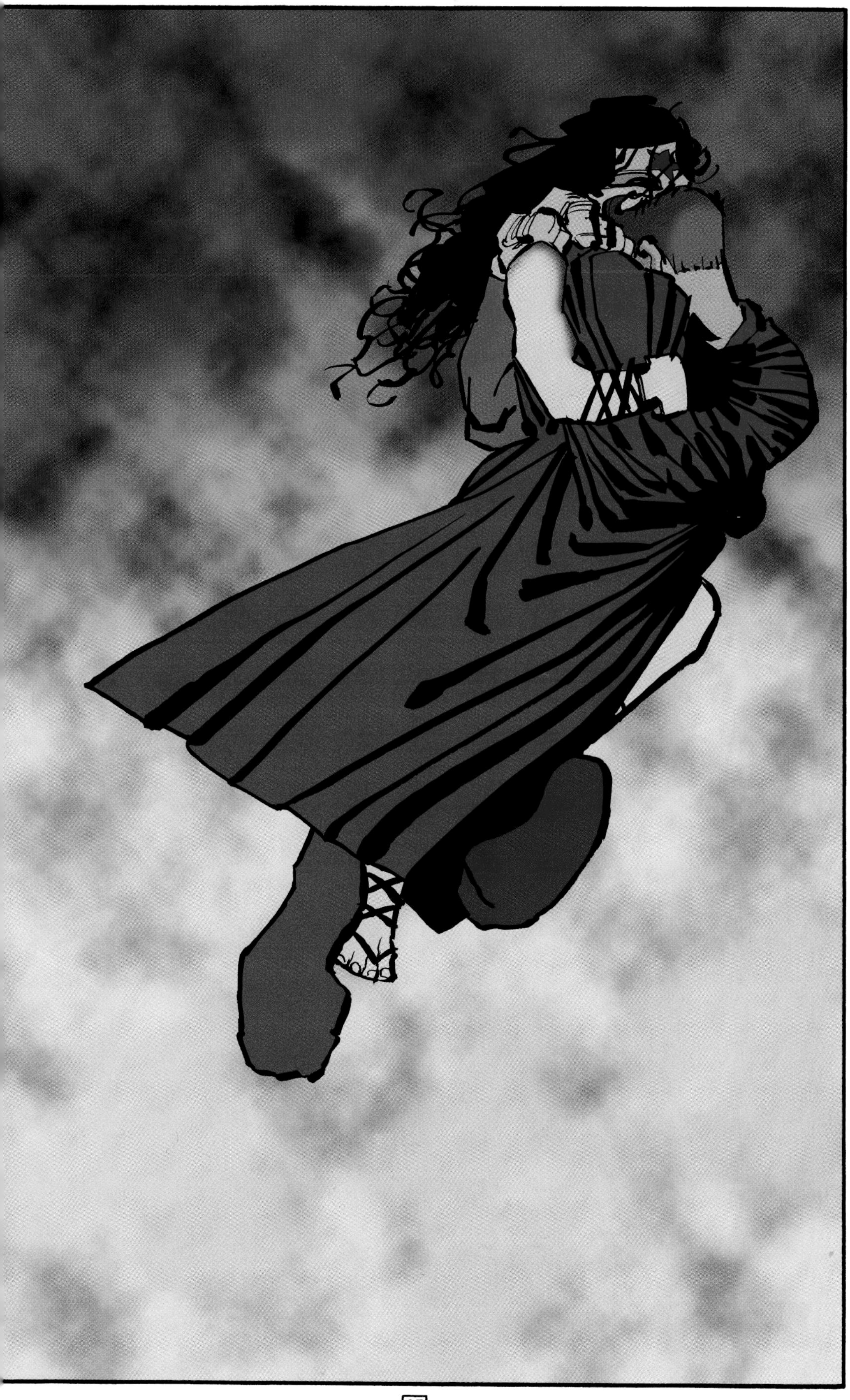

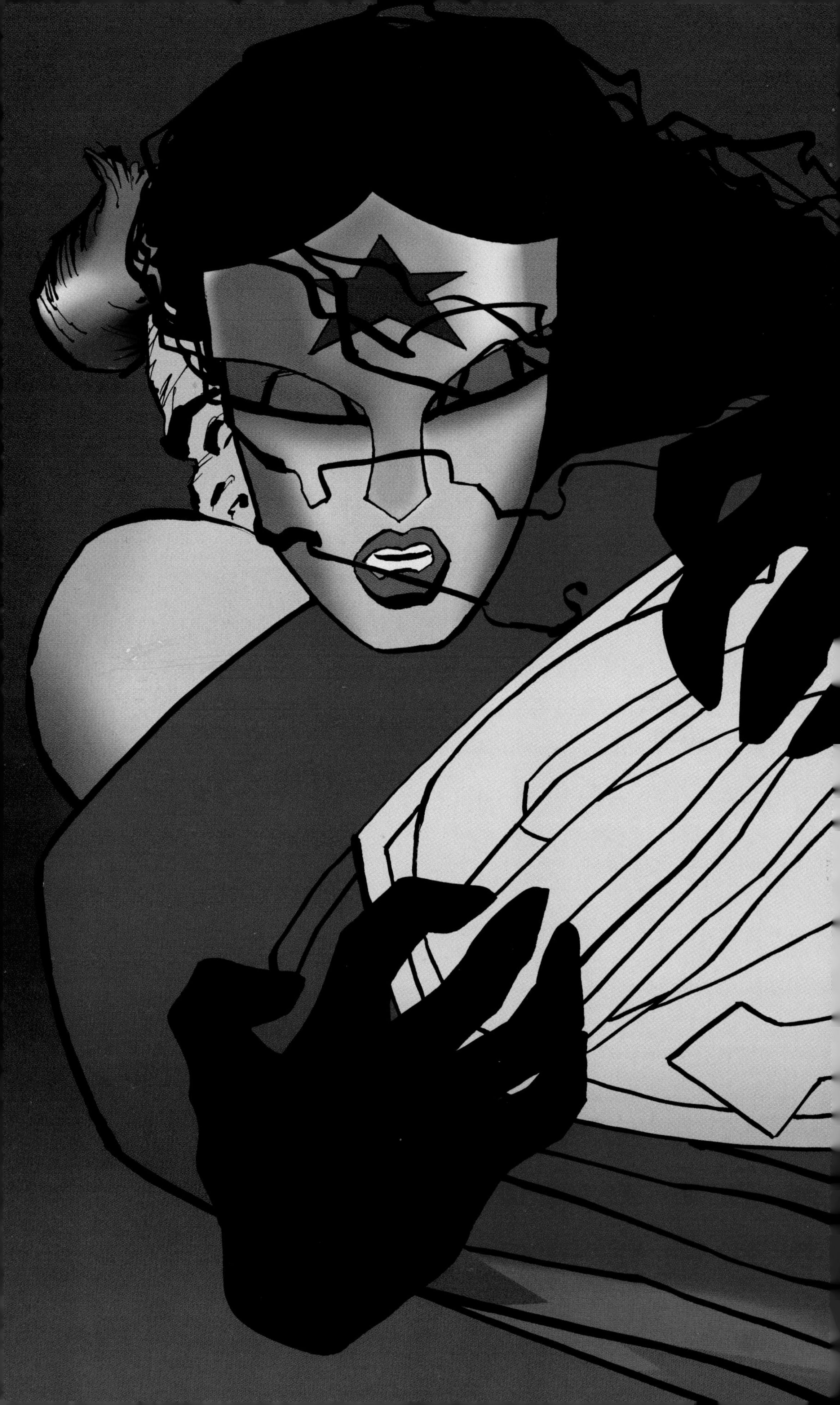

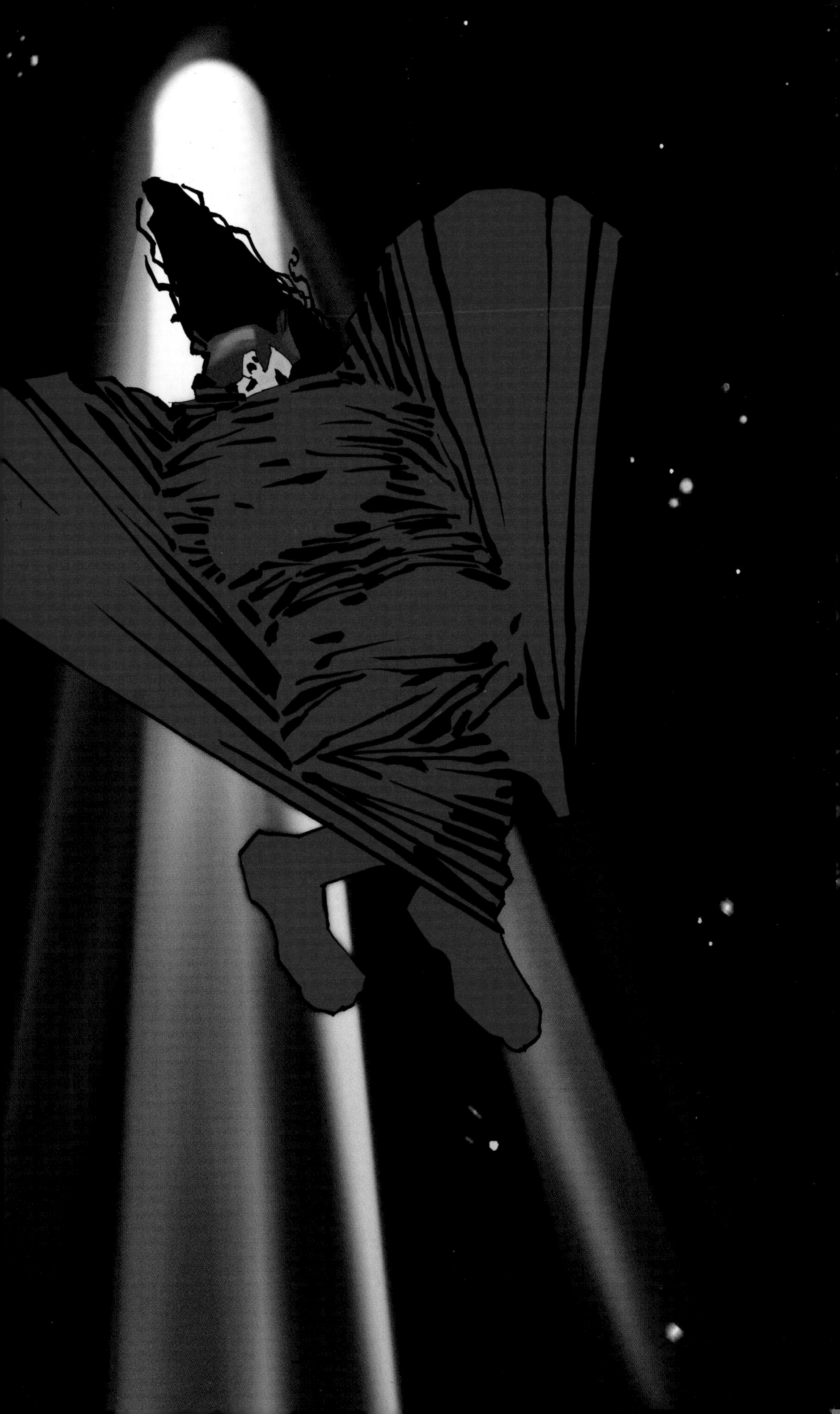

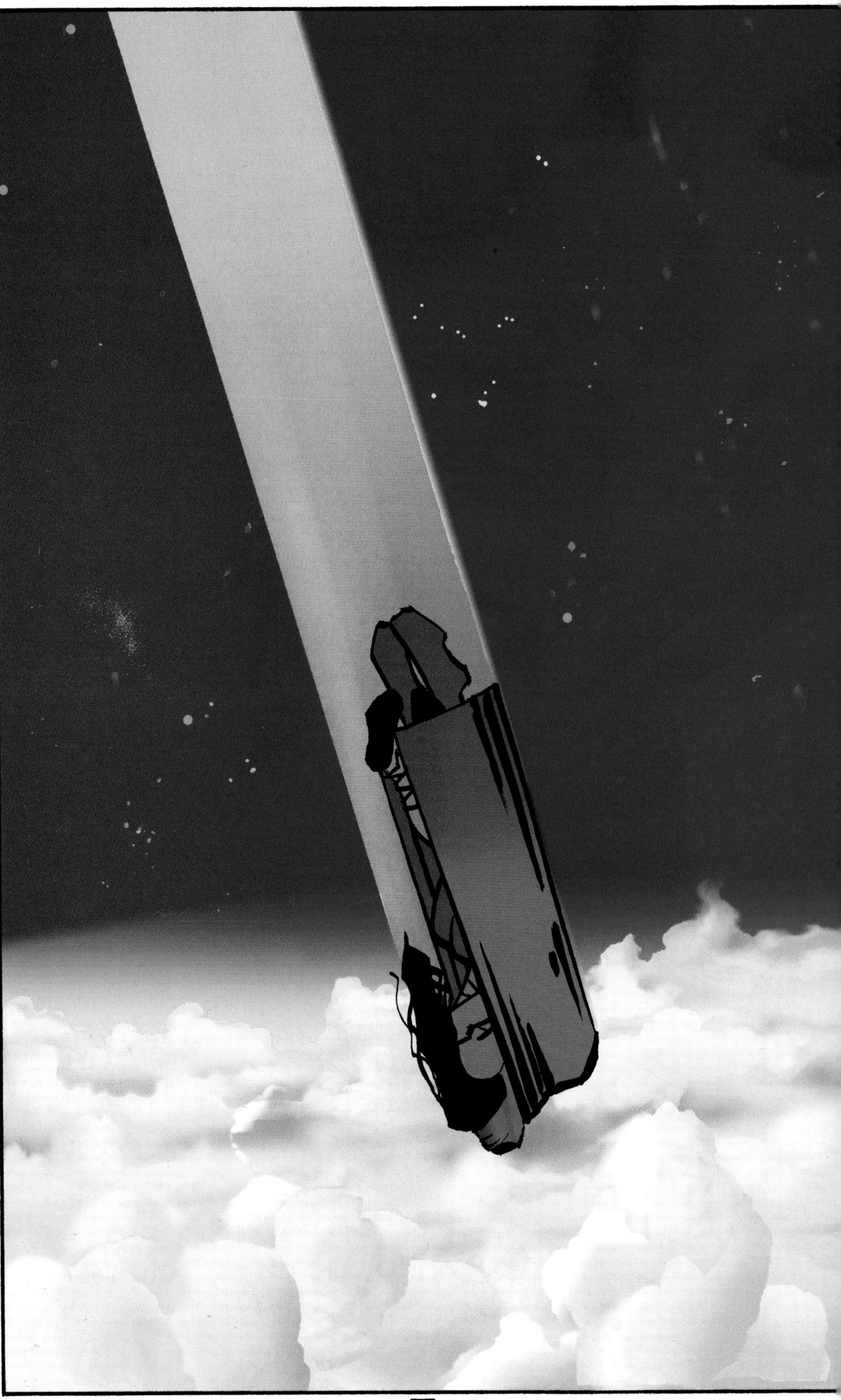

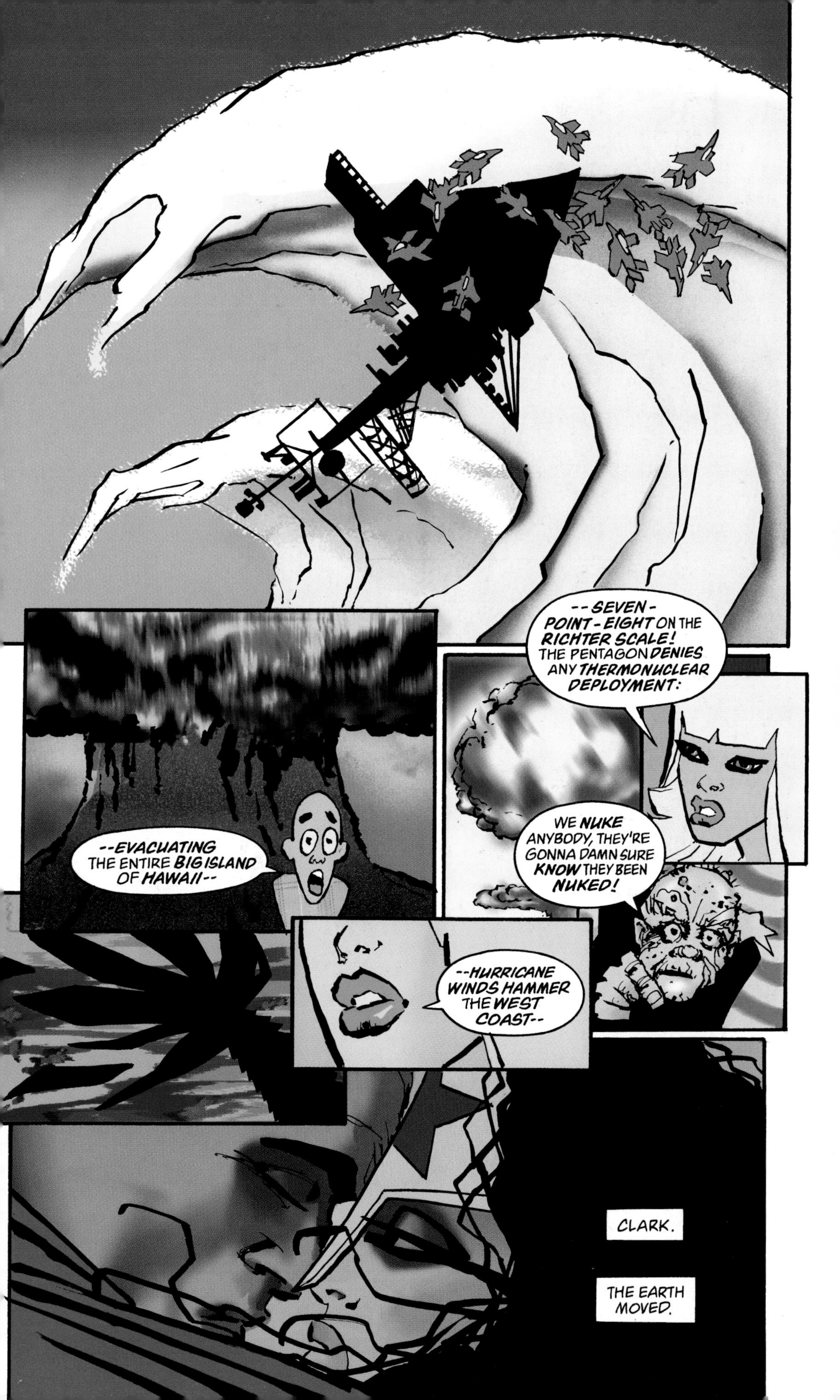
--SEVEN-POINT-EIGHT ON THE RICHTER SCALE! THE PENTAGON DENIES ANY THERMONUCLEAR DEPLOYMENT:
--EVACUATING THE ENTIRE BIG ISLAND OF HAWAII--
WE NUKE ANYBODY, THEY'RE GONNA DAMN SURE KNOW THEY BEEN NUKED!
--HURRICANE WINDS HAMMER THE WEST COAST--
CLARK.
THE EARTH MOVED.

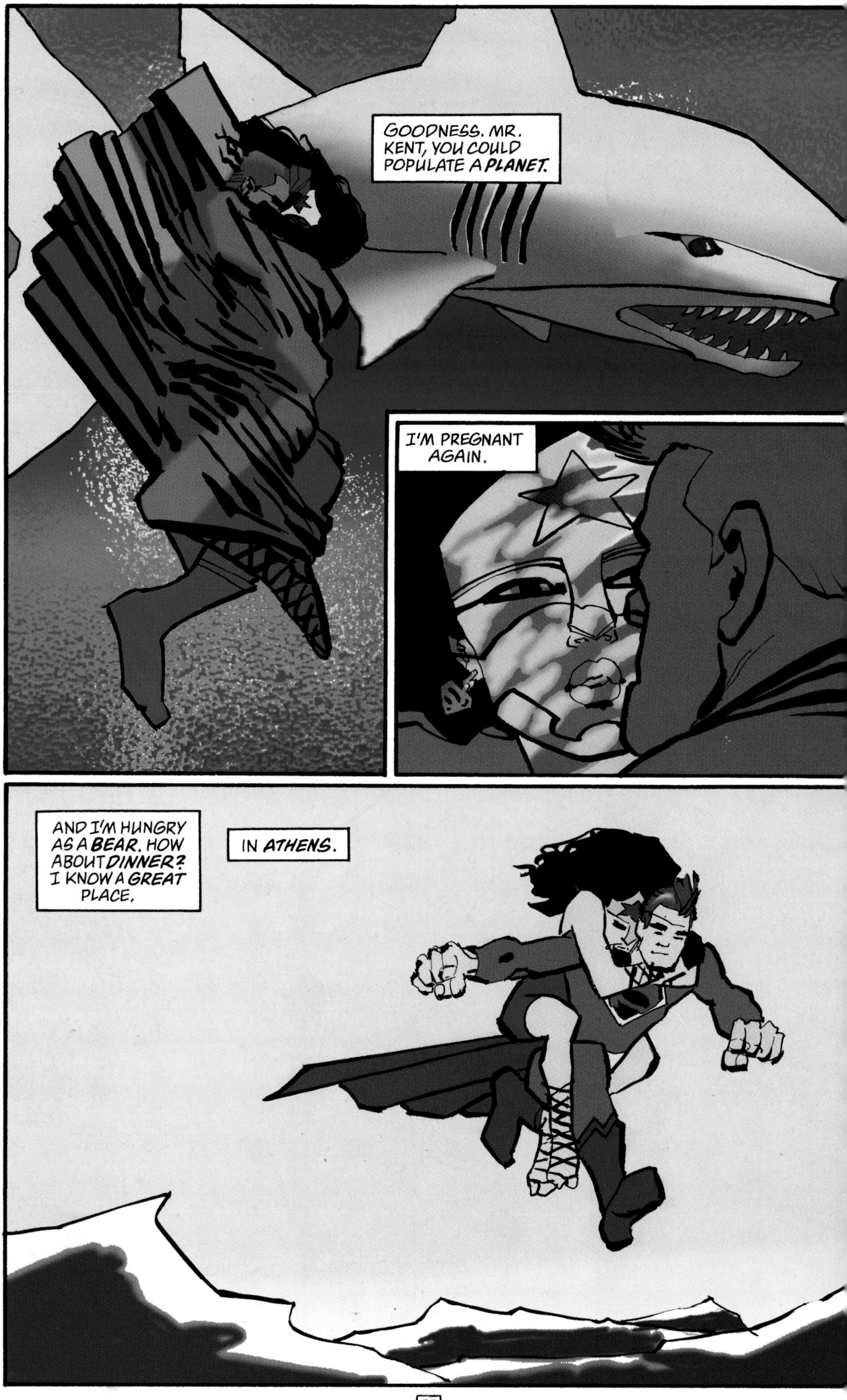
GOODNESS. MR. KENT, YOU COULD POPULATE A PLANET.
I'M PREGNANT AGAIN.
AND I'M HUNGRY AS A BEAR. HOW ABOUT DINNER? I KNOW A GREAT PLACE.
IN ATHENS.

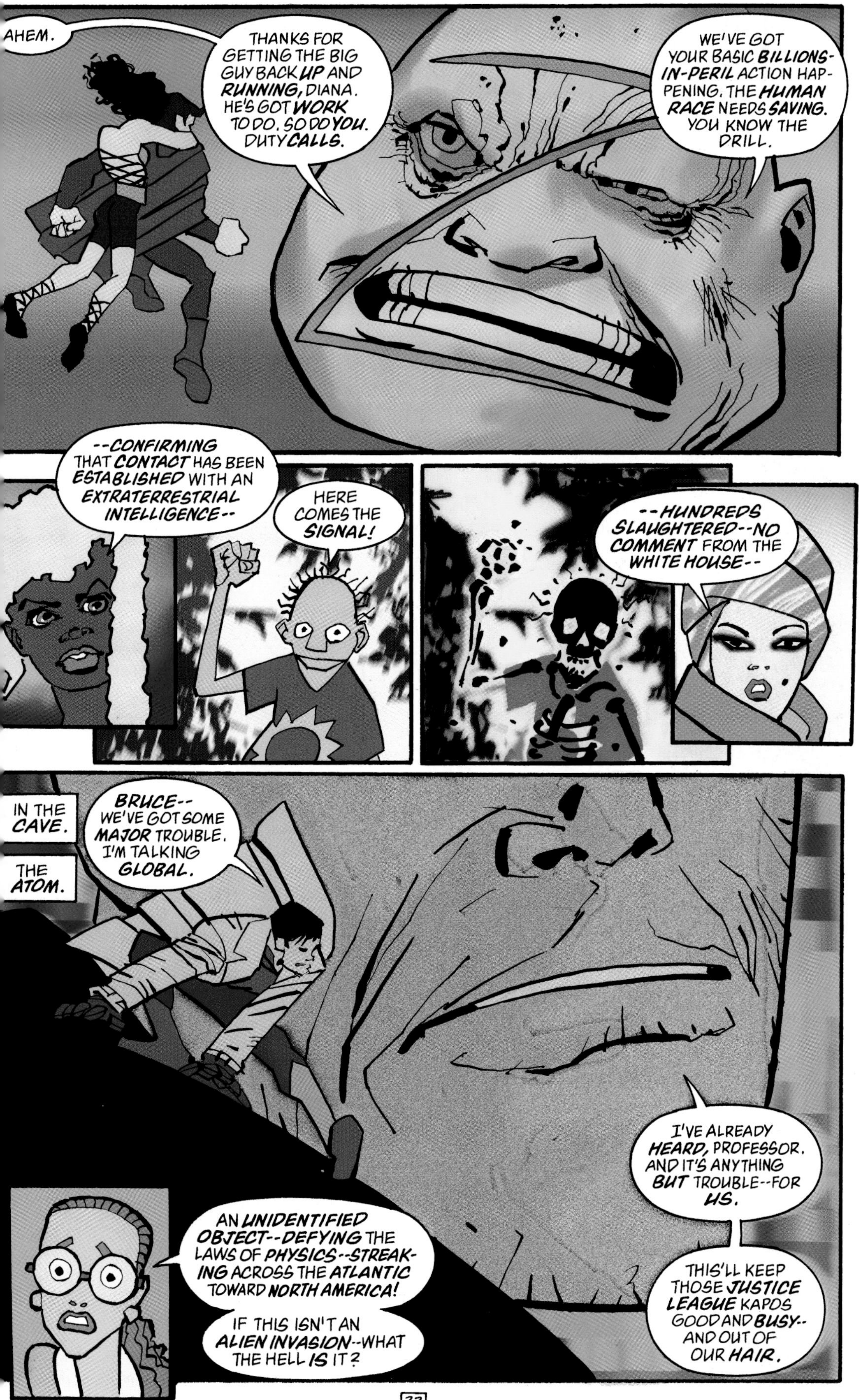
AHEM.
THANKS FOR GETTING THE BIG GUY BACK UP AND RUNNING, DIANA. HE'S GOT WORK TO DO. SO DO YOU. DUTY CALLS.
WE'VE GOT YOUR BASIC BILLIONS-IN-PERIL ACTION HAP-PENING. THE HUMAN RACE NEEDS SAVING. YOU KNOW THE DRILL.
--CONFIRMING THAT CONTACT HAS BEEN ESTABLISHED WITH AN EXTRATERRESTRIAL INTELLIGENCE--
HERE COMES THE SIGNAL!
--HUNDREDS SLAUGHTERED--NO COMMENT FROM THE WHITE HOUSE--
IN THE CAVE.
THE ATOM.
BRUCE-- WE'VE GOT SOME MAJOR TROUBLE. I'M TALKING GLOBAL.
I'VE ALREADY HEARD, PROFESSOR. AND IT'S ANYTHING BUT TROUBLE--FOR US.
AN UNIDENTIFIED OBJECT--DEFYING THE LAWS OF PHYSICS--STREAK-ING ACROSS THE ATLANTIC TOWARD NORTH AMERICA!
IF THIS ISN'T AN ALIEN INVASION--WHAT THE HELL IS IT?
THIS'LL KEEP THOSE JUSTICE LEAGUE KAPOS GOOD AND BUSY-- AND OUT OF OUR HAIR.

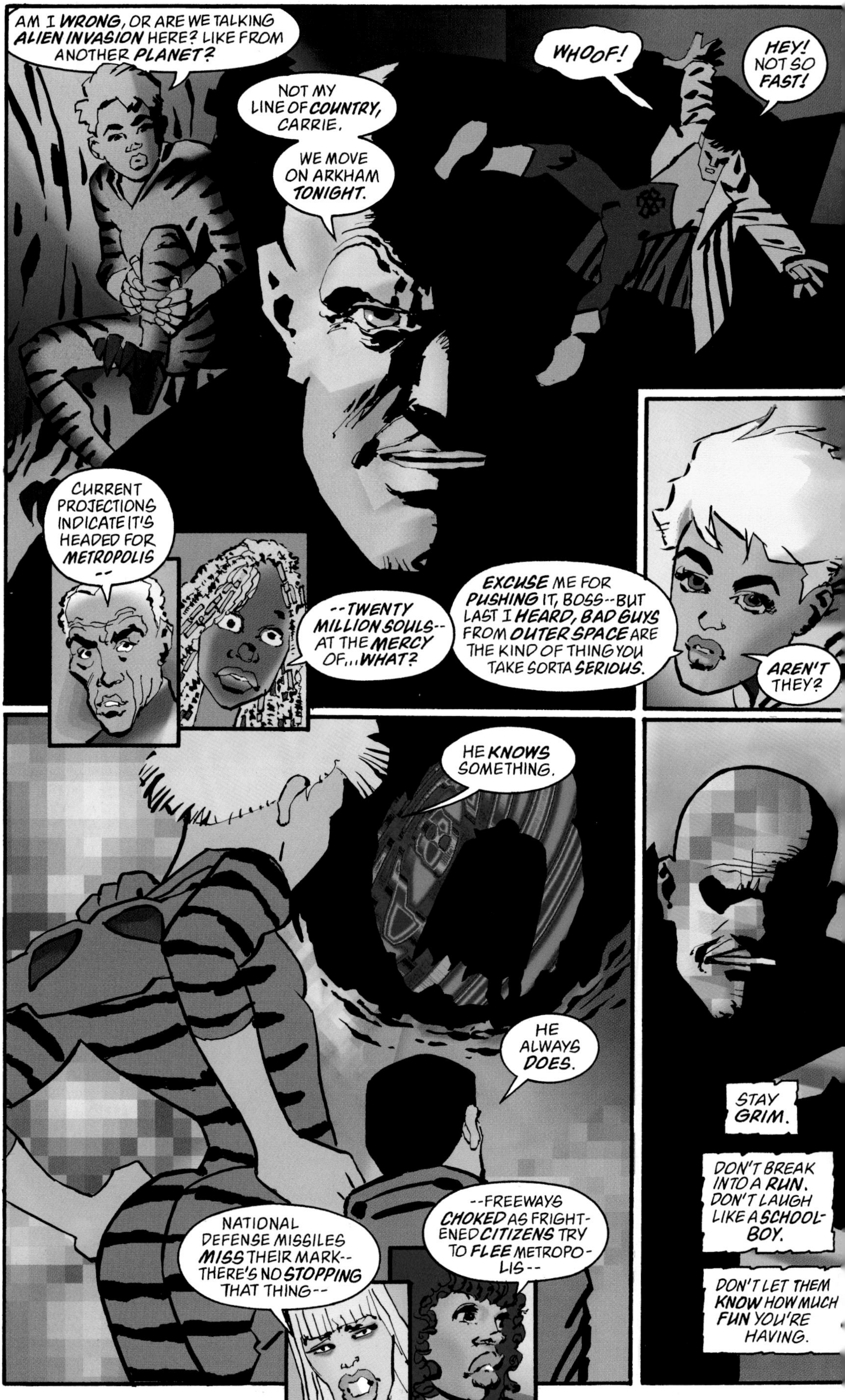
AM I WRONG, OR ARE WE TALKING ALIEN INVASION HERE? LIKE FROM ANOTHER PLANET?
NOT MY LINE OF COUNTRY, CARRIE.
WE MOVE ON ARKHAM TONIGHT.
WHOOF!
HEY! NOT SO FAST!
CURRENT PROJECTIONS INDICATE IT'S HEADED FOR METROPOLIS --
--TWENTY MILLION SOULS-- AT THE MERCY OF...WHAT?
EXCUSE ME FOR PUSHING IT, BOSS--BUT LAST I HEARD, BAD GUYS FROM OUTER SPACE ARE THE KIND OF THING YOU TAKE SORTA SERIOUS.
AREN'T THEY?
HE KNOWS SOMETHING.
HE ALWAYS DOES.
NATIONAL DEFENSE MISSILES MISS THEIR MARK-- THERE'S NO STOPPING THAT THING--
--FREEWAYS CHOKED AS FRIGHT-ENED CITIZENS TRY TO FLEE METROPO-LIS--
STAY GRIM.
DON'T BREAK INTO A RUN. DON'T LAUGH LIKE A SCHOOL-BOY.
DON'T LET THEM KNOW HOW MUCH FUN YOU'RE HAVING.

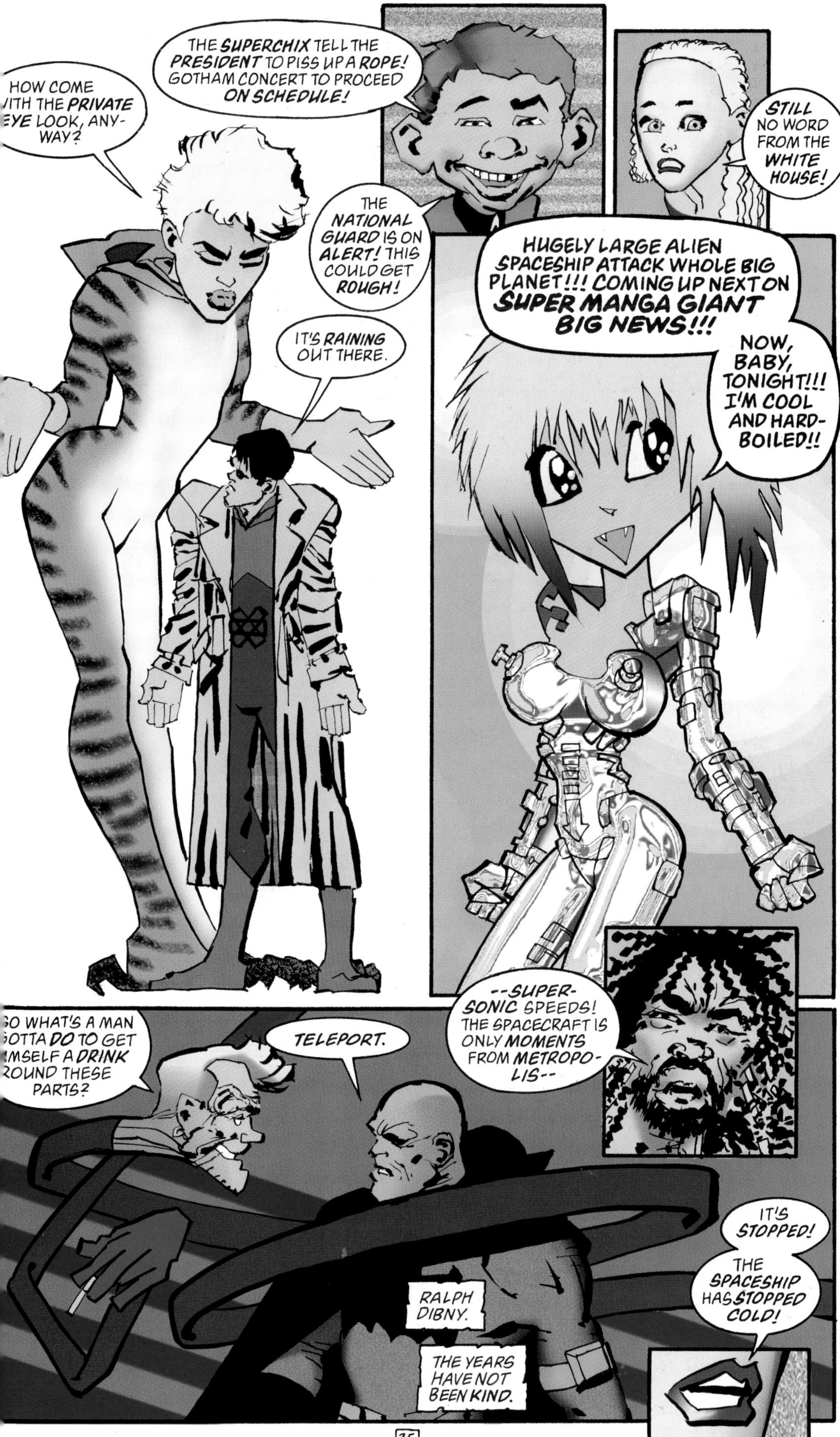
HOW COME WITH THE PRIVATE EYE LOOK, ANYWAY?
THE SUPERCHIX TELL THE PRESIDENT TO PISS UP A ROPE! GOTHAM CONCERT TO PROCEED ON SCHEDULE!
THE NATIONAL GUARD IS ON ALERT! THIS COULD GET ROUGH!
STILL NO WORD FROM THE WHITE HOUSE!
IT'S RAINING OUT THERE.
HUGELY LARGE ALIEN SPACESHIP ATTACK WHOLE BIG PLANET!!! COMING UP NEXT ON SUPER MANGA GIANT BIG NEWS!!!
NOW, BABY, TONIGHT!!! I'M COOL AND HARD-BOILED!!
--SUPERSONIC SPEEDS! THE SPACECRAFT IS ONLY MOMENTS FROM METROPOLIS--
SO WHAT'S A MAN GOTTA DO TO GET HIMSELF A DRINK 'ROUND THESE PARTS?
TELEPORT.
RALPH DIBNY.
THE YEARS HAVE NOT BEEN KIND.
IT'S STOPPED!
THE SPACESHIP HAS STOPPED COLD!

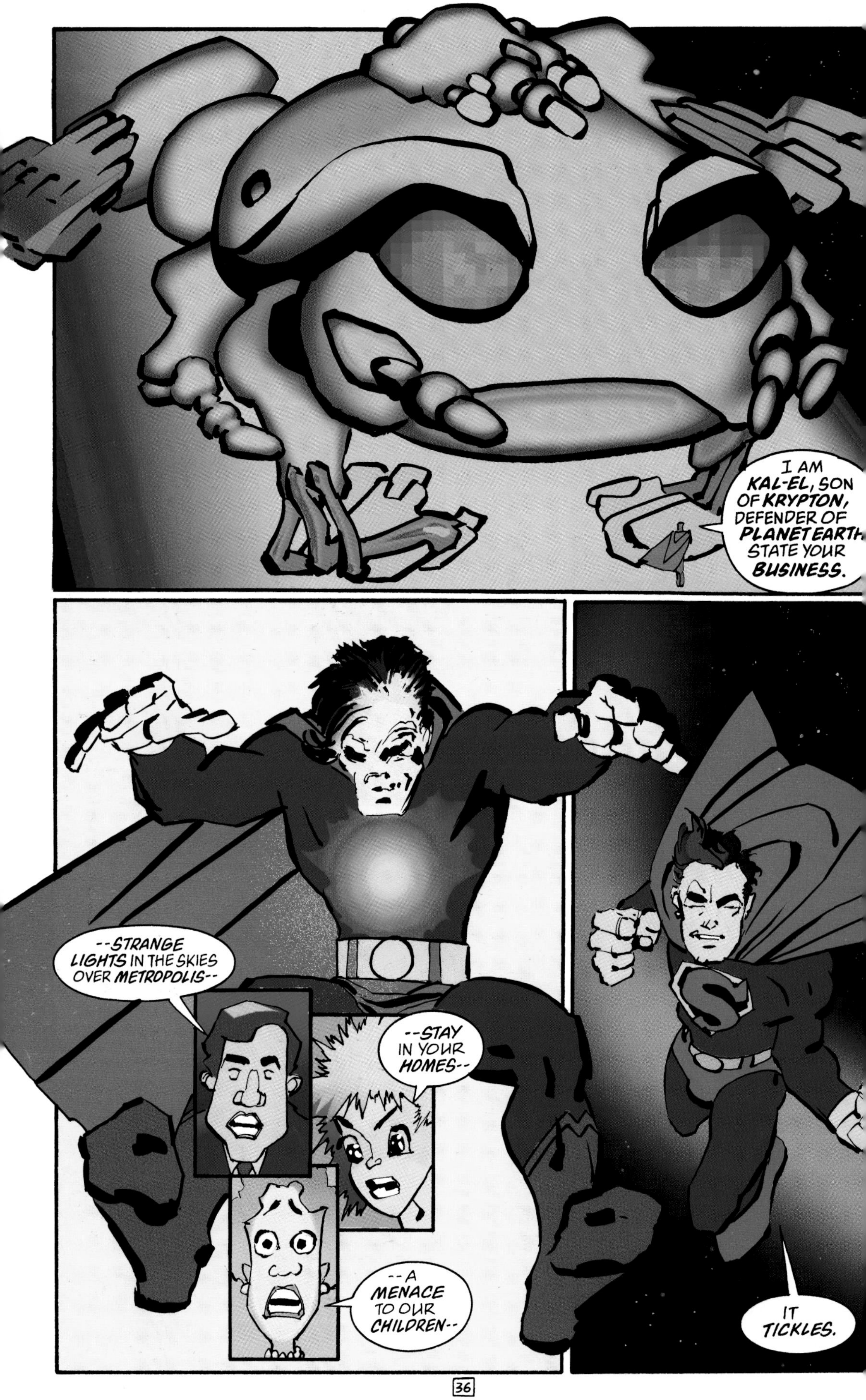
I AM KAL-EL, SON OF KRYPTON, DEFENDER OF PLANET EARTH. STATE YOUR BUSINESS.
--STRANGE LIGHTS IN THE SKIES OVER METROPOLIS--
--STAY IN YOUR HOMES--
--A MENACE TO OUR CHILDREN--
IT TICKLES.

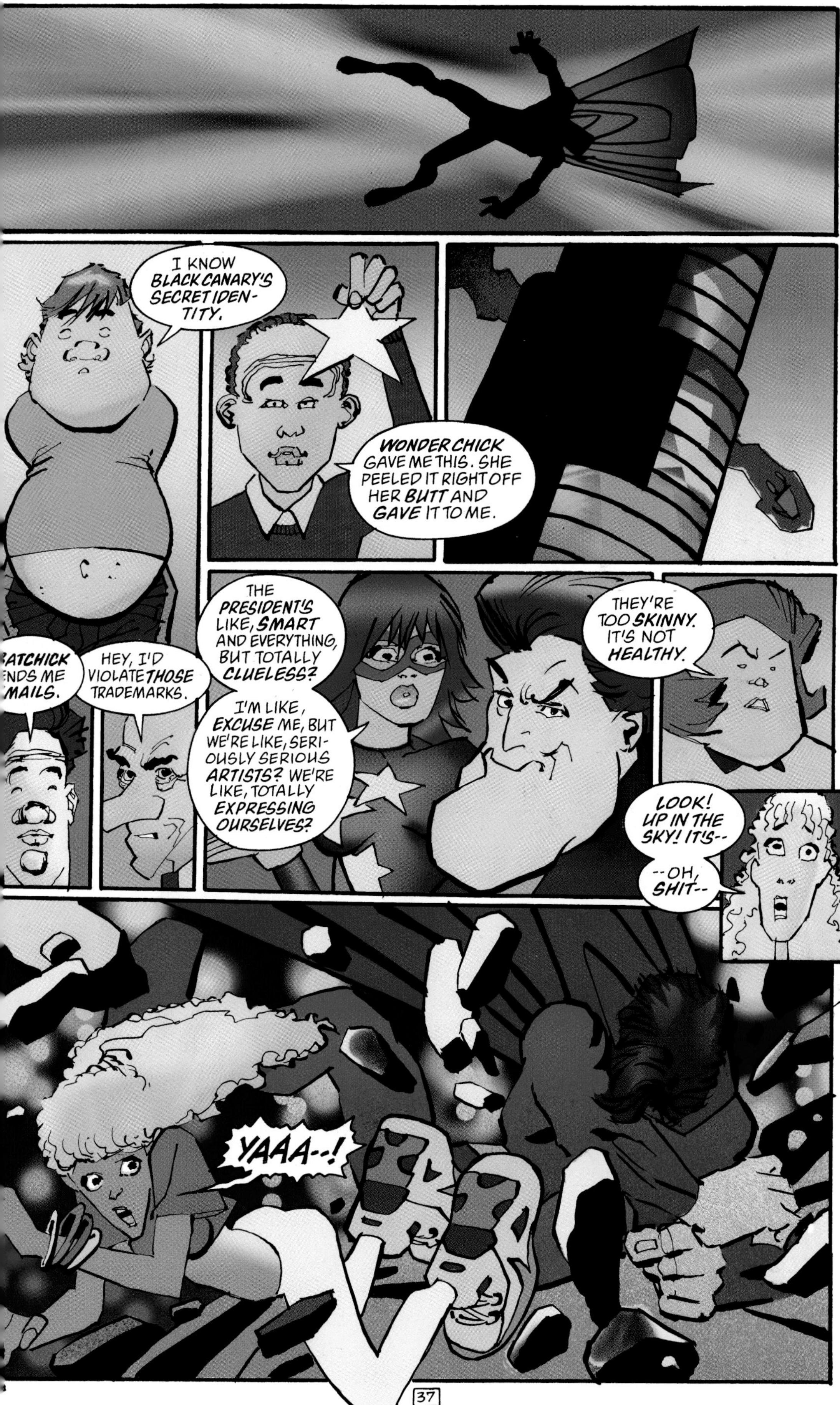
I KNOW BLACK CANARY'S SECRET IDEN-TITY.
WONDER CHICK GAVE ME THIS. SHE PEELED IT RIGHT OFF HER BUTT AND GAVE IT TO ME.
ATCHICK ENDS ME MAILS.
HEY, I'D VIOLATE THOSE TRADEMARKS.
THE PRESIDENT'S LIKE, SMART AND EVERYTHING, BUT TOTALLY CLUELESS?
I'M LIKE, EXCUSE ME, BUT WE'RE LIKE, SERI-OUSLY SERIOUS ARTISTS? WE'RE LIKE, TOTALLY EXPRESSING OURSELVES?
THEY'RE TOO SKINNY. IT'S NOT HEALTHY.
LOOK! UP IN THE SKY! IT'S--
--OH, SHIT--
YAAA--!

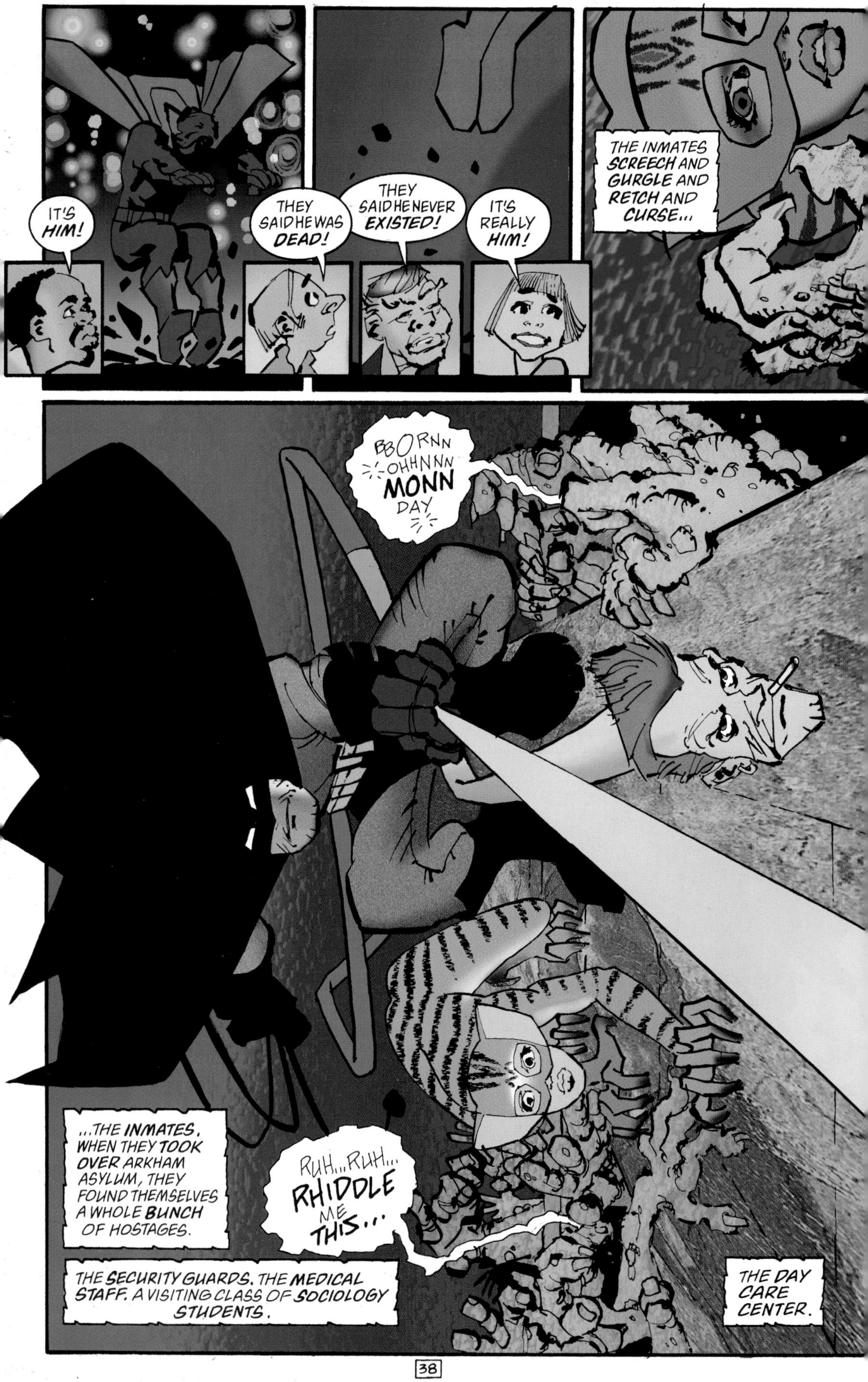

IT'S HIM!
THEY SAID HE WAS DEAD!
THEY SAID HE NEVER EXISTED!
IT'S REALLY HIM!
THE INMATES SCREECH AND GURGLE AND RETCH AND CURSE...
BBORNN OHHNNN MONN DAY
...THE INMATES, WHEN THEY TOOK OVER ARKHAM ASYLUM, THEY FOUND THEMSELVES A WHOLE BUNCH OF HOSTAGES.
RUH... RUH... RHIDDLE ME THIS...
THE SECURITY GUARDS. THE MEDICAL STAFF. A VISITING CLASS OF SOCIOLOGY STUDENTS.
THE DAY CARE CENTER.

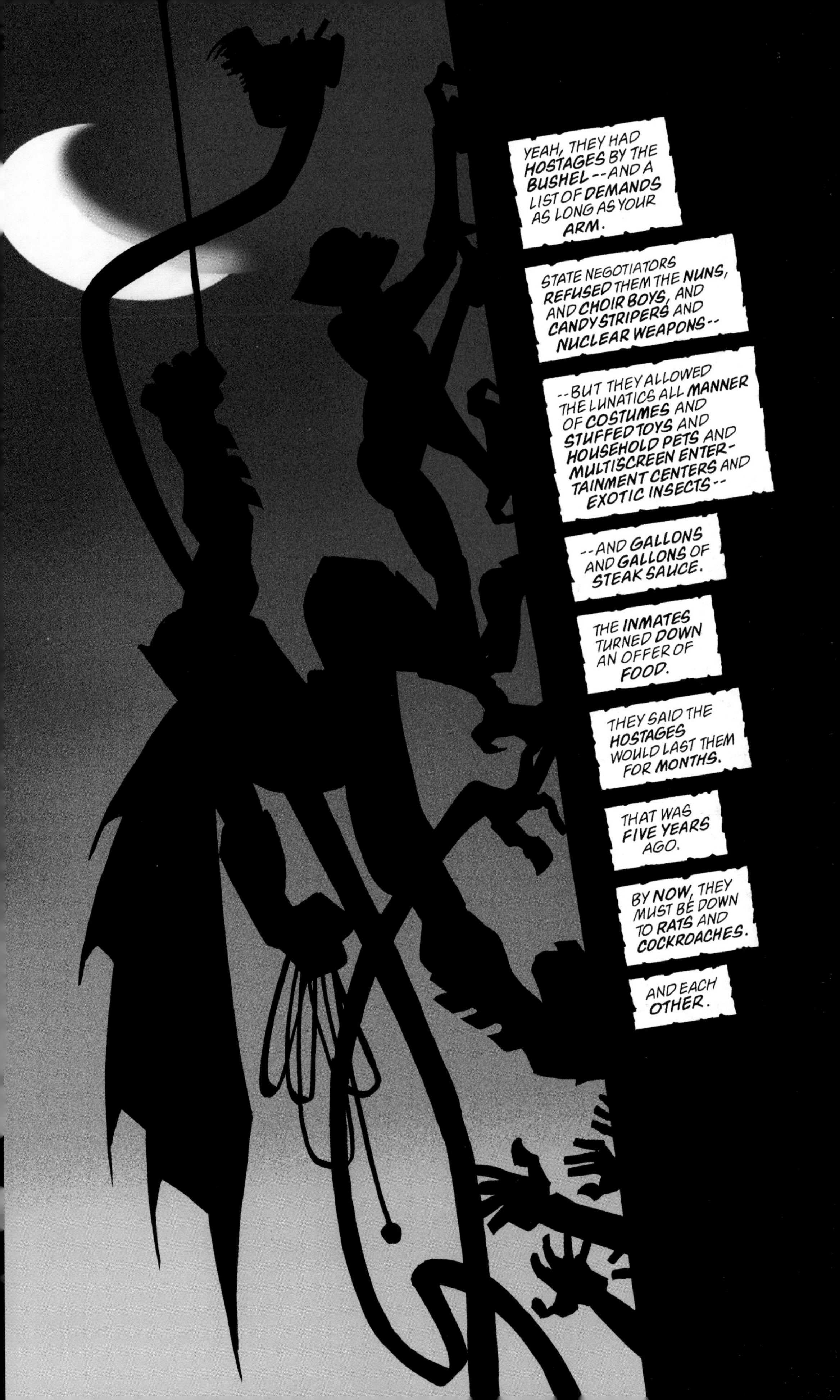
YEAH, THEY HAD HOSTAGES BY THE BUSHEL--AND A LIST OF DEMANDS AS LONG AS YOUR ARM.
STATE NEGOTIATORS REFUSED THEM THE NUNS, AND CHOIR BOYS, AND CANDY STRIPERS AND NUCLEAR WEAPONS--
--BUT THEY ALLOWED THE LUNATICS ALL MANNER OF COSTUMES AND STUFFED TOYS AND HOUSEHOLD PETS AND MULTISCREEN ENTER-TAINMENT CENTERS AND EXOTIC INSECTS--
--AND GALLONS AND GALLONS OF STEAK SAUCE.
THE INMATES TURNED DOWN AN OFFER OF FOOD.
THEY SAID THE HOSTAGES WOULD LAST THEM FOR MONTHS.
THAT WAS FIVE YEARS AGO.
BY NOW, THEY MUST BE DOWN TO RATS AND COCKROACHES.
AND EACH OTHER.

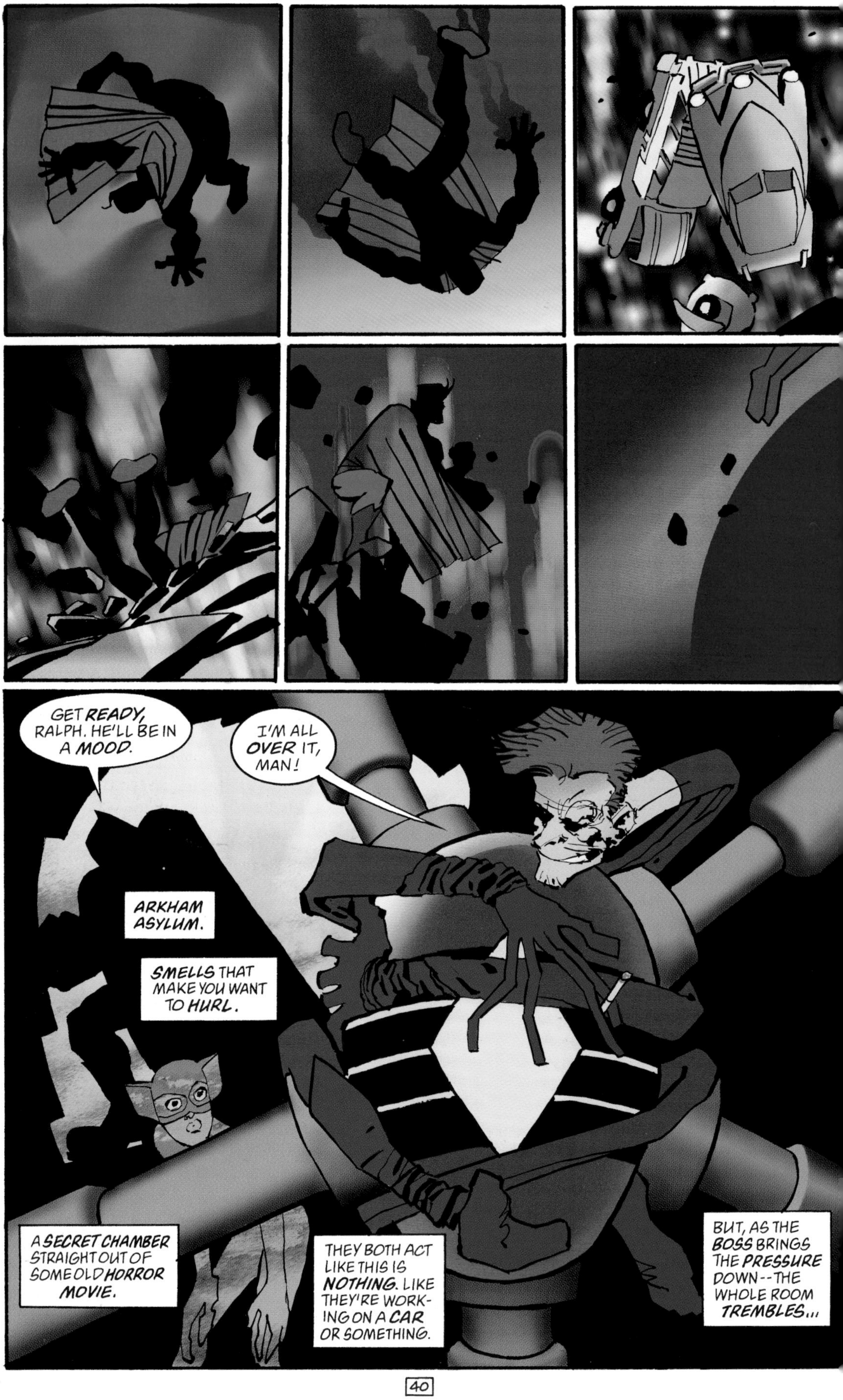

GET READY, RALPH. HE'LL BE IN A MOOD.
I'M ALL OVER IT, MAN!
ARKHAM ASYLUM.
SMELLS THAT MAKE YOU WANT TO HURL.
A SECRET CHAMBER STRAIGHT OUT OF SOME OLD HORROR MOVIE.
THEY BOTH ACT LIKE THIS IS NOTHING. LIKE THEY'RE WORKING ON A CAR OR SOMETHING.
BUT, AS THE BOSS BRINGS THE PRESSURE DOWN--THE WHOLE ROOM TREMBLES...

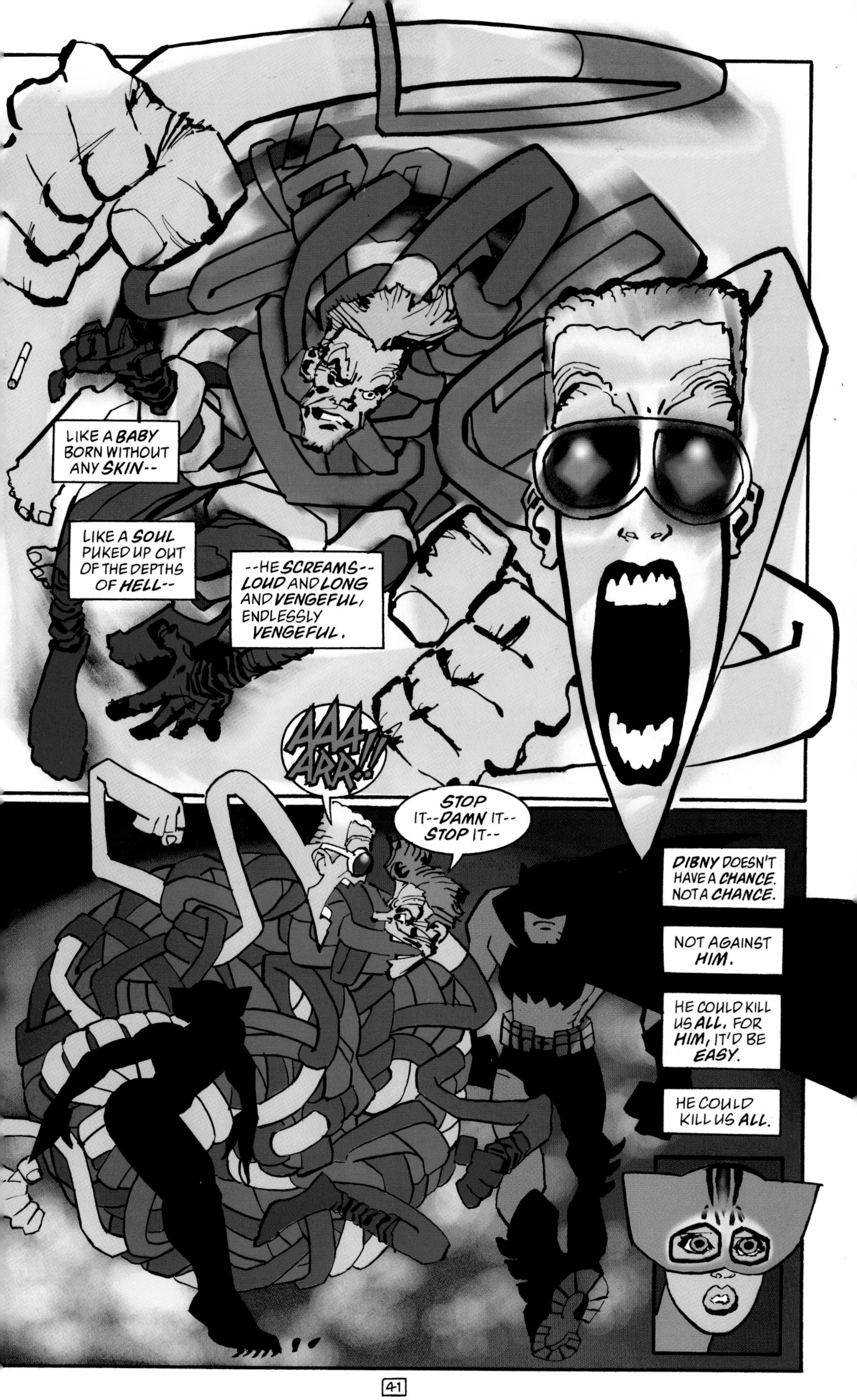
LIKE A BABY BORN WITHOUT ANY SKIN--
LIKE A SOUL PUKED UP OUT OF THE DEPTHS OF HELL--
--HE SCREAMS-- LOUD AND LONG AND VENGEFUL, ENDLESSLY VENGEFUL.
AAAARR!!
STOP IT--DAMN IT-- STOP IT--
DIBNY DOESN'T HAVE A CHANCE. NOT A CHANCE.
NOT AGAINST HIM.
HE COULD KILL US ALL. FOR HIM, IT'D BE EASY.
HE COULD KILL US ALL.

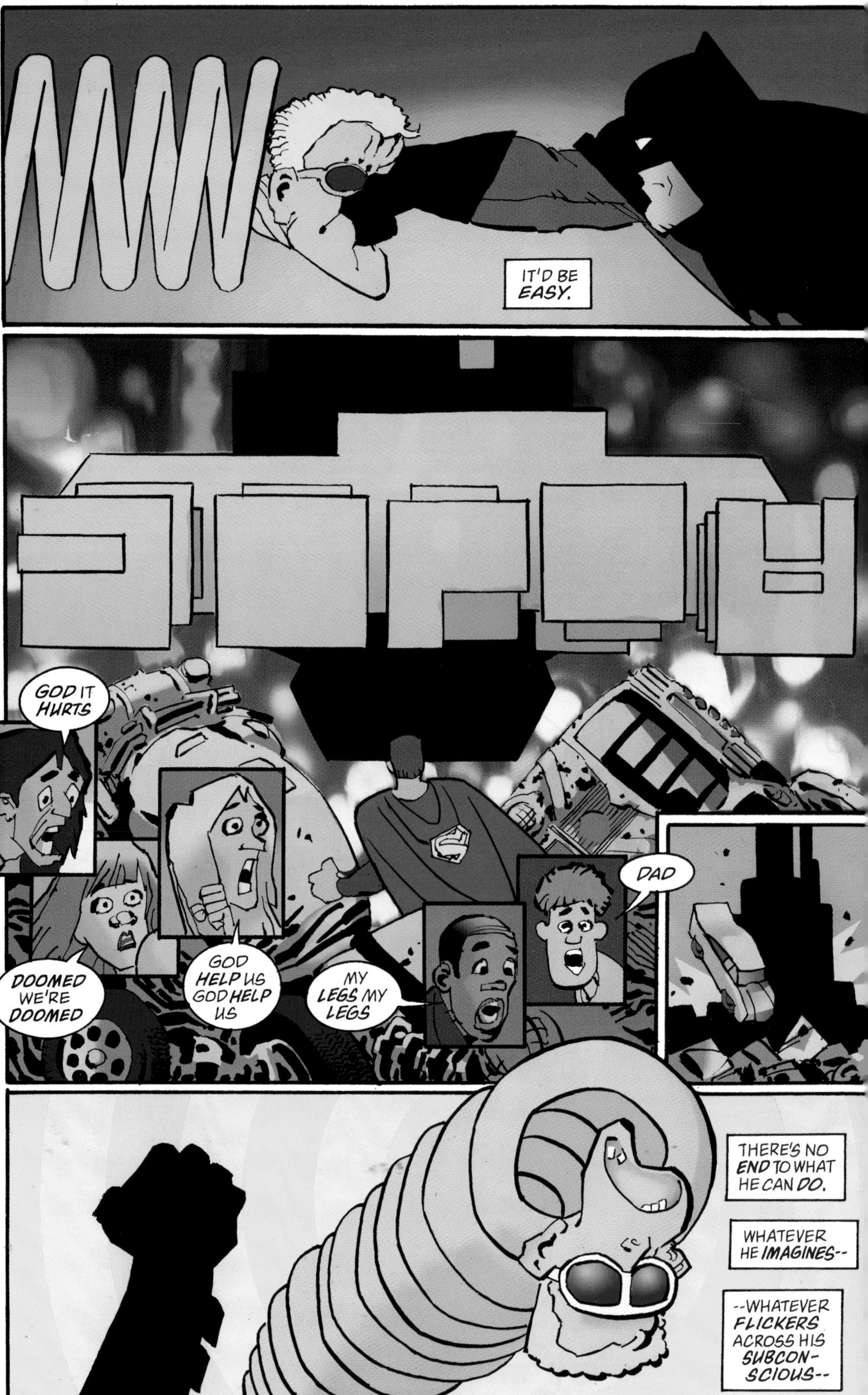
IT'D BE EASY.
GOD IT HURTS
DOOMED WE'RE DOOMED
GOD HELP US GOD HELP US
MY LEGS MY LEGS
DAD
THERE'S NO END TO WHAT HE CAN DO.
WHATEVER HE IMAGINES--
--WHATEVER FLICKERS ACROSS HIS SUBCON-SCIOUS--

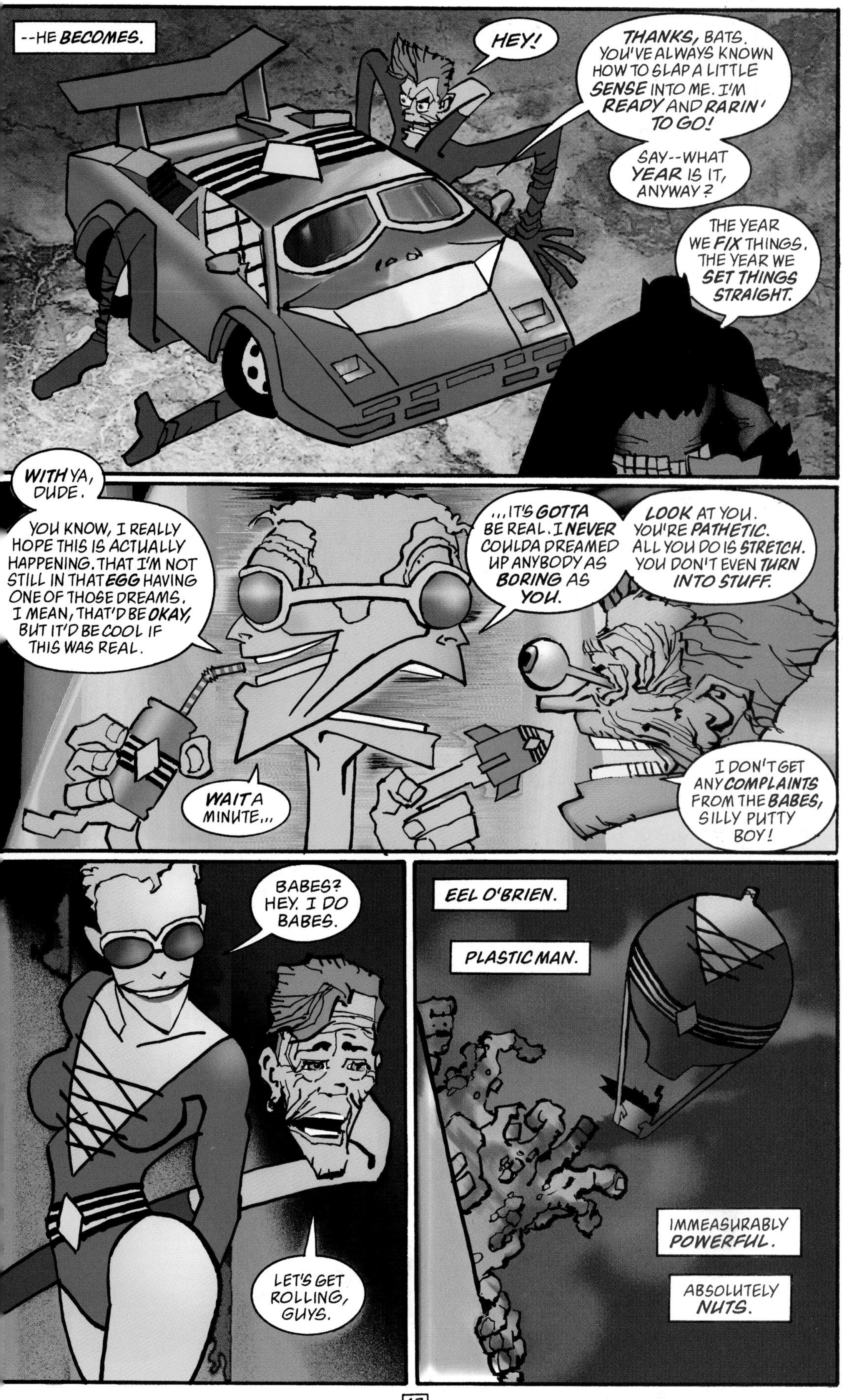
--HE BECOMES.
HEY!
THANKS, BATS. YOU'VE ALWAYS KNOWN HOW TO SLAP A LITTLE SENSE INTO ME. I'M READY AND RARIN' TO GO!
SAY--WHAT YEAR IS IT, ANYWAY?
THE YEAR WE FIX THINGS. THE YEAR WE SET THINGS STRAIGHT.
WITH YA, DUDE.
YOU KNOW, I REALLY HOPE THIS IS ACTUALLY HAPPENING. THAT I'M NOT STILL IN THAT EGG HAVING ONE OF THOSE DREAMS. I MEAN, THAT'D BE OKAY, BUT IT'D BE COOL IF THIS WAS REAL.
WAIT A MINUTE...
...IT'S GOTTA BE REAL. I NEVER COULDA DREAMED UP ANYBODY AS BORING AS YOU.
LOOK AT YOU. YOU'RE PATHETIC. ALL YOU DO IS STRETCH. YOU DON'T EVEN TURN INTO STUFF.
I DON'T GET ANY COMPLAINTS FROM THE BABES, SILLY PUTTY BOY!
BABES? HEY. I DO BABES.
LET'S GET ROLLING, GUYS.
EEL O'BRIEN.
PLASTIC MAN.
IMMEASURABLY POWERFUL.
ABSOLUTELY NUTS.

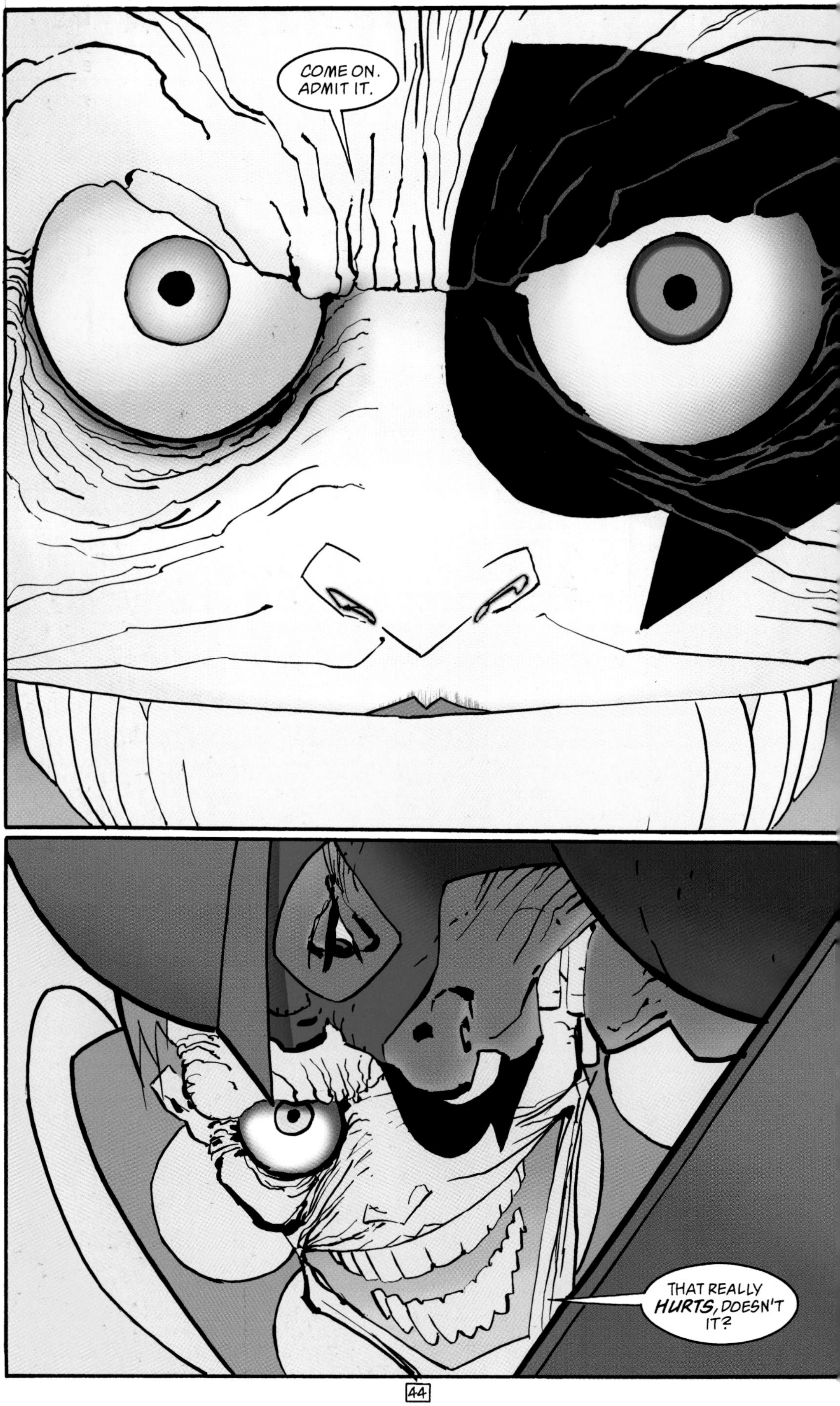
COME ON. ADMIT IT.
THAT REALLY *HURTS*, DOESN'T IT?

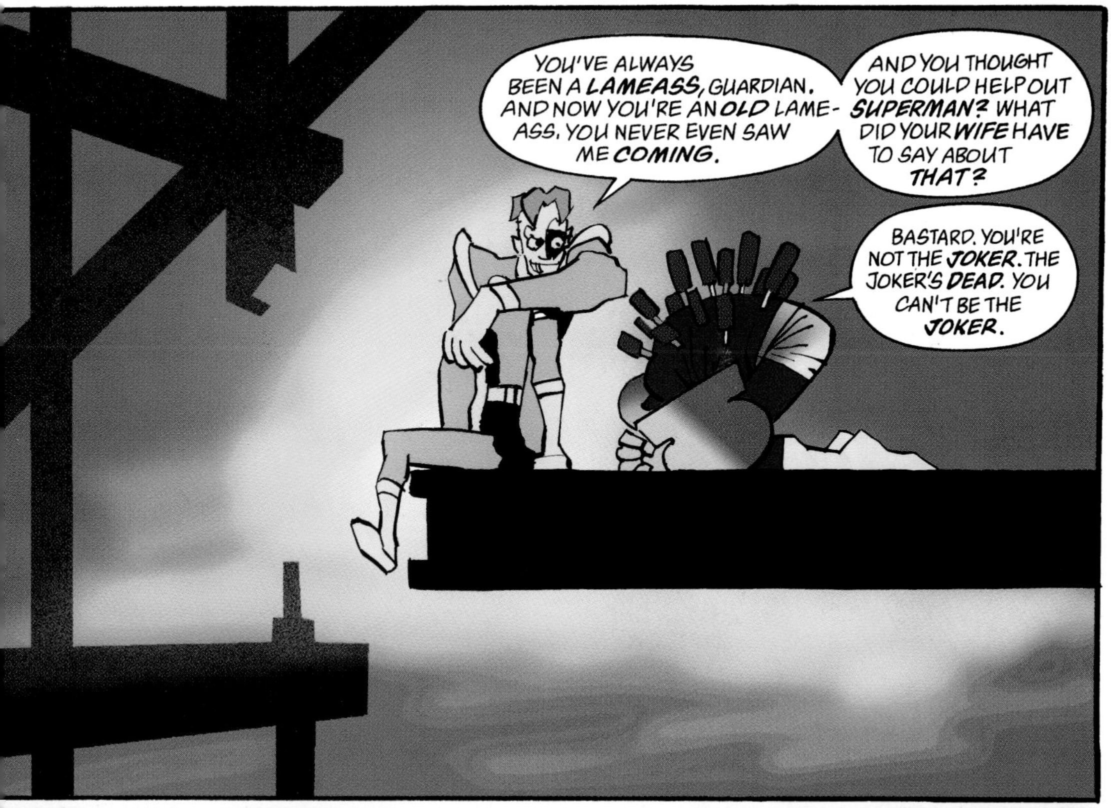
YOU'VE ALWAYS BEEN A LAMEASS, GUARDIAN. AND NOW YOU'RE AN OLD LAME-ASS. YOU NEVER EVEN SAW ME COMING.
AND YOU THOUGHT YOU COULD HELP OUT SUPERMAN? WHAT DID YOUR WIFE HAVE TO SAY ABOUT THAT?
BASTARD. YOU'RE NOT THE JOKER. THE JOKER'S DEAD. YOU CAN'T BE THE JOKER.

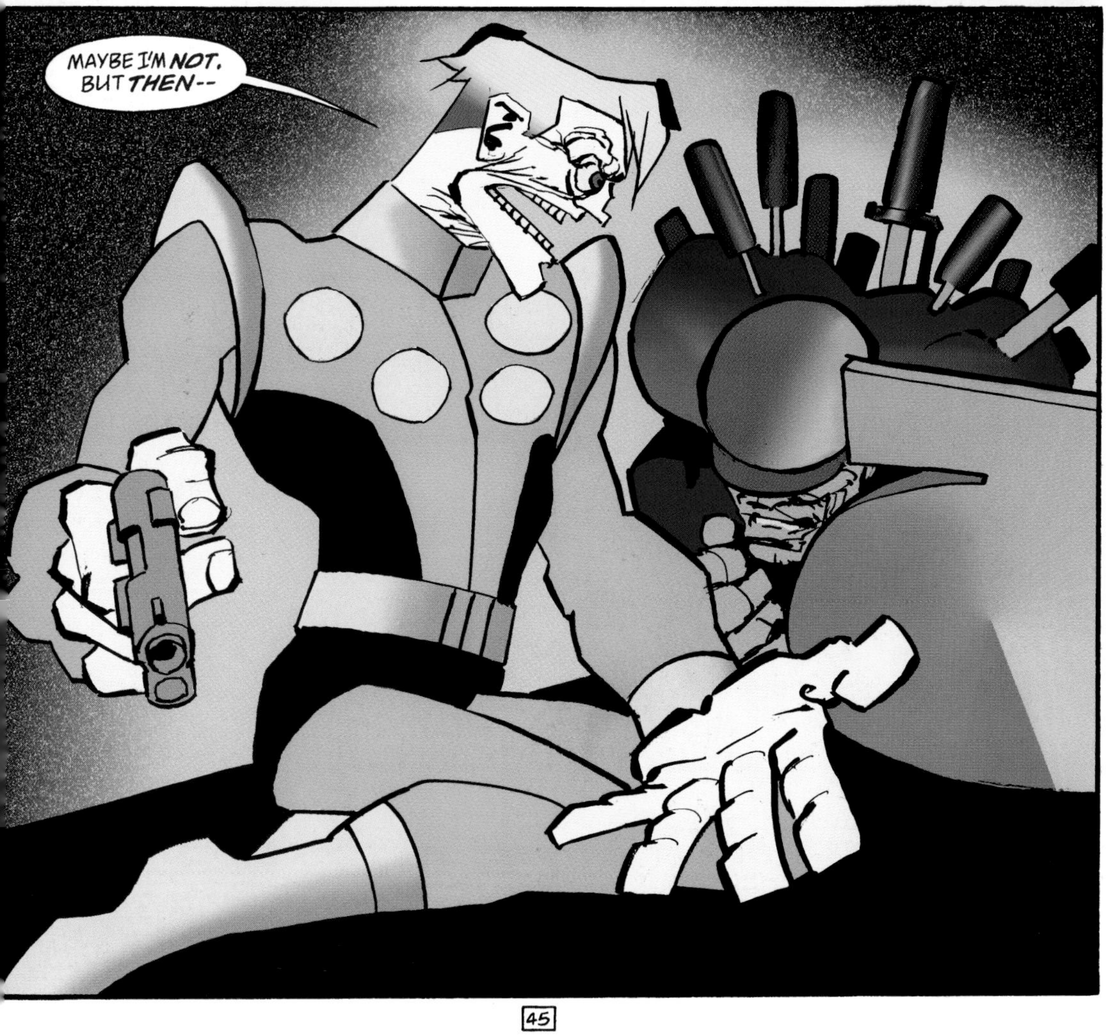
MAYBE I'M NOT. BUT THEN--

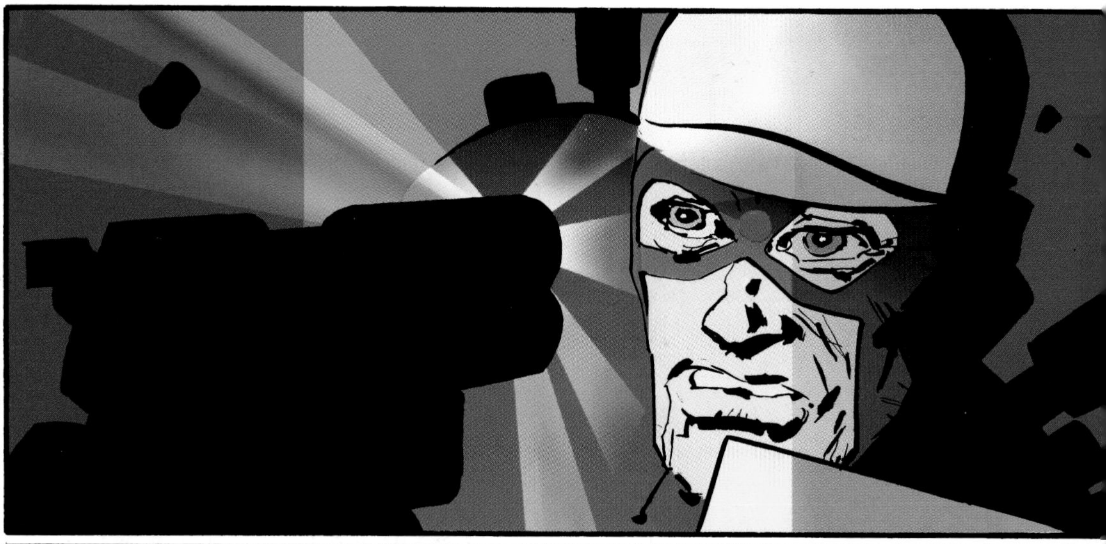

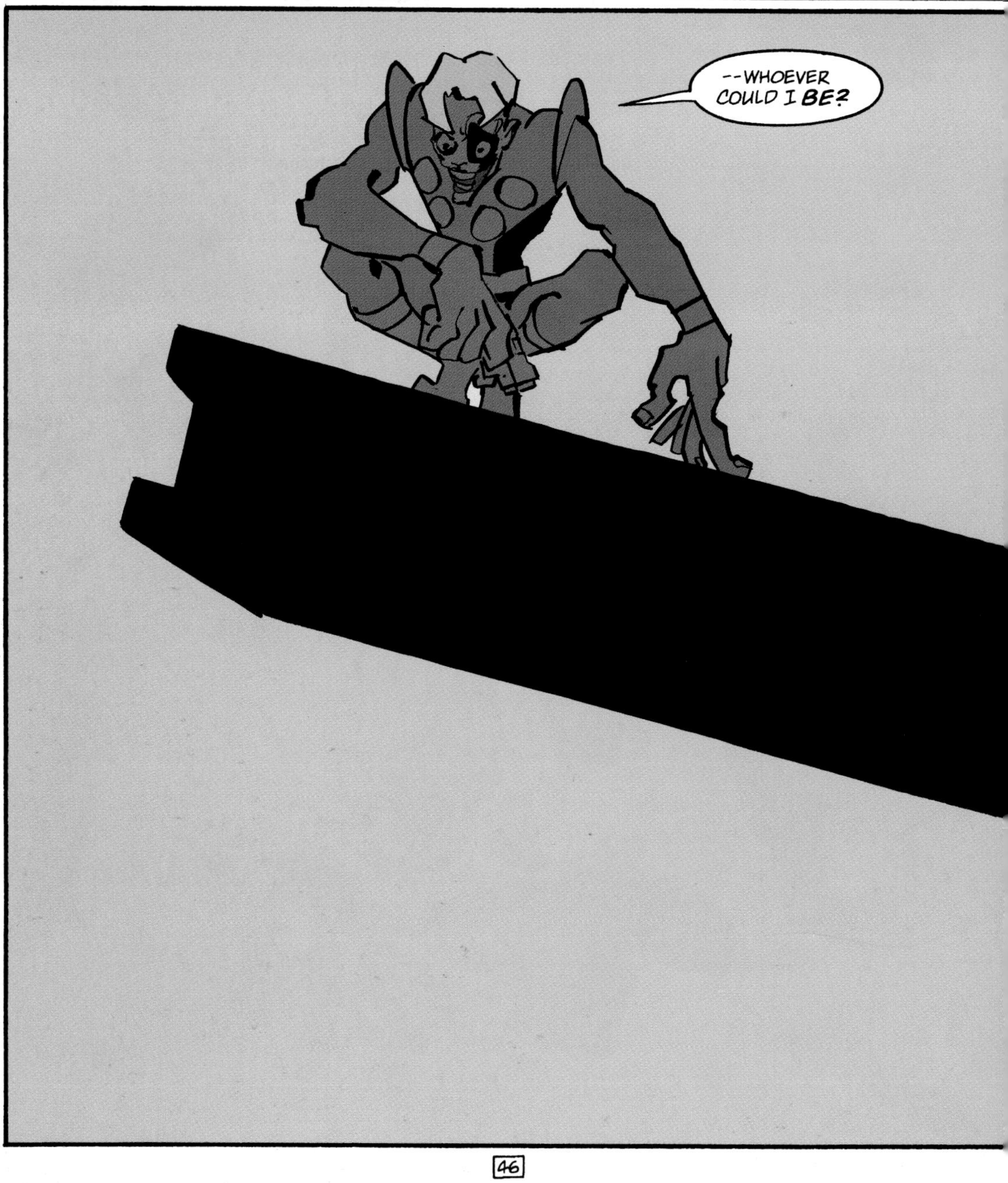
--WHOEVER COULD I BE?

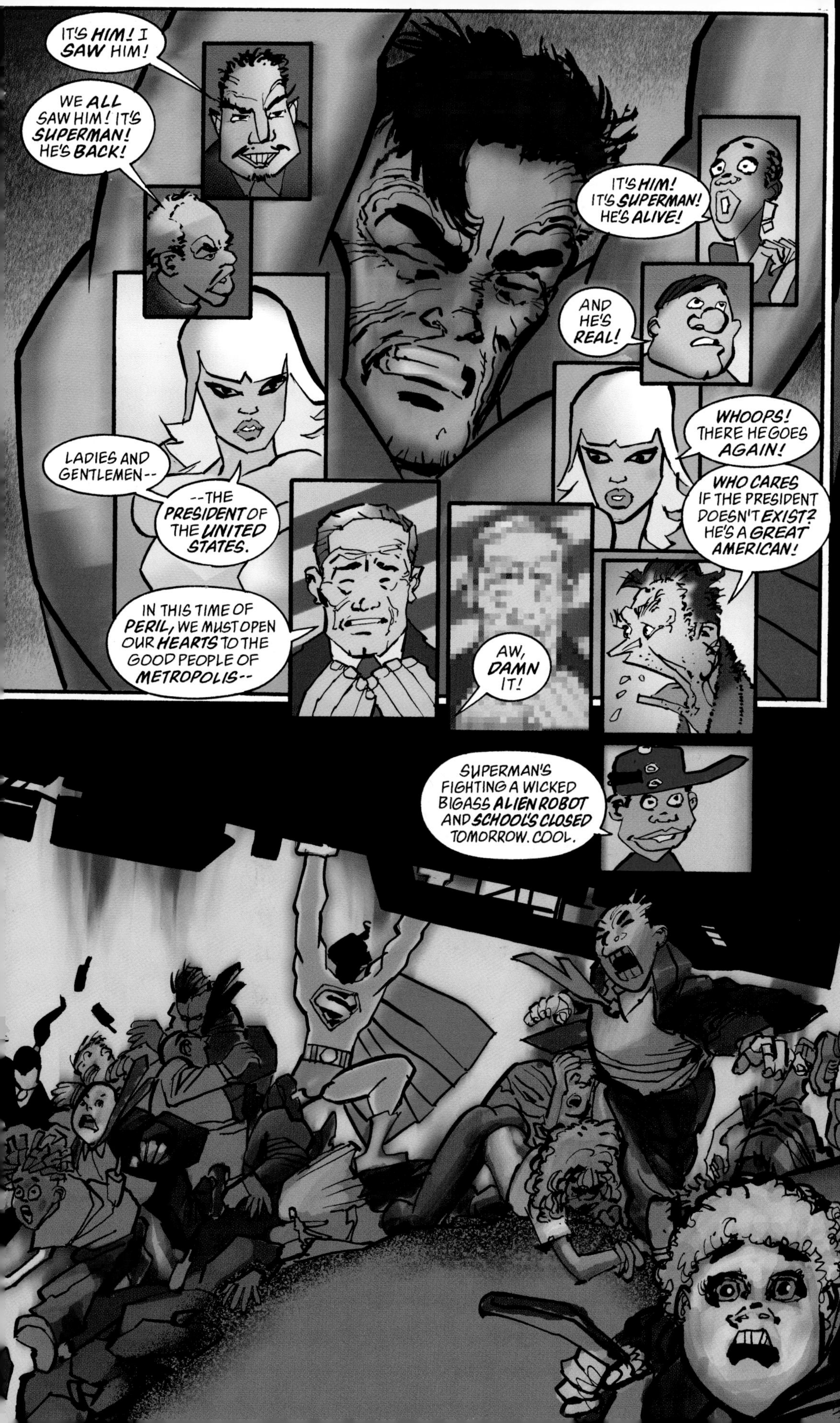
IT'S HIM! I SAW HIM!
WE ALL SAW HIM! IT'S SUPERMAN! HE'S BACK!
IT'S HIM! IT'S SUPERMAN! HE'S ALIVE!
AND HE'S REAL!
LADIES AND GENTLEMEN--
--THE PRESIDENT OF THE UNITED STATES.
WHOOPS! THERE HE GOES AGAIN!
WHO CARES IF THE PRESIDENT DOESN'T EXIST? HE'S A GREAT AMERICAN!
IN THIS TIME OF PERIL, WE MUST OPEN OUR HEARTS TO THE GOOD PEOPLE OF METROPOLIS--
AW, DAMN IT!
SUPERMAN'S FIGHTING A WICKED BIGASS ALIEN ROBOT AND SCHOOL'S CLOSED TOMORROW. COOL.

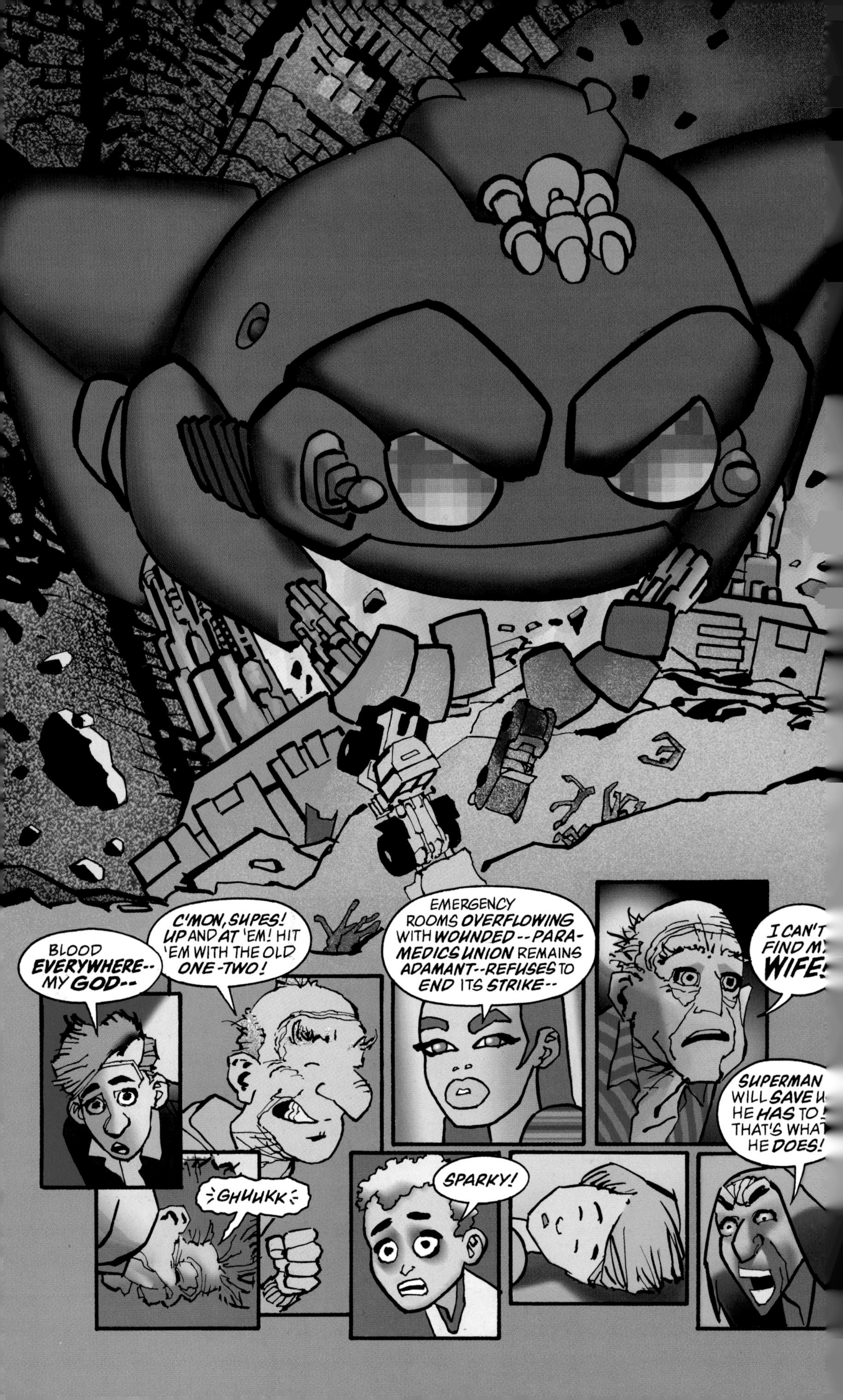
BLOOD EVERYWHERE-- MY GOD--
C'MON, SUPES! UP AND AT 'EM! HIT 'EM WITH THE OLD ONE-TWO!
EMERGENCY ROOMS OVERFLOWING WITH WOUNDED--PARAMEDICS UNION REMAINS ADAMANT--REFUSES TO END ITS STRIKE--
I CAN'T FIND MY WIFE!
GHUUKK
SPARKY!
SUPERMAN WILL SAVE US! HE HAS TO! THAT'S WHAT HE DOES!

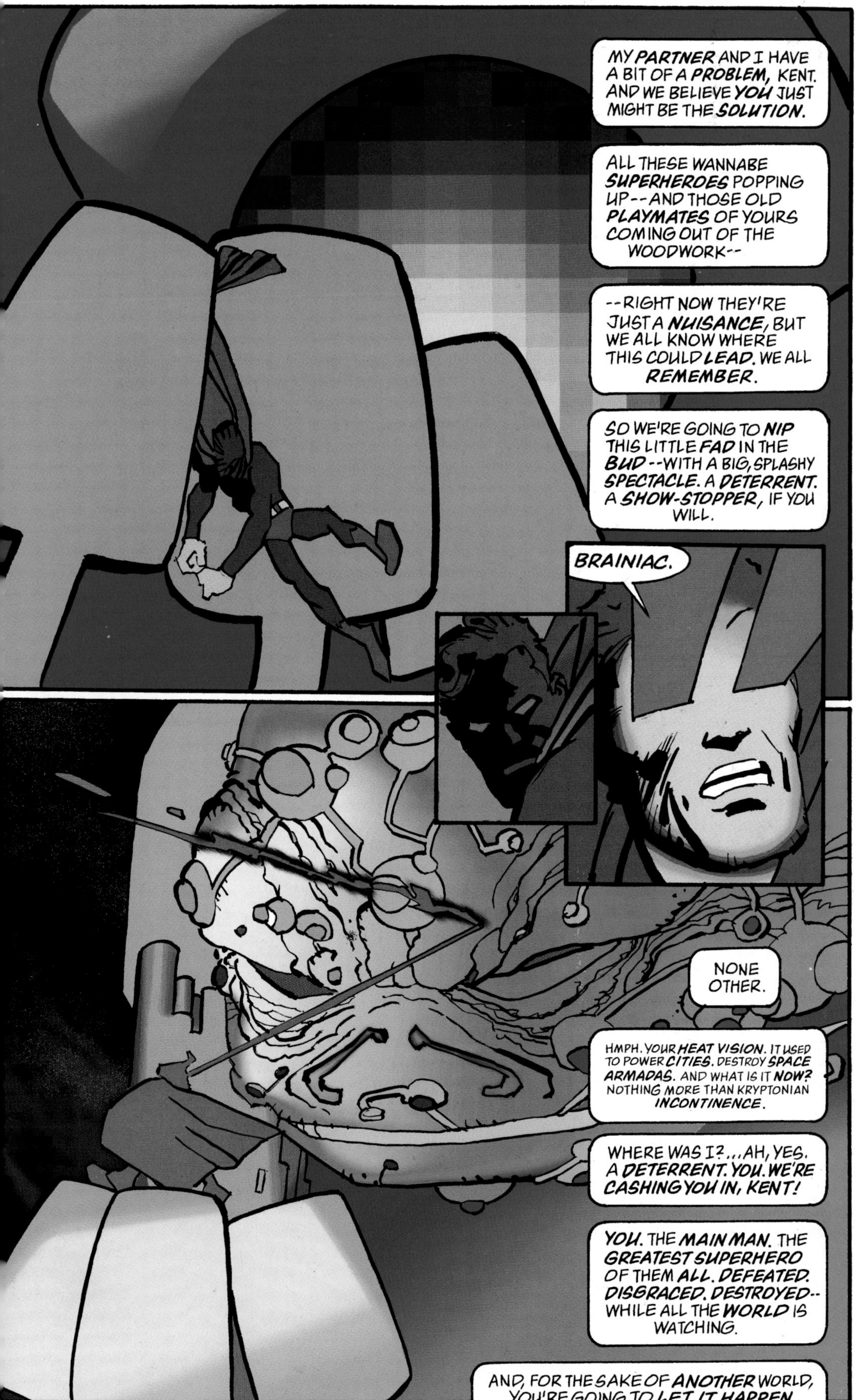
MY PARTNER AND I HAVE A BIT OF A PROBLEM, KENT. AND WE BELIEVE YOU JUST MIGHT BE THE SOLUTION.
ALL THESE WANNABE SUPERHEROES POPPING UP--AND THOSE OLD PLAYMATES OF YOURS COMING OUT OF THE WOODWORK--
--RIGHT NOW THEY'RE JUST A NUISANCE, BUT WE ALL KNOW WHERE THIS COULD LEAD. WE ALL REMEMBER.
SO WE'RE GOING TO NIP THIS LITTLE FAD IN THE BUD--WITH A BIG, SPLASHY SPECTACLE. A DETERRENT. A SHOW-STOPPER, IF YOU WILL.
BRAINIAC.
NONE OTHER.
HMPH. YOUR HEAT VISION. IT USED TO POWER CITIES. DESTROY SPACE ARMADAS. AND WHAT IS IT NOW? NOTHING MORE THAN KRYPTONIAN INCONTINENCE.
WHERE WAS I?...AH, YES. A DETERRENT. YOU. WE'RE CASHING YOU IN, KENT!
YOU. THE MAIN MAN. THE GREATEST SUPERHERO OF THEM ALL. DEFEATED. DISGRACED. DESTROYED--WHILE ALL THE WORLD IS WATCHING.
AND, FOR THE SAKE OF ANOTHER WORLD, YOU'RE GOING TO LET IT HAPPEN.

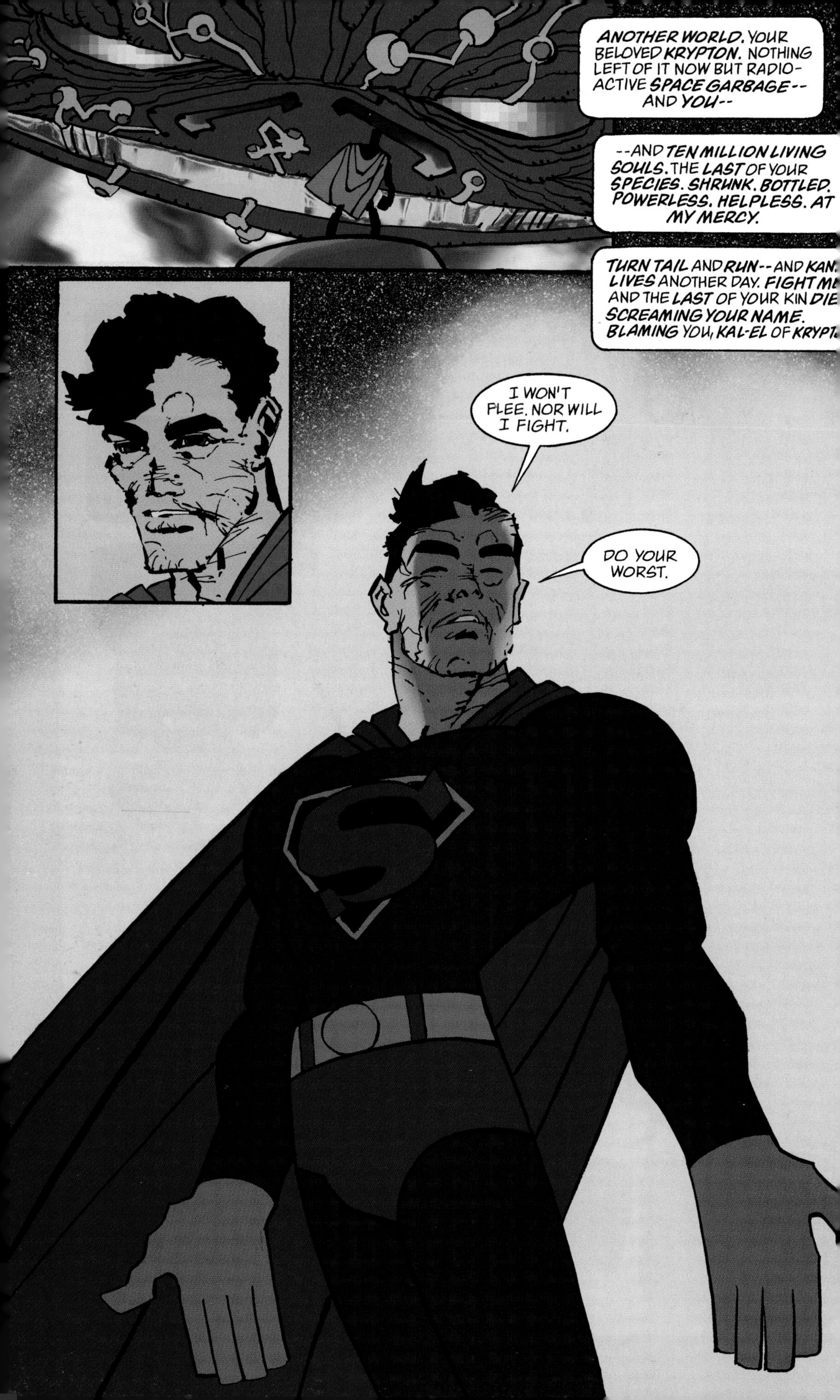

ANOTHER WORLD. YOUR BELOVED KRYPTON. NOTHING LEFT OF IT NOW BUT RADIO-ACTIVE SPACE GARBAGE-- AND YOU--
--AND TEN MILLION LIVING SOULS. THE LAST OF YOUR SPECIES. SHRUNK. BOTTLED. POWERLESS. HELPLESS. AT MY MERCY.
TURN TAIL AND RUN--AND KAN LIVES ANOTHER DAY. FIGHT M AND THE LAST OF YOUR KIN DIE SCREAMING YOUR NAME. BLAMING YOU, KAL-EL OF KRYPT
I WON'T FLEE. NOR WILL I FIGHT.
DO YOUR WORST.

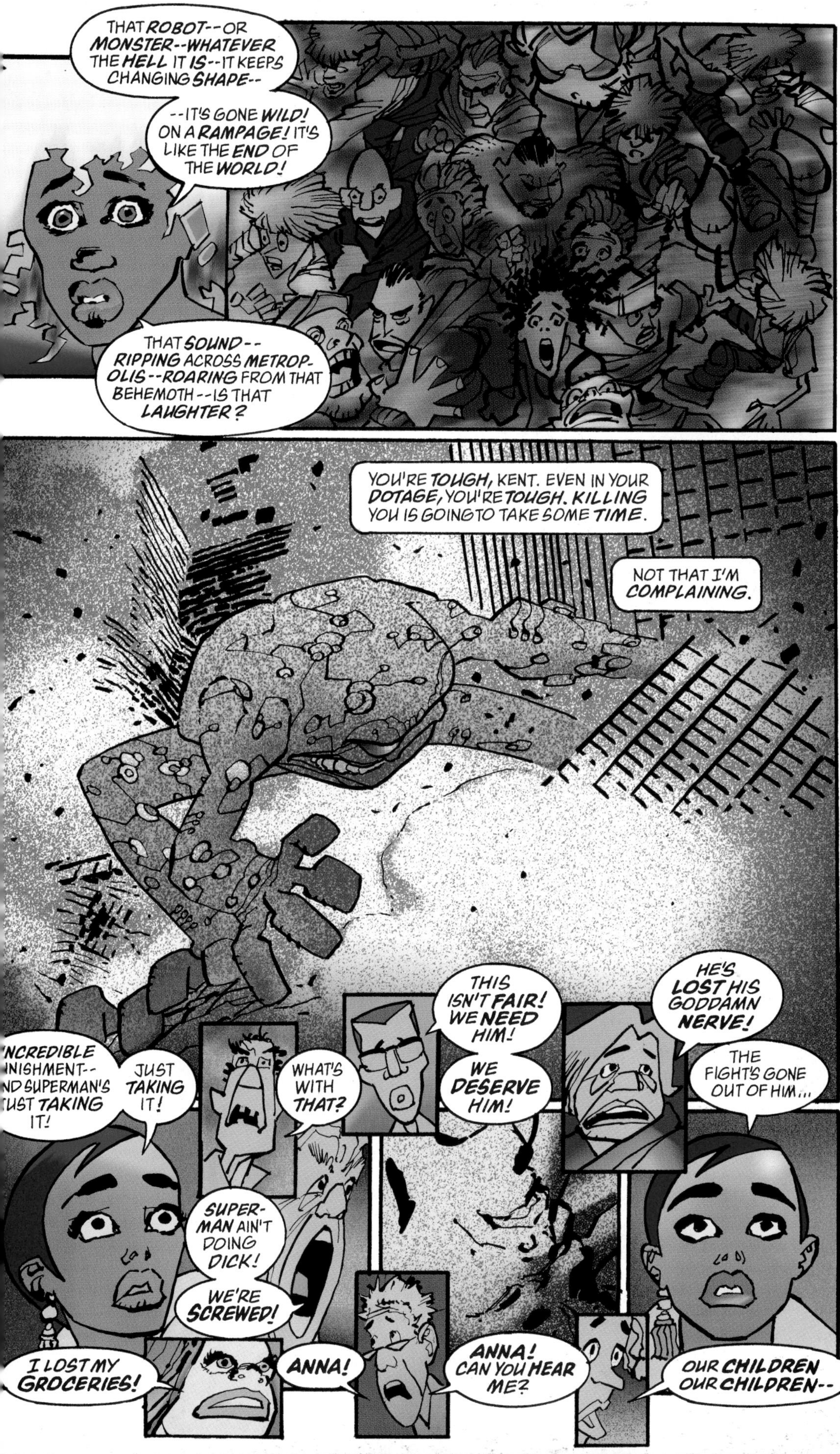

THAT ROBOT--OR MONSTER--WHATEVER THE HELL IT IS--IT KEEPS CHANGING SHAPE--
--IT'S GONE WILD! ON A RAMPAGE! IT'S LIKE THE END OF THE WORLD!
THAT SOUND--RIPPING ACROSS METROPOLIS--ROARING FROM THAT BEHEMOTH--IS THAT LAUGHTER?
YOU'RE TOUGH, KENT. EVEN IN YOUR DOTAGE, YOU'RE TOUGH. KILLING YOU IS GOING TO TAKE SOME TIME.
NOT THAT I'M COMPLAINING.
JUST TAKING IT!
WHAT'S WITH THAT?
THIS ISN'T FAIR! WE NEED HIM!
WE DESERVE HIM!
HE'S LOST HIS GODDAMN NERVE!
THE FIGHT'S GONE OUT OF HIM...
SUPERMAN AIN'T DOING DICK!
WE'RE SCREWED!
I LOST MY GROCERIES!
ANNA!
ANNA! CAN YOU HEAR ME?
OUR CHILDREN OUR CHILDREN--

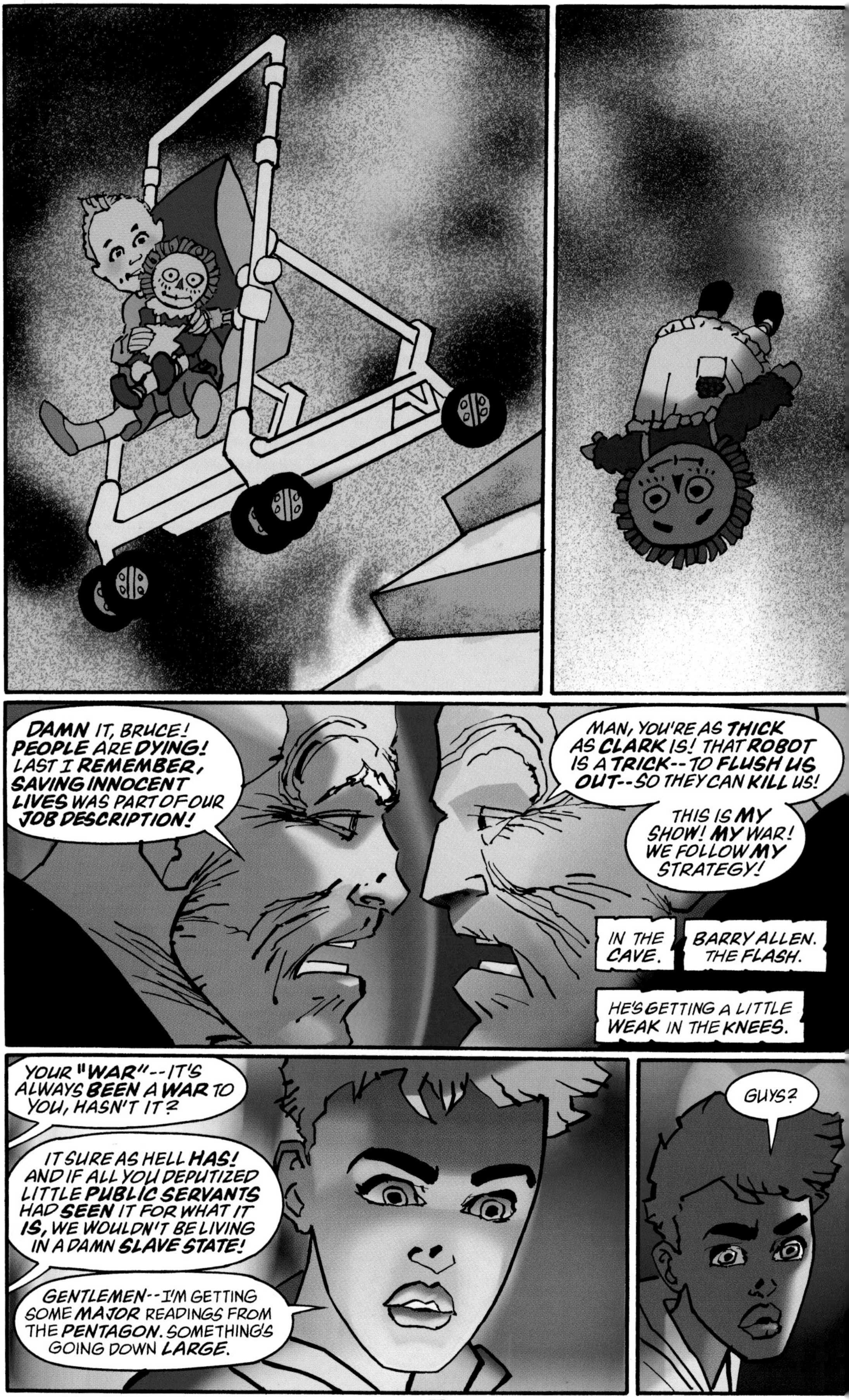
DAMN IT, BRUCE! PEOPLE ARE DYING! LAST I REMEMBER, SAVING INNOCENT LIVES WAS PART OF OUR JOB DESCRIPTION!
MAN, YOU'RE AS THICK AS CLARK IS! THAT ROBOT IS A TRICK--TO FLUSH US OUT--SO THEY CAN KILL US!
THIS IS MY SHOW! MY WAR! WE FOLLOW MY STRATEGY!
IN THE CAVE.
BARRY ALLEN. THE FLASH.
HE'S GETTING A LITTLE WEAK IN THE KNEES.
YOUR "WAR"--IT'S ALWAYS BEEN A WAR TO YOU, HASN'T IT?
IT SURE AS HELL HAS! AND IF ALL YOU DEPUTIZED LITTLE PUBLIC SERVANTS HAD SEEN IT FOR WHAT IT IS, WE WOULDN'T BE LIVING IN A DAMN SLAVE STATE!
GENTLEMEN--I'M GETTING SOME MAJOR READINGS FROM THE PENTAGON. SOMETHING'S GOING DOWN LARGE.
GUYS?

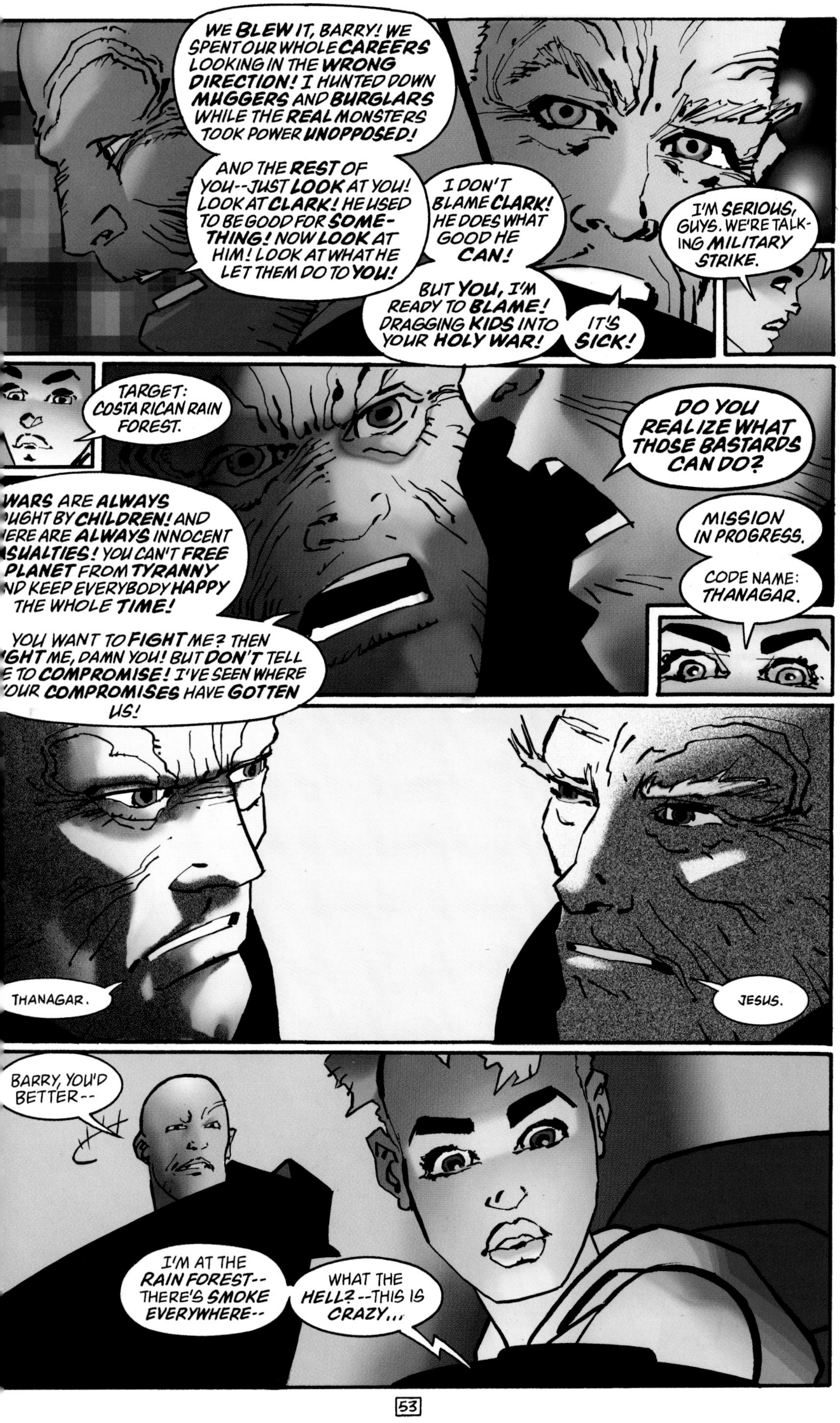
WE BLEW IT, BARRY! WE SPENT OUR WHOLE CAREERS LOOKING IN THE WRONG DIRECTION! I HUNTED DOWN MUGGERS AND BURGLARS WHILE THE REAL MONSTERS TOOK POWER UNOPPOSED!
AND THE REST OF YOU--JUST LOOK AT YOU! LOOK AT CLARK! HE USED TO BE GOOD FOR SOME-THING! NOW LOOK AT HIM! LOOK AT WHAT HE LET THEM DO TO YOU!
I DON'T BLAME CLARK! HE DOES WHAT GOOD HE CAN!
BUT YOU, I'M READY TO BLAME! DRAGGING KIDS INTO YOUR HOLY WAR!
IT'S SICK!
I'M SERIOUS, GUYS. WE'RE TALK-ING MILITARY STRIKE.
TARGET: COSTA RICAN RAIN FOREST.
DO YOU REALIZE WHAT THOSE BASTARDS CAN DO?
WARS ARE ALWAYS UGHT BY CHILDREN! AND ERE ARE ALWAYS INNOCENT SUALTIES! YOU CAN'T FREE PLANET FROM TYRANNY ND KEEP EVERYBODY HAPPY THE WHOLE TIME!
YOU WANT TO FIGHT ME? THEN GHT ME, DAMN YOU! BUT DON'T TELL E TO COMPROMISE! I'VE SEEN WHERE OUR COMPROMISES HAVE GOTTEN US!
MISSION IN PROGRESS.
CODE NAME: THANAGAR.
THANAGAR.
JESUS.
BARRY, YOU'D BETTER--
I'M AT THE RAIN FOREST-- THERE'S SMOKE EVERYWHERE--
WHAT THE HELL? --THIS IS CRAZY...

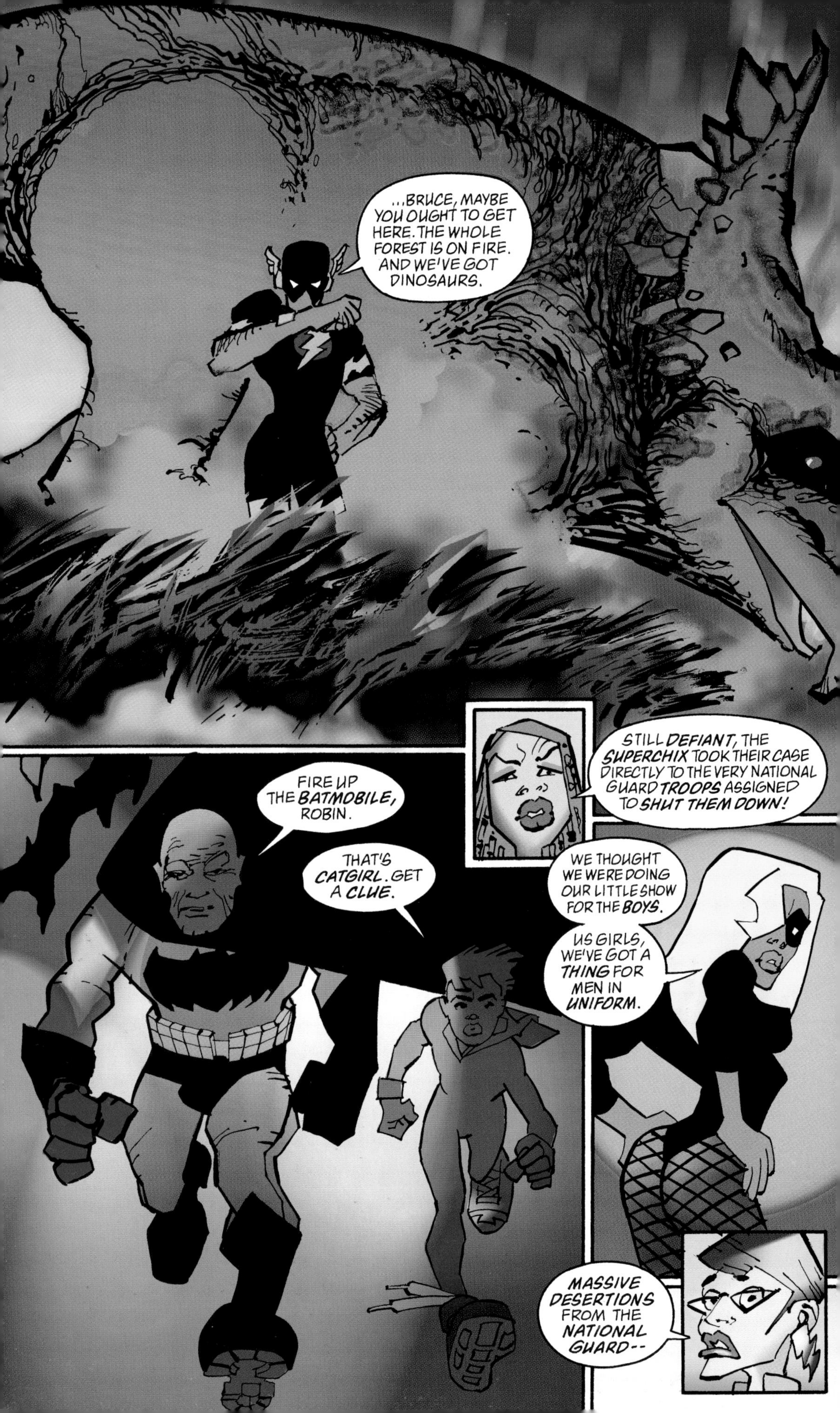

...BRUCE, MAYBE YOU OUGHT TO GET HERE. THE WHOLE FOREST IS ON FIRE. AND WE'VE GOT DINOSAURS.
FIRE UP THE BATMOBILE, ROBIN.
THAT'S CATGIRL. GET A CLUE.
STILL DEFIANT, THE SUPERCHIX TOOK THEIR CASE DIRECTLY TO THE VERY NATIONAL GUARD TROOPS ASSIGNED TO SHUT THEM DOWN!
WE THOUGHT WE WERE DOING OUR LITTLE SHOW FOR THE BOYS.
US GIRLS, WE'VE GOT A THING FOR MEN IN UNIFORM.
MASSIVE DESERTIONS FROM THE NATIONAL GUARD--

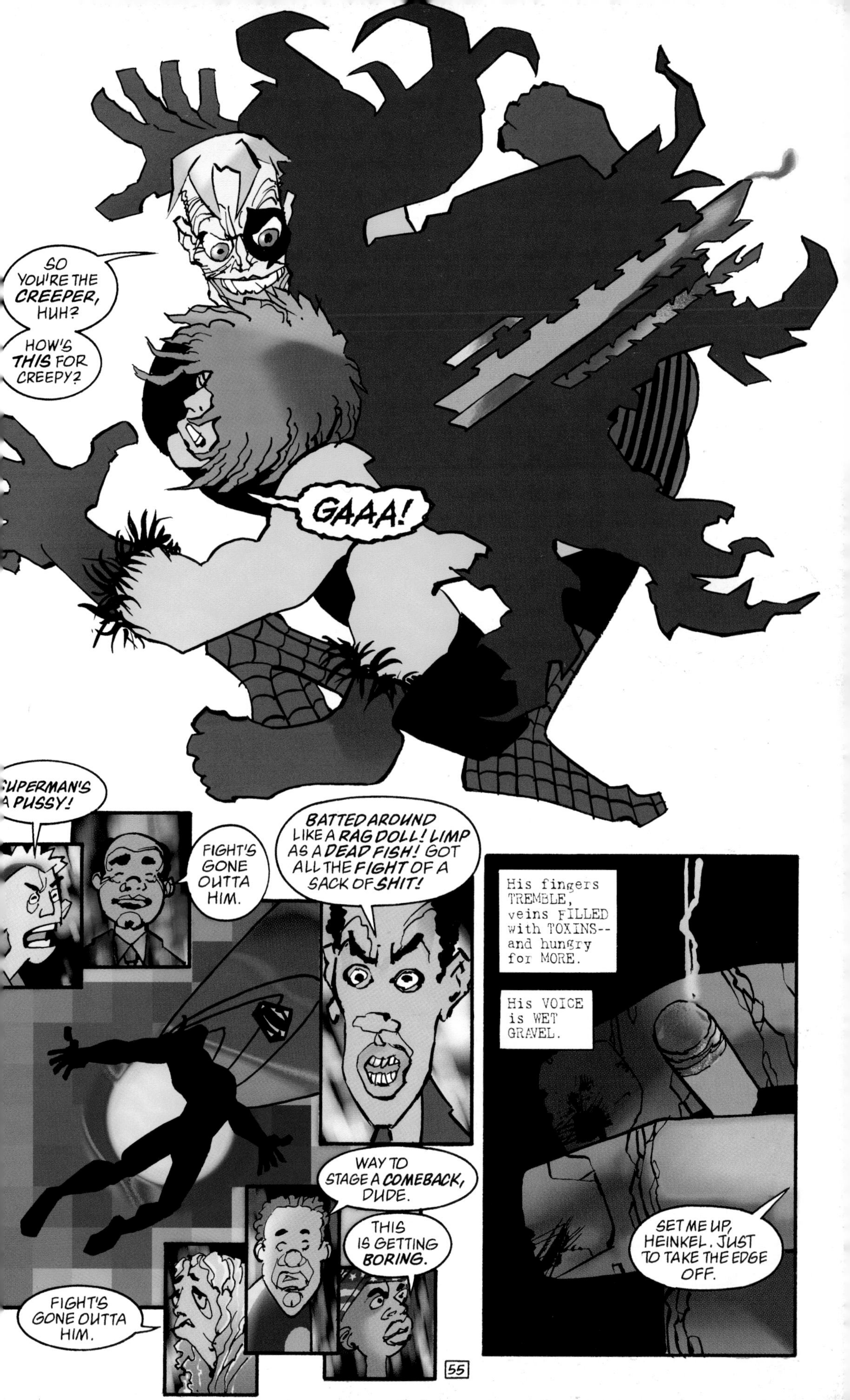
SO YOU'RE THE CREEPER, HUH?
HOW'S THIS FOR CREEPY?
GAAA!
SUPERMAN'S A PUSSY!
FIGHT'S GONE OUTTA HIM.
BATTED AROUND LIKE A RAG DOLL! LIMP AS A DEAD FISH! GOT ALL THE FIGHT OF A SACK OF SHIT!
WAY TO STAGE A COMEBACK, DUDE.
THIS IS GETTING BORING.
FIGHT'S GONE OUTTA HIM.
His fingers TREMBLE, veins FILLED with TOXINS-- and hungry for MORE.
His VOICE is WET GRAVEL.
SET ME UP, HEINKEL. JUST TO TAKE THE EDGE OFF.

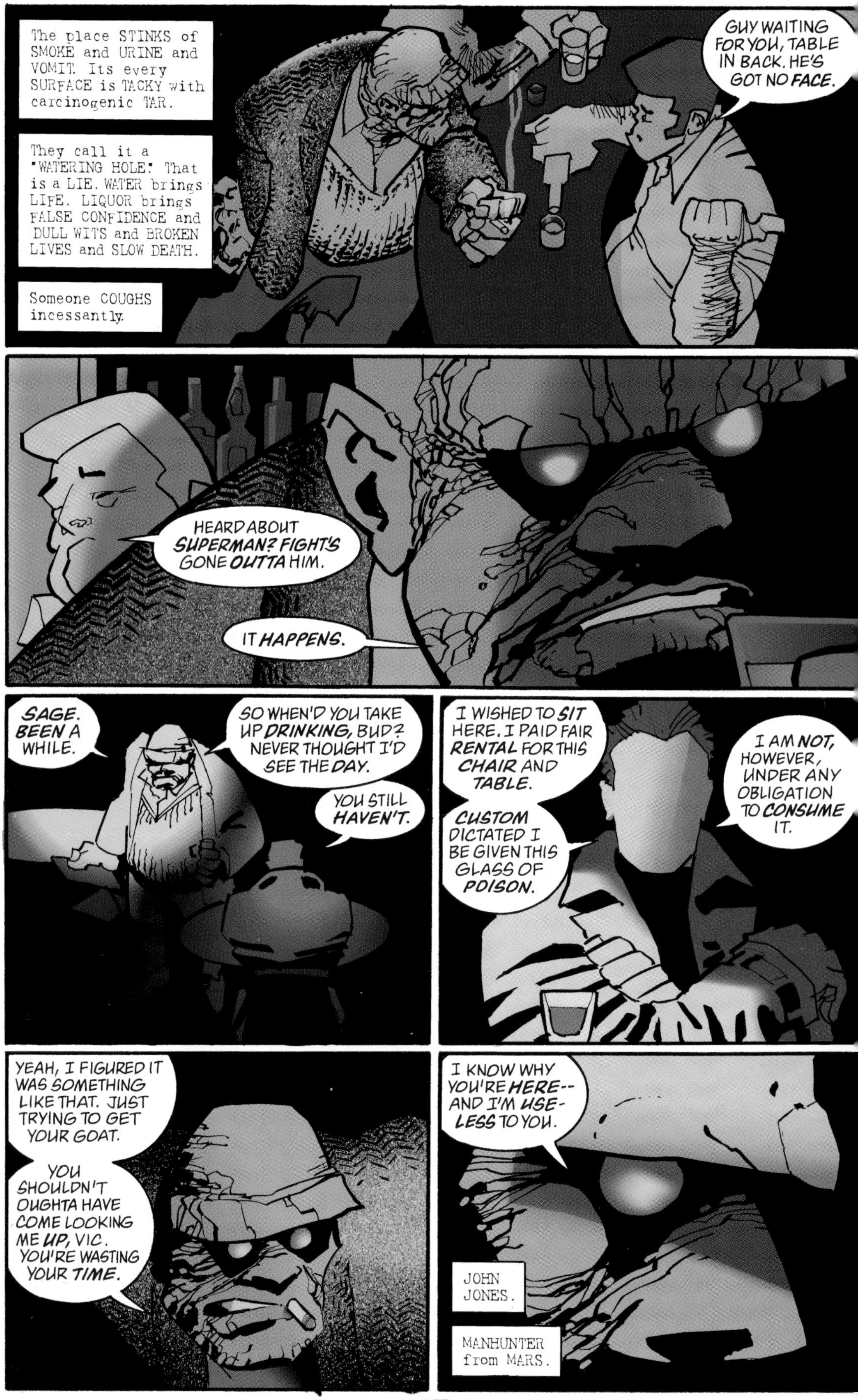

The place STINKS of SMOKE and URINE and VOMIT. Its every SURFACE is TACKY with carcinogenic TAR.
They call it a "WATERING HOLE." That is a LIE. WATER brings LIFE. LIQUOR brings FALSE CONFIDENCE and DULL WITS and BROKEN LIVES and SLOW DEATH.
Someone COUGHS incessantly.
GUY WAITING FOR YOU, TABLE IN BACK. HE'S GOT NO FACE.
HEARD ABOUT SUPERMAN? FIGHT'S GONE OUTTA HIM.
IT HAPPENS.
SAGE. BEEN A WHILE.
SO WHEN'D YOU TAKE UP DRINKING, BUD? NEVER THOUGHT I'D SEE THE DAY.
YOU STILL HAVEN'T.
I WISHED TO SIT HERE. I PAID FAIR RENTAL FOR THIS CHAIR AND TABLE.
CUSTOM DICTATED I BE GIVEN THIS GLASS OF POISON.
I AM NOT, HOWEVER, UNDER ANY OBLIGATION TO CONSUME IT.
YEAH, I FIGURED IT WAS SOMETHING LIKE THAT. JUST TRYING TO GET YOUR GOAT.
YOU SHOULDN'T OUGHTA HAVE COME LOOKING ME UP, VIC. YOU'RE WASTING YOUR TIME.
I KNOW WHY YOU'RE HERE-- AND I'M USELESS TO YOU.
JOHN JONES.
MANHUNTER from MARS.

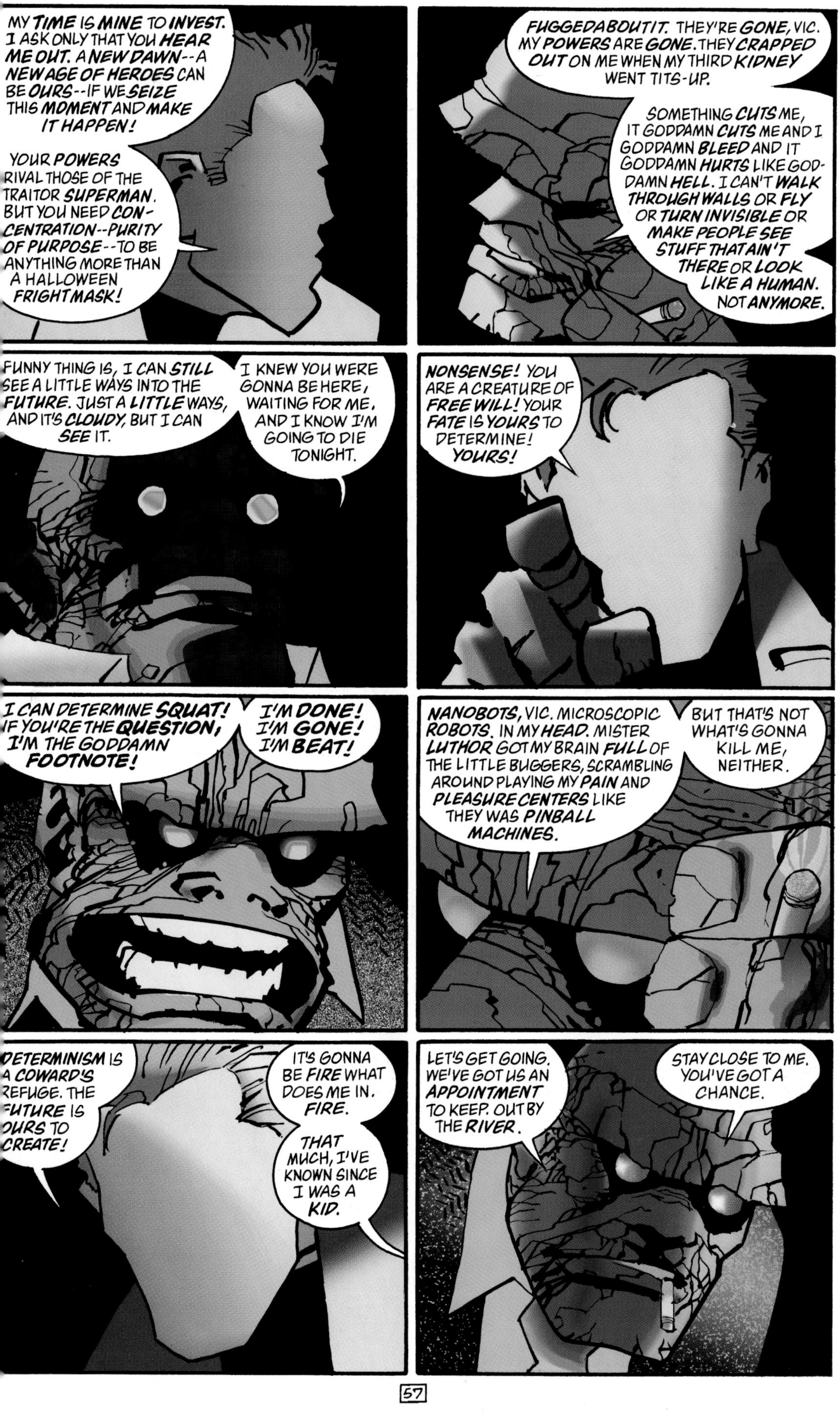
MY TIME IS MINE TO INVEST. I ASK ONLY THAT YOU HEAR ME OUT. A NEW DAWN--A NEW AGE OF HEROES CAN BE OURS--IF WE SEIZE THIS MOMENT AND MAKE IT HAPPEN!
YOUR POWERS RIVAL THOSE OF THE TRAITOR SUPERMAN. BUT YOU NEED CON-CENTRATION--PURITY OF PURPOSE--TO BE ANYTHING MORE THAN A HALLOWEEN FRIGHTMASK!
FUGGEDABOUTIT. THEY'RE GONE, VIC. MY POWERS ARE GONE. THEY CRAPPED OUT ON ME WHEN MY THIRD KIDNEY WENT TITS-UP.
SOMETHING CUTS ME, IT GODDAMN CUTS ME AND I GODDAMN BLEED AND IT GODDAMN HURTS LIKE GOD-DAMN HELL. I CAN'T WALK THROUGH WALLS OR FLY OR TURN INVISIBLE OR MAKE PEOPLE SEE STUFF THAT AIN'T THERE OR LOOK LIKE A HUMAN. NOT ANYMORE.
FUNNY THING IS, I CAN STILL SEE A LITTLE WAYS INTO THE FUTURE. JUST A LITTLE WAYS, AND IT'S CLOUDY, BUT I CAN SEE IT.
I KNEW YOU WERE GONNA BE HERE, WAITING FOR ME. AND I KNOW I'M GOING TO DIE TONIGHT.
NONSENSE! YOU ARE A CREATURE OF FREE WILL! YOUR FATE IS YOURS TO DETERMINE! YOURS!
I CAN DETERMINE SQUAT! IF YOU'RE THE QUESTION, I'M THE GODDAMN FOOTNOTE!
I'M DONE! I'M GONE! I'M BEAT!
NANOBOTS, VIC. MICROSCOPIC ROBOTS. IN MY HEAD. MISTER LUTHOR GOT MY BRAIN FULL OF THE LITTLE BUGGERS, SCRAMBLING AROUND PLAYING MY PAIN AND PLEASURE CENTERS LIKE THEY WAS PINBALL MACHINES.
BUT THAT'S NOT WHAT'S GONNA KILL ME, NEITHER.
DETERMINISM IS A COWARD'S REFUGE. THE FUTURE IS OURS TO CREATE!
IT'S GONNA BE FIRE WHAT DOES ME IN. FIRE.
THAT MUCH, I'VE KNOWN SINCE I WAS A KID.
LET'S GET GOING. WE'VE GOT US AN APPOINTMENT TO KEEP. OUT BY THE RIVER.
STAY CLOSE TO ME. YOU'VE GOT A CHANCE.

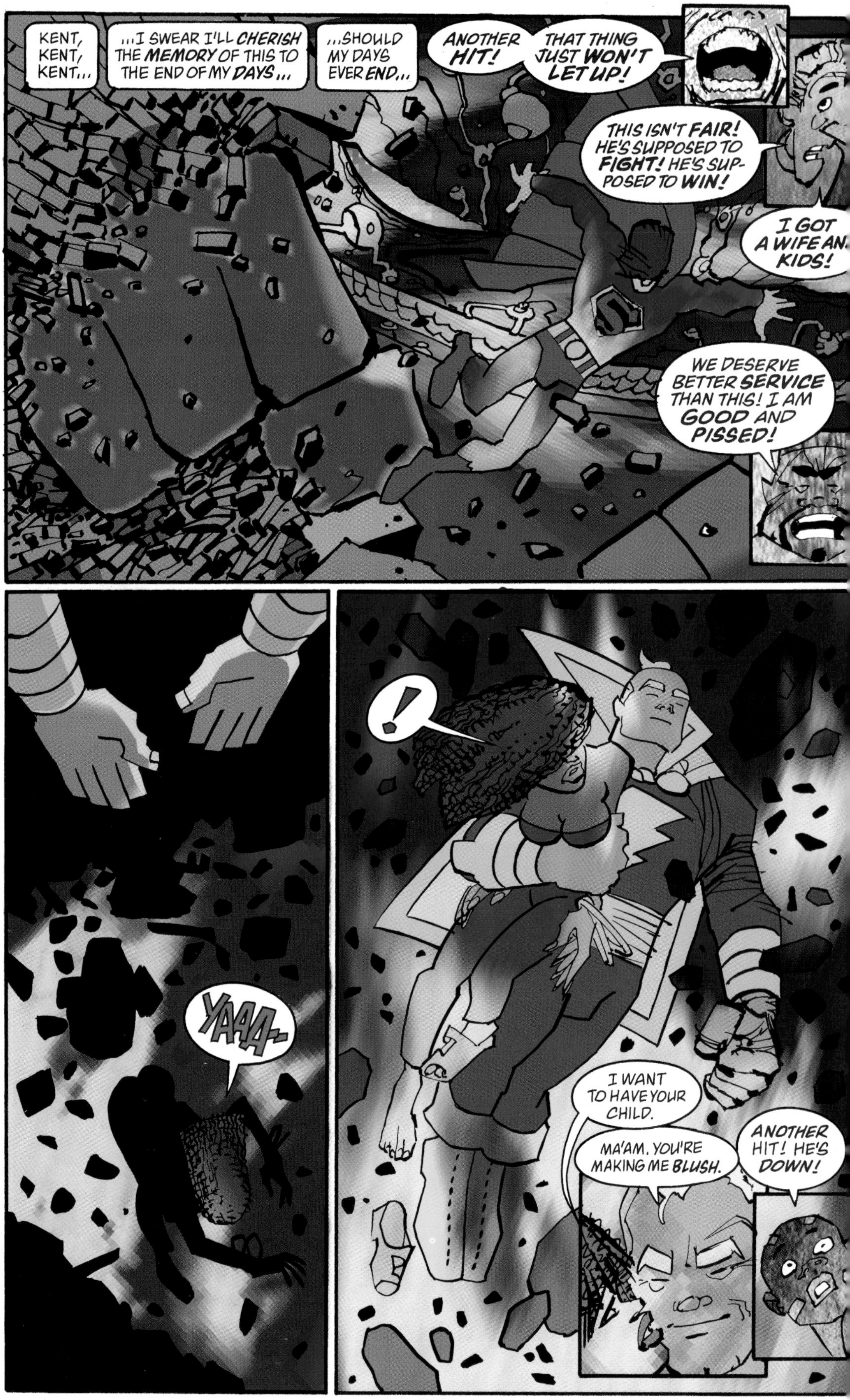
KENT, KENT, KENT...
...I SWEAR I'LL CHERISH THE MEMORY OF THIS TO THE END OF MY DAYS...
...SHOULD MY DAYS EVER END...
ANOTHER HIT!
THAT THING JUST WON'T LET UP!
THIS ISN'T FAIR! HE'S SUPPOSED TO FIGHT! HE'S SUPPOSED TO WIN!
I GOT A WIFE AN KIDS!
WE DESERVE BETTER SERVICE THAN THIS! I AM GOOD AND PISSED!
YAAA-
!
I WANT TO HAVE YOUR CHILD.
MA'AM. YOU'RE MAKING ME BLUSH.
ANOTHER HIT! HE'S DOWN!

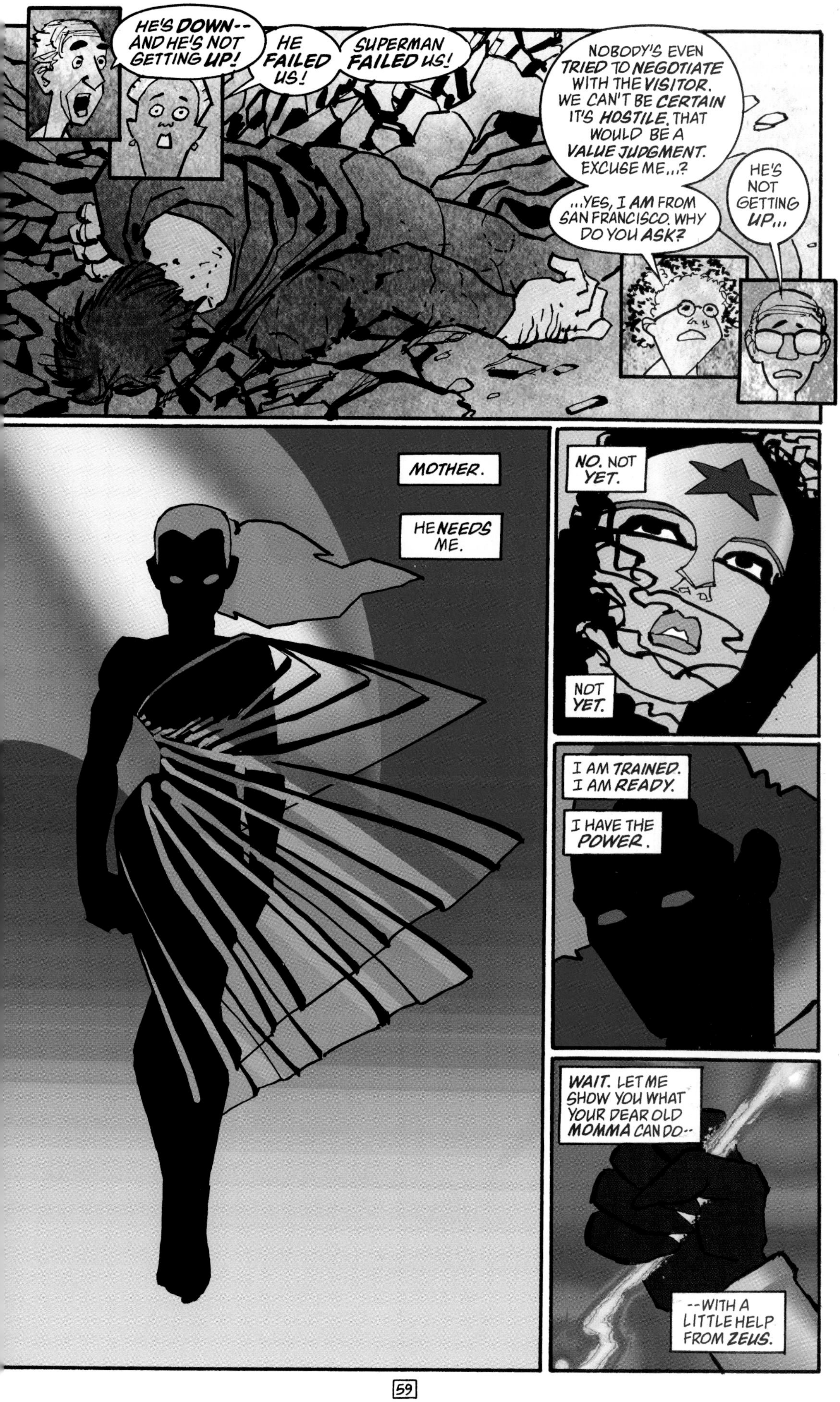
HE'S DOWN--
AND HE'S NOT GETTING UP!
HE FAILED US!
SUPERMAN FAILED US!
NOBODY'S EVEN TRIED TO NEGOTIATE WITH THE VISITOR. WE CAN'T BE CERTAIN IT'S HOSTILE. THAT WOULD BE A VALUE JUDGMENT. EXCUSE ME...?
...YES, I AM FROM SAN FRANCISCO. WHY DO YOU ASK?
HE'S NOT GETTING UP...
MOTHER.
HE NEEDS ME.
NO. NOT YET.
NOT YET.
I AM TRAINED. I AM READY.
I HAVE THE POWER.
WAIT. LET ME SHOW YOU WHAT YOUR DEAR OLD MOMMA CAN DO--
--WITH A LITTLE HELP FROM ZEUS.

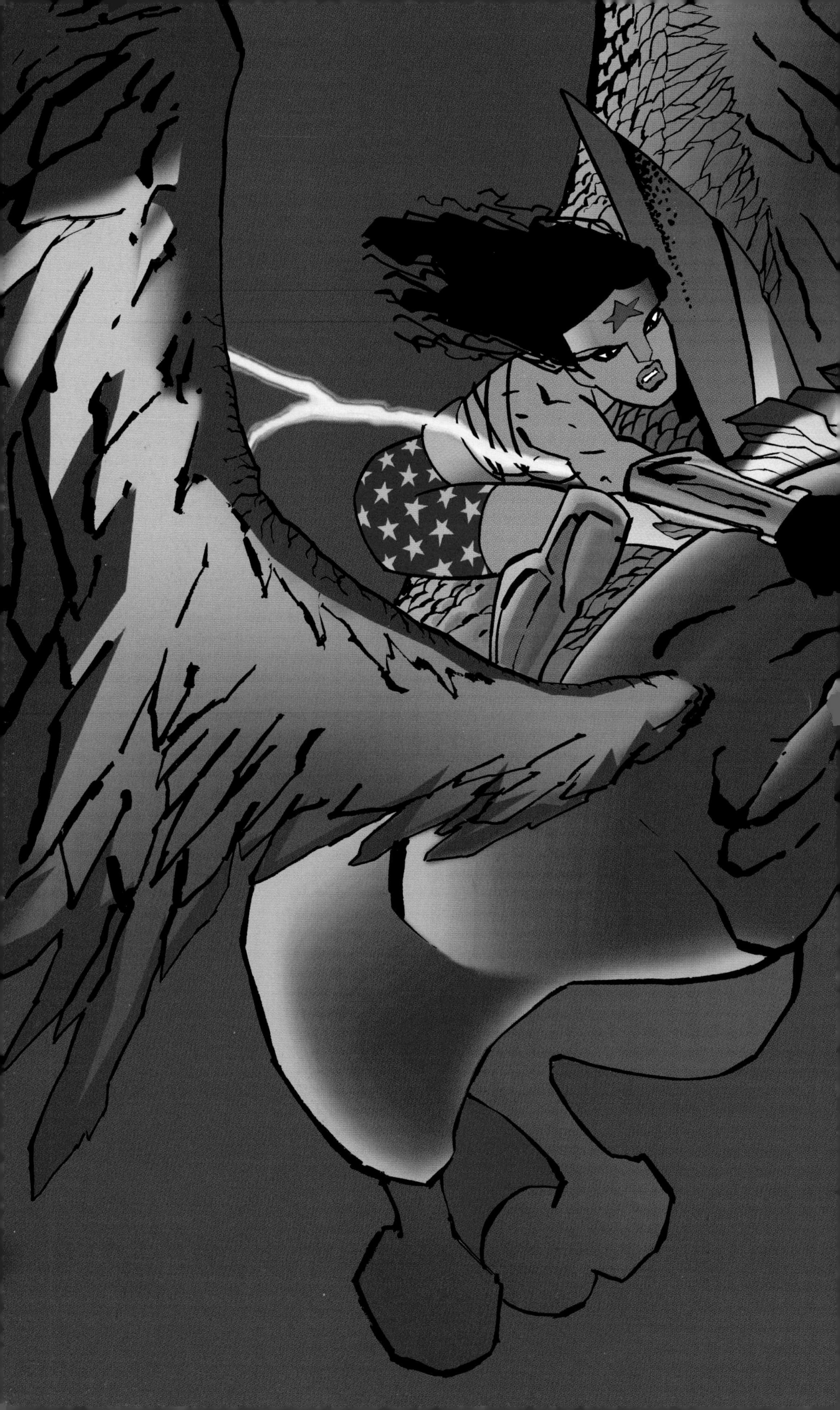

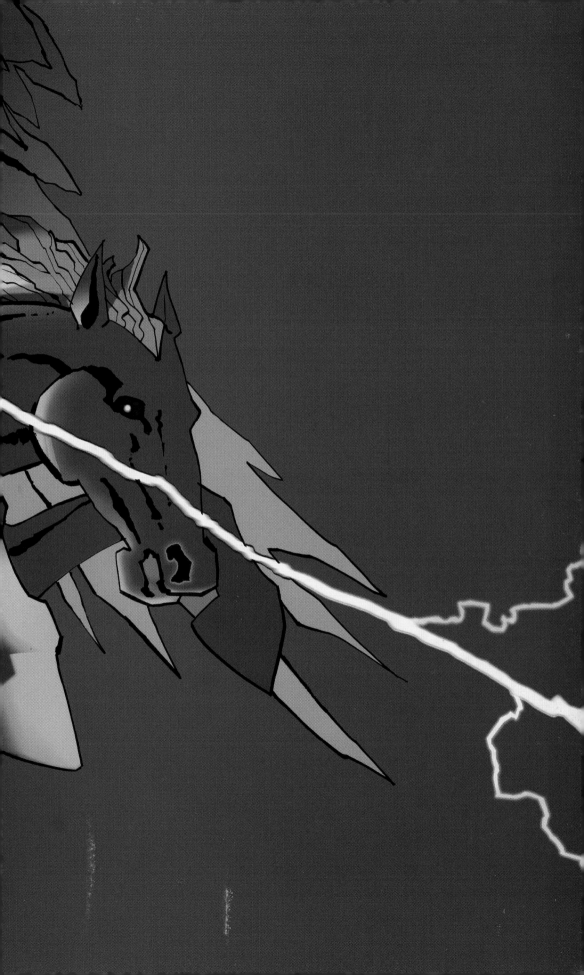

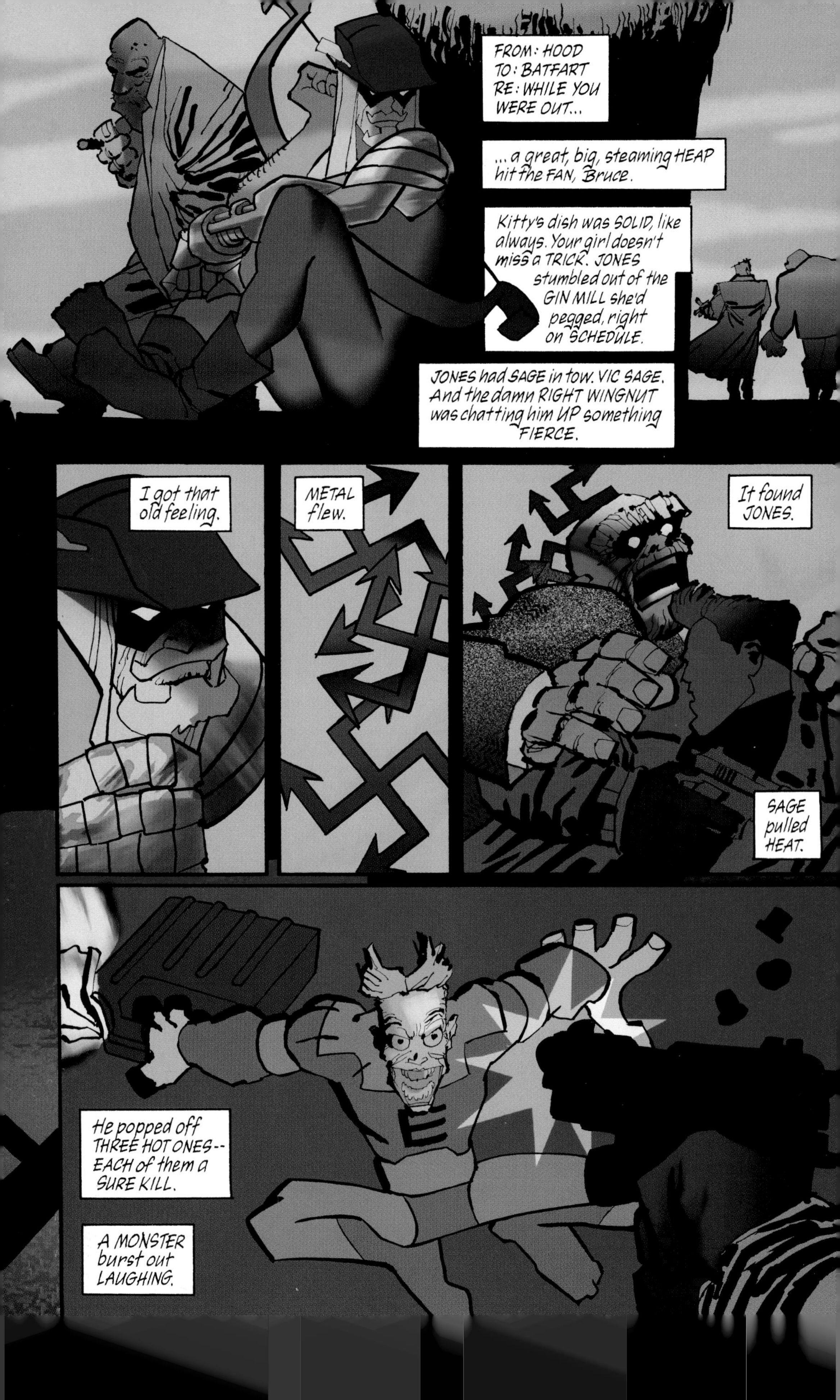
FROM: HOOD
TO: BATFART
RE: WHILE YOU WERE OUT...
...a great, big, steaming HEAP hit the FAN, Bruce.
Kitty's dish was SOLID, like always. Your girl doesn't miss a TRICK. JONES stumbled out of the GIN MILL she'd pegged, right on SCHEDULE.
JONES had SAGE in tow. VIC SAGE. And the damn RIGHT WINGNUT was chatting him UP something FIERCE.
I got that old feeling.
METAL flew.
It found JONES.
SAGE pulled HEAT.
He popped off THREE HOT ONES-- EACH of them a SURE KILL.
A MONSTER burst out LAUGHING.

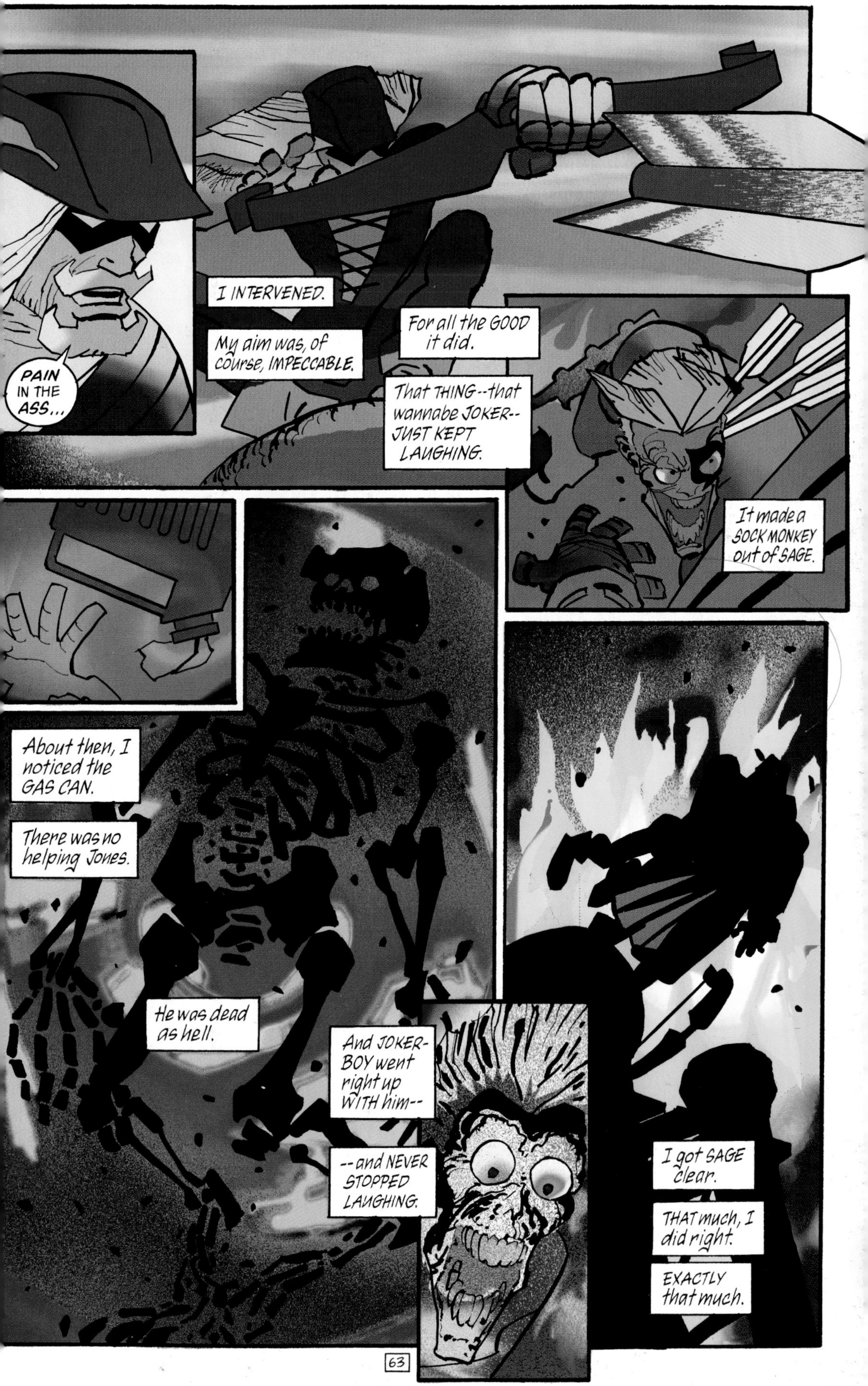

PAIN IN THE ASS...
I INTERVENED.
My aim was, of course, IMPECCABLE.
For all the GOOD it did.
That THING--that wannabe JOKER--JUST KEPT LAUGHING.
It made a SOCK MONKEY out of SAGE.
About then, I noticed the GAS CAN.
There was no helping Jones.
He was dead as hell.
And JOKER-BOY went right up WITH him--
--and NEVER STOPPED LAUGHING.
I got SAGE clear.
THAT much, I did right.
EXACTLY that much.

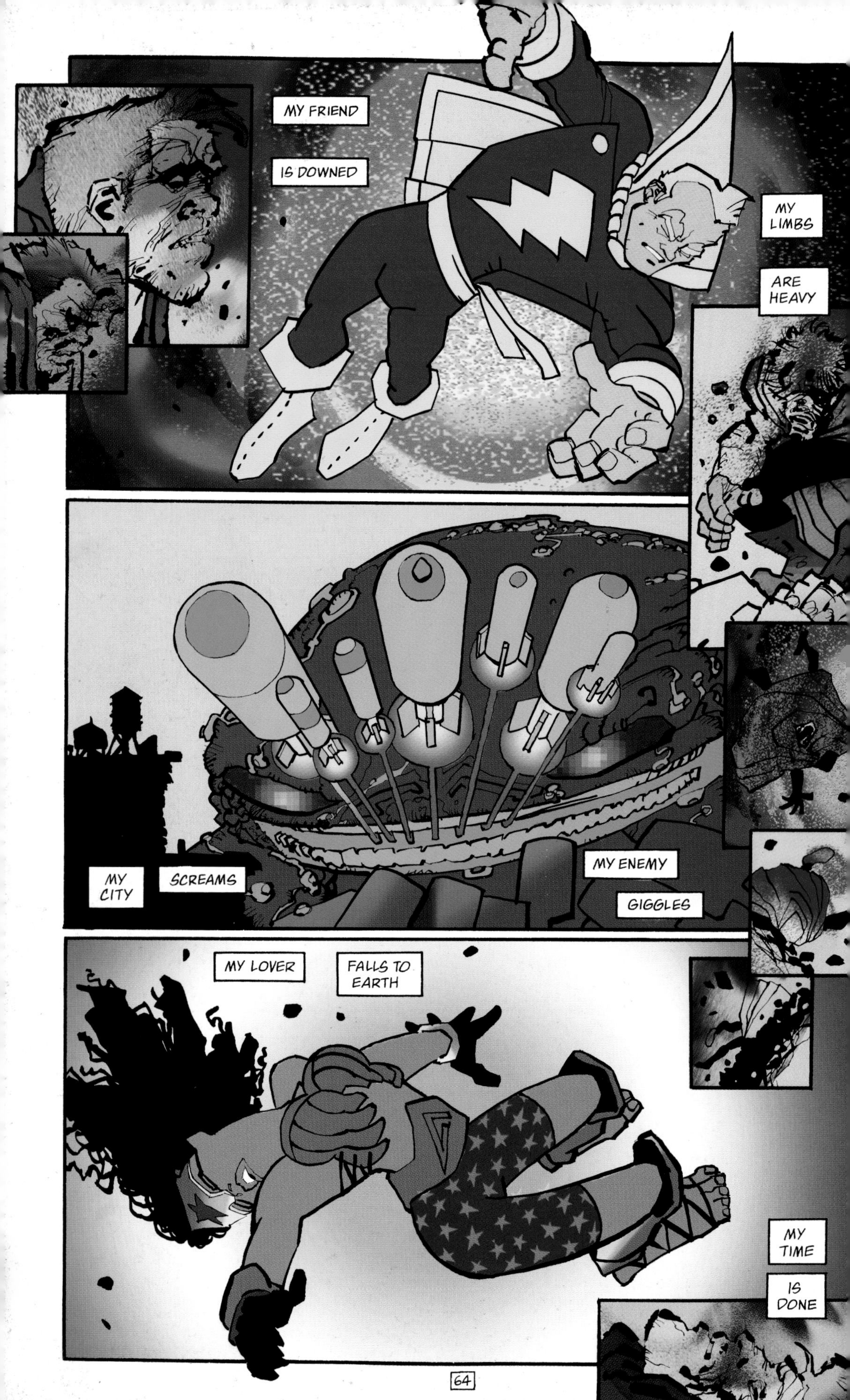
MY FRIEND
IS DOWNED
MY LIMBS
ARE HEAVY
MY CITY
SCREAMS
MY ENEMY
GIGGLES
MY LOVER
FALLS TO EARTH
MY TIME
IS DONE

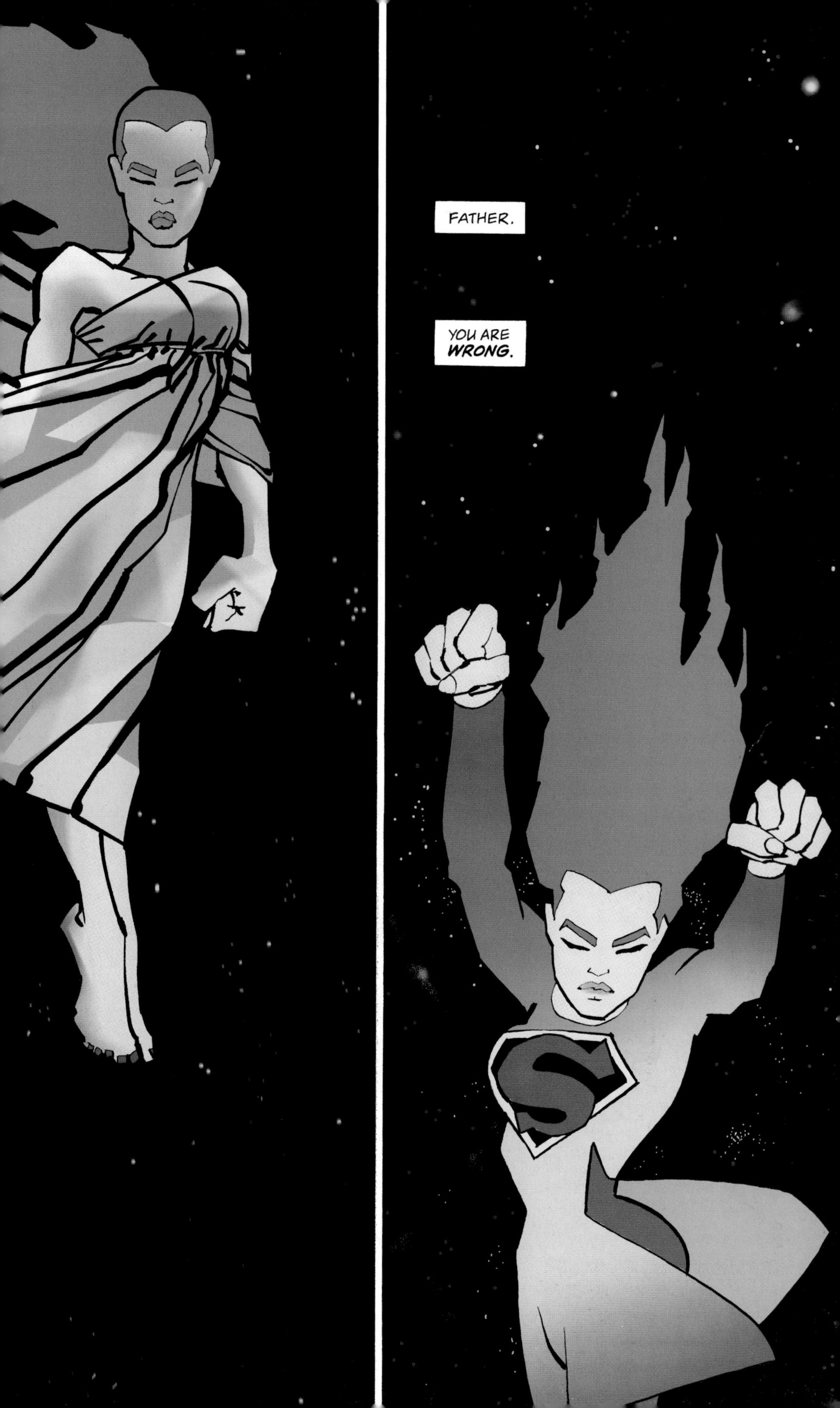
FATHER.
YOU ARE WRONG.

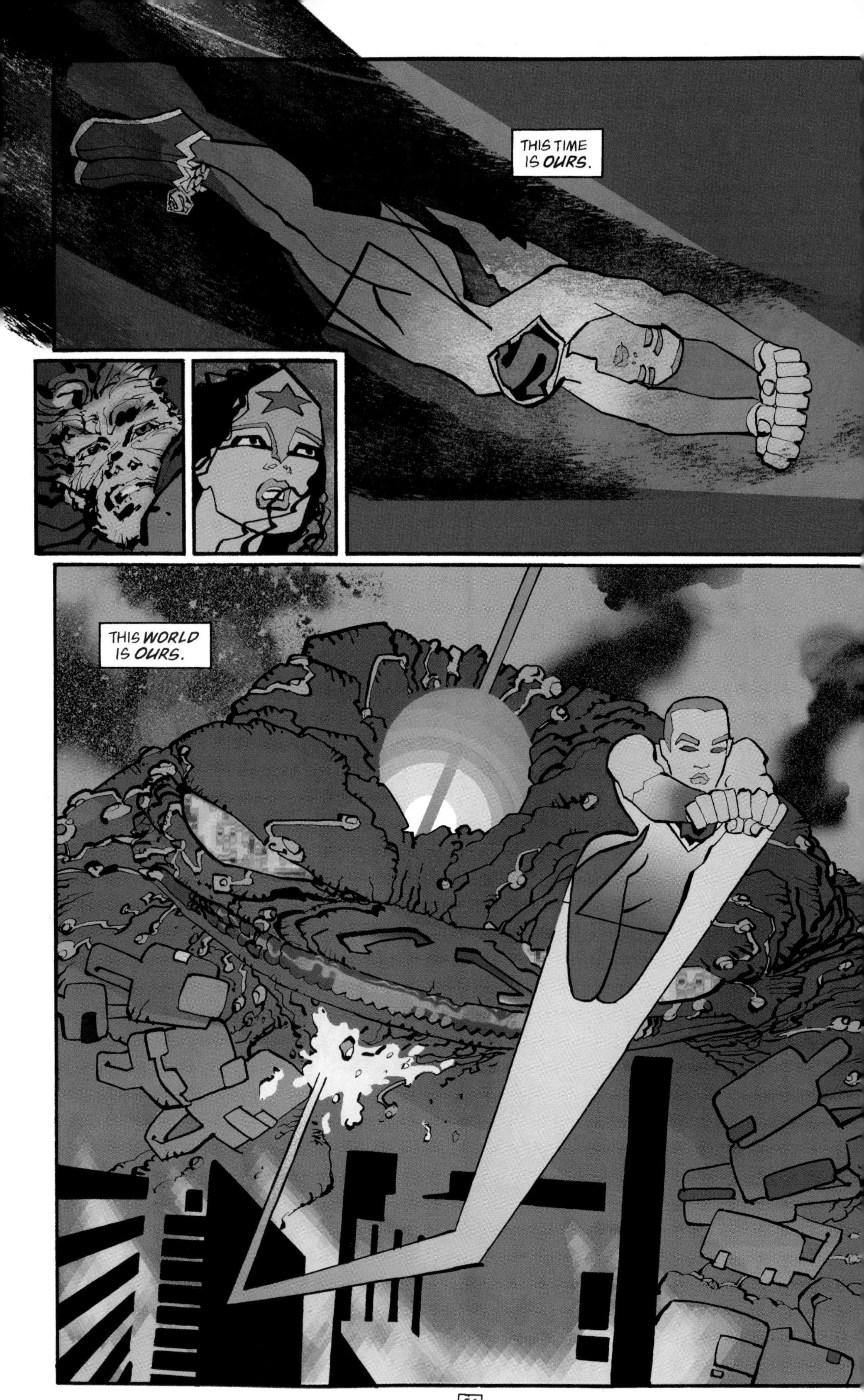
THIS TIME
IS OURS.
THIS WORLD
IS OURS.

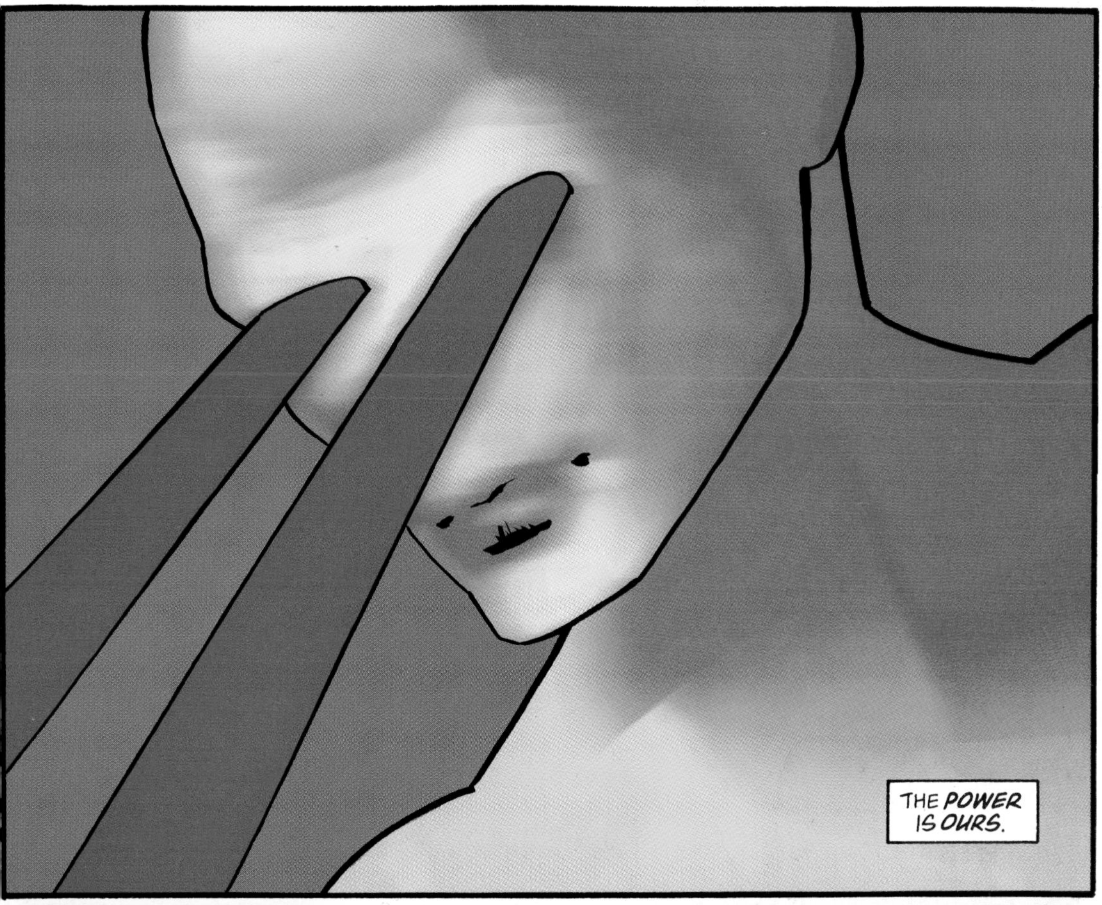
THE *POWER* IS *OURS*.

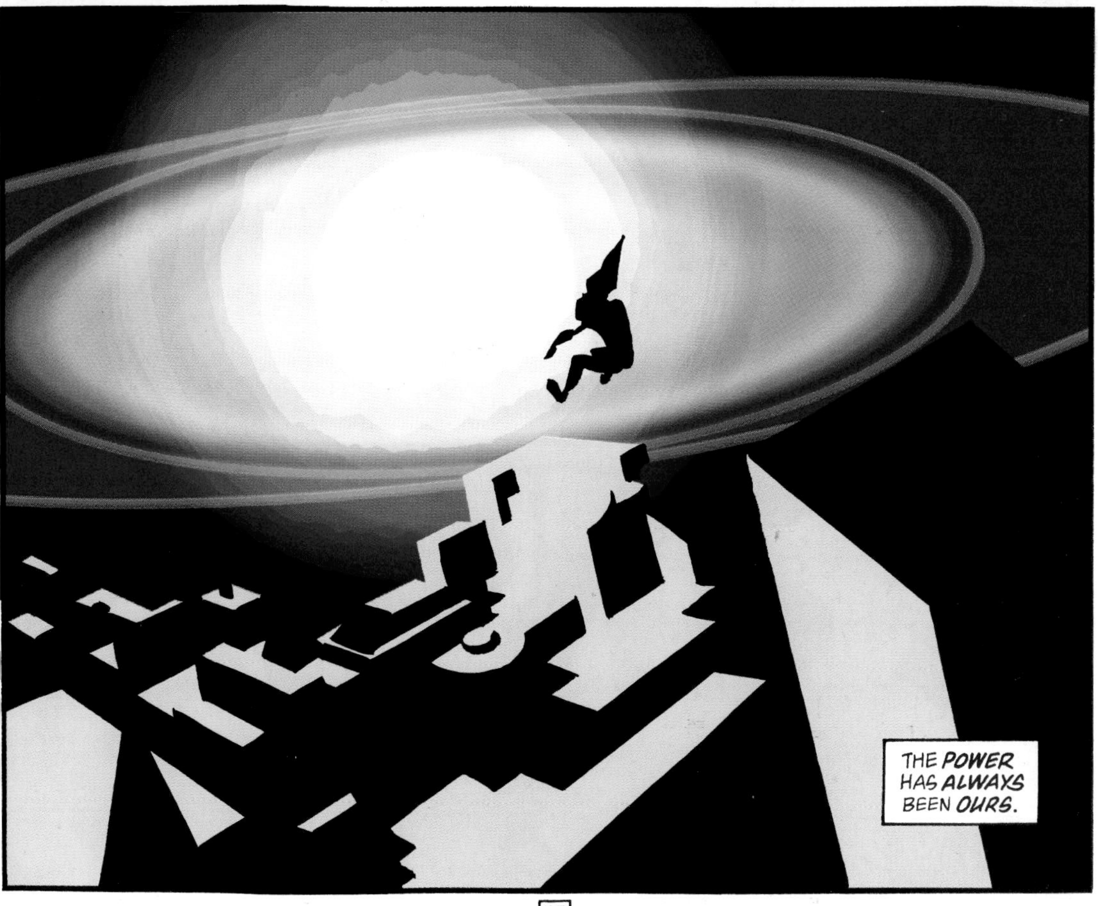
THE *POWER* HAS *ALWAYS* BEEN *OURS*.

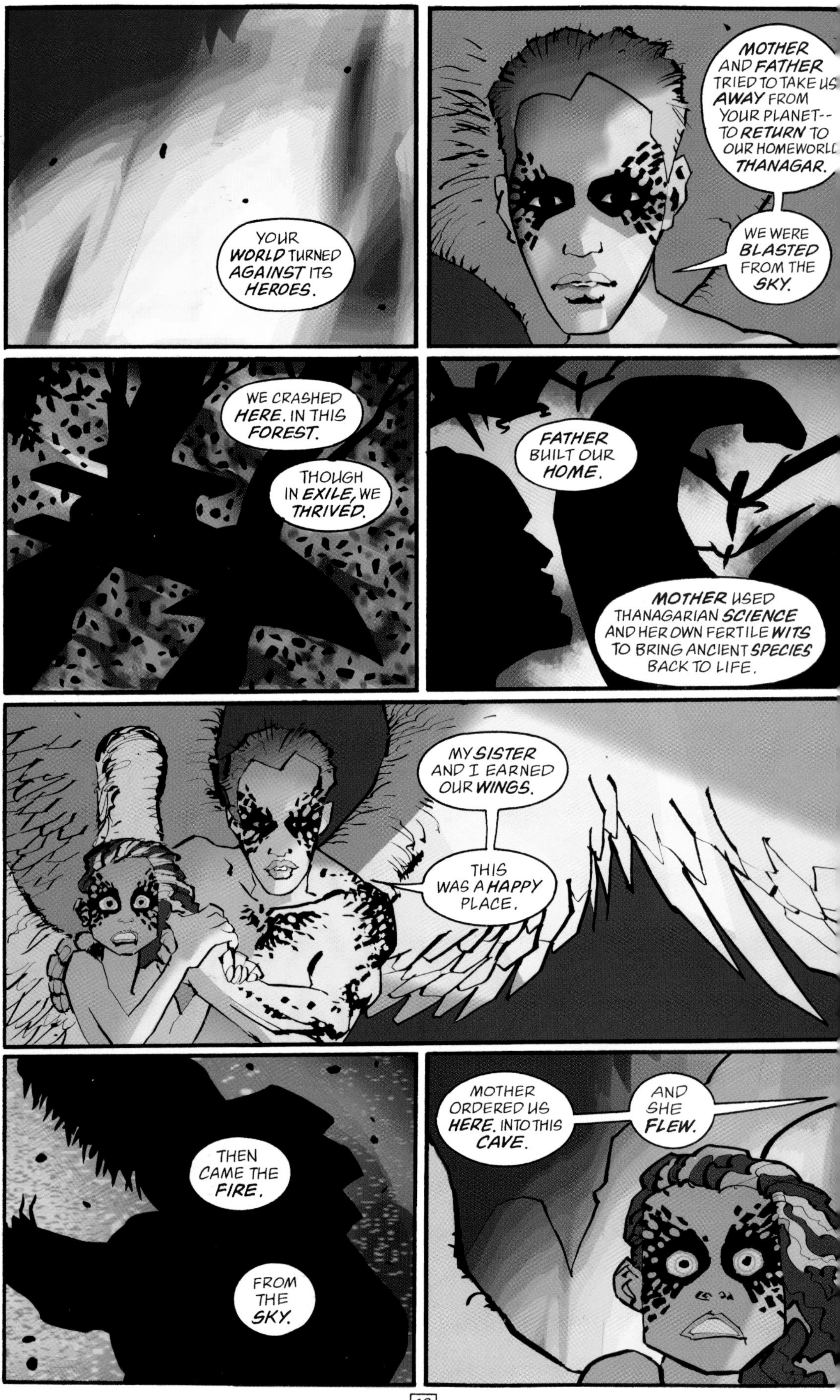

YOUR WORLD TURNED AGAINST ITS HEROES.
MOTHER AND FATHER TRIED TO TAKE US AWAY FROM YOUR PLANET-- TO RETURN TO OUR HOMEWORLD THANAGAR.
WE WERE BLASTED FROM THE SKY.
WE CRASHED HERE. IN THIS FOREST.
THOUGH IN EXILE, WE THRIVED.
FATHER BUILT OUR HOME.
MOTHER USED THANAGARIAN SCIENCE AND HER OWN FERTILE WITS TO BRING ANCIENT SPECIES BACK TO LIFE.
MY SISTER AND I EARNED OUR WINGS.
THIS WAS A HAPPY PLACE.
THEN CAME THE FIRE.
FROM THE SKY.
MOTHER ORDERED US HERE. INTO THIS CAVE.
AND SHE FLEW.

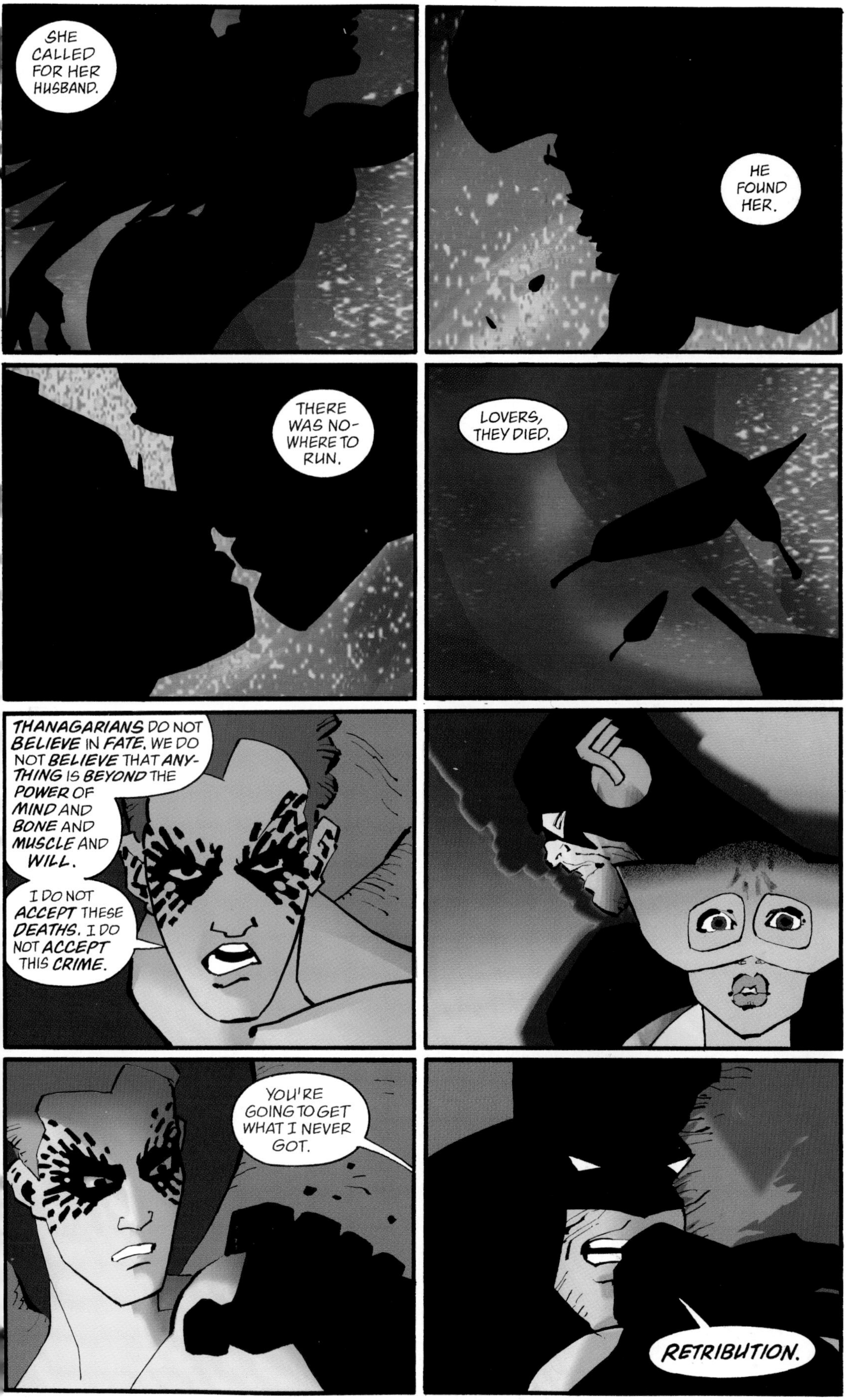
SHE CALLED FOR HER HUSBAND.
HE FOUND HER.
THERE WAS NO-WHERE TO RUN.
LOVERS, THEY DIED.
THANAGARIANS DO NOT BELIEVE IN FATE. WE DO NOT BELIEVE THAT ANY-THING IS BEYOND THE POWER OF MIND AND BONE AND MUSCLE AND WILL.
I DO NOT ACCEPT THESE DEATHS. I DO NOT ACCEPT THIS CRIME.
YOU'RE GOING TO GET WHAT I NEVER GOT.
RETRIBUTION.

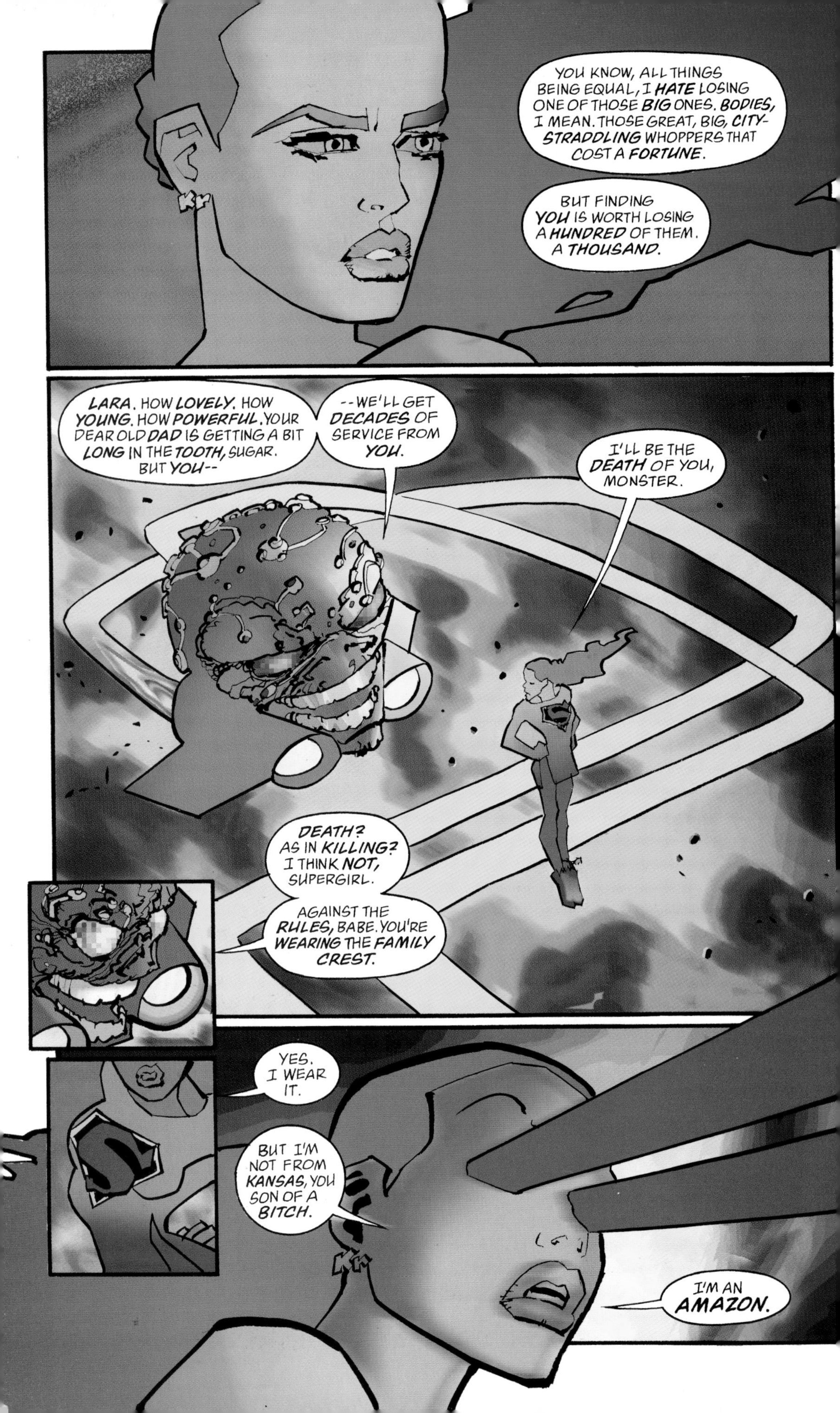
YOU KNOW, ALL THINGS BEING EQUAL, I HATE LOSING ONE OF THOSE BIG ONES. BODIES, I MEAN. THOSE GREAT, BIG, CITY-STRADDLING WHOPPERS THAT COST A FORTUNE.
BUT FINDING YOU IS WORTH LOSING A HUNDRED OF THEM. A THOUSAND.
LARA. HOW LOVELY. HOW YOUNG. HOW POWERFUL. YOUR DEAR OLD DAD IS GETTING A BIT LONG IN THE TOOTH, SUGAR. BUT YOU--
--WE'LL GET DECADES OF SERVICE FROM YOU.
I'LL BE THE DEATH OF YOU, MONSTER.
DEATH? AS IN KILLING? I THINK NOT, SUPERGIRL.
AGAINST THE RULES, BABE. YOU'RE WEARING THE FAMILY CREST.
YES. I WEAR IT.
BUT I'M NOT FROM KANSAS, YOU SON OF A BITCH.
I'M AN AMAZON.

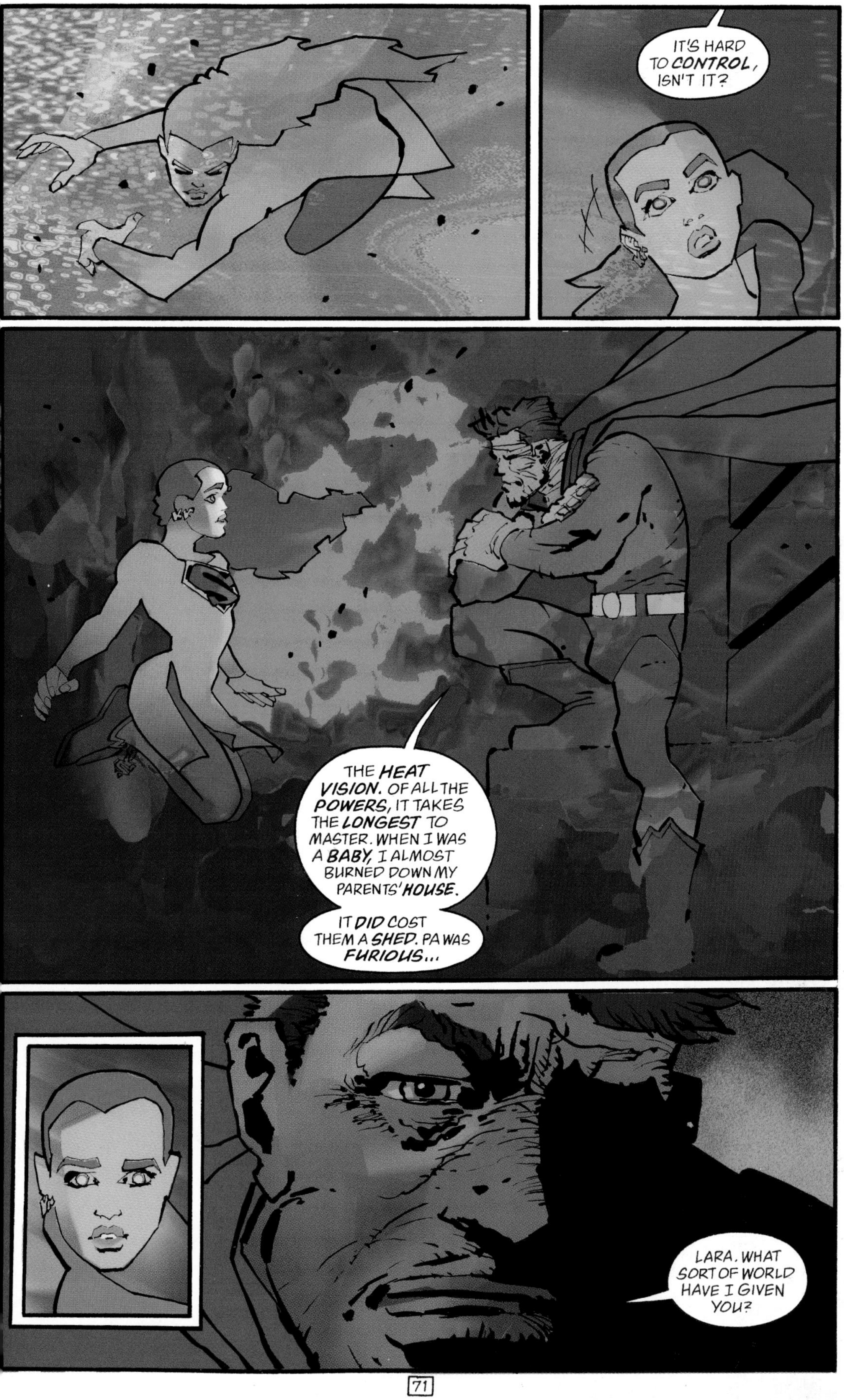

IT'S HARD TO **CONTROL**, ISN'T IT?
THE **HEAT VISION**. OF ALL THE **POWERS**, IT TAKES THE **LONGEST** TO MASTER. WHEN I WAS A **BABY**, I ALMOST BURNED DOWN MY PARENTS' **HOUSE**.
IT **DID** COST THEM A **SHED**. PA WAS **FURIOUS**...
LARA. WHAT SORT OF WORLD HAVE I GIVEN YOU?

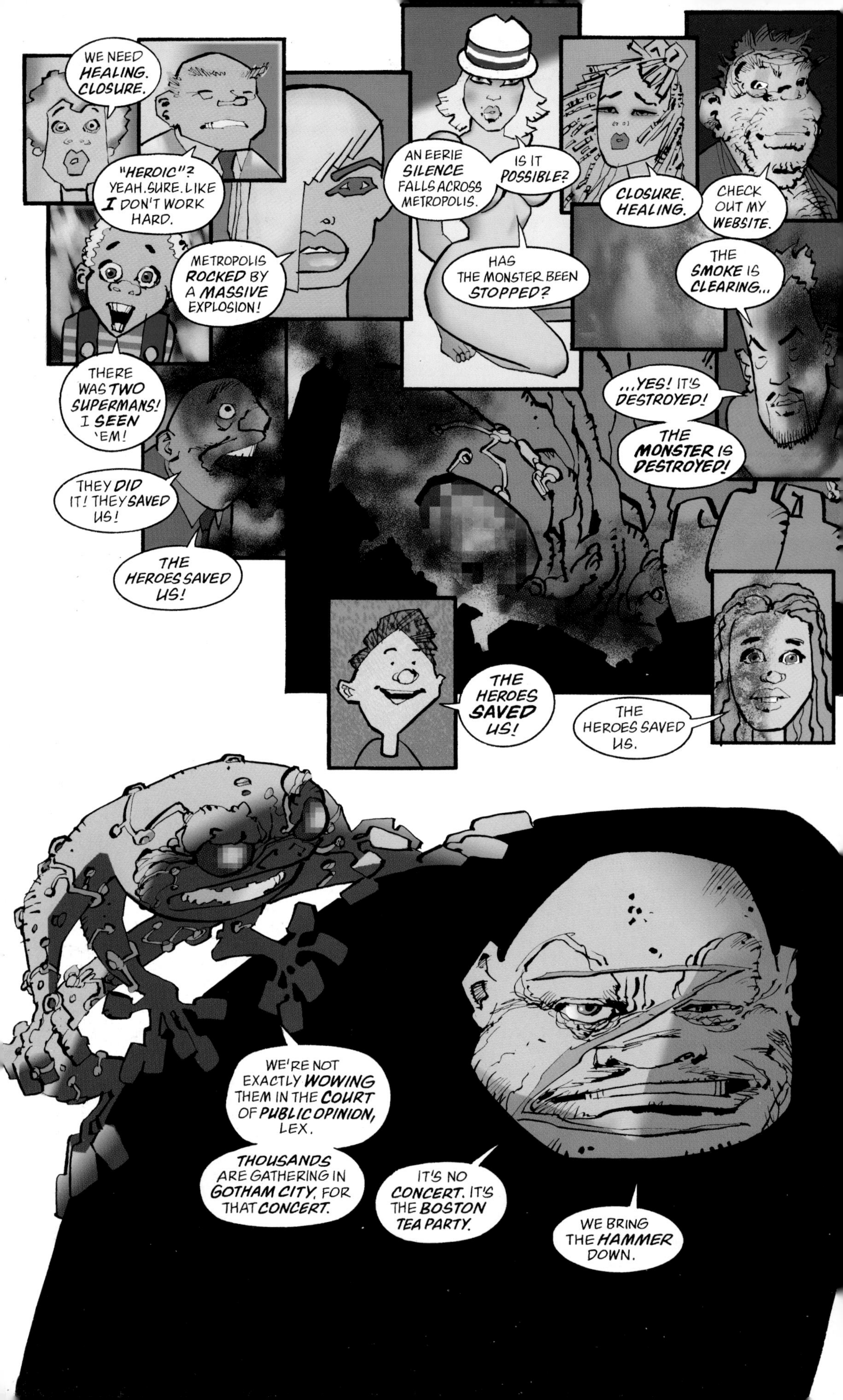

WE NEED HEALING. CLOSURE.
"HEROIC"? YEAH. SURE. LIKE I DON'T WORK HARD.
METROPOLIS ROCKED BY A MASSIVE EXPLOSION!
AN EERIE SILENCE FALLS ACROSS METROPOLIS.
IS IT POSSIBLE?
HAS THE MONSTER BEEN STOPPED?
CLOSURE. HEALING.
CHECK OUT MY WEBSITE.
THE SMOKE IS CLEARING...
THERE WAS TWO SUPERMANS! I SEEN 'EM!
THEY DID IT! THEY SAVED US!
THE HEROES SAVED US!
...YES! IT'S DESTROYED!
THE MONSTER IS DESTROYED!
THE HEROES SAVED US!
THE HEROES SAVED US.
WE'RE NOT EXACTLY WOWING THEM IN THE COURT OF PUBLIC OPINION, LEX.
THOUSANDS ARE GATHERING IN GOTHAM CITY, FOR THAT CONCERT.
IT'S NO CONCERT. IT'S THE BOSTON TEA PARTY.
WE BRING THE HAMMER DOWN.

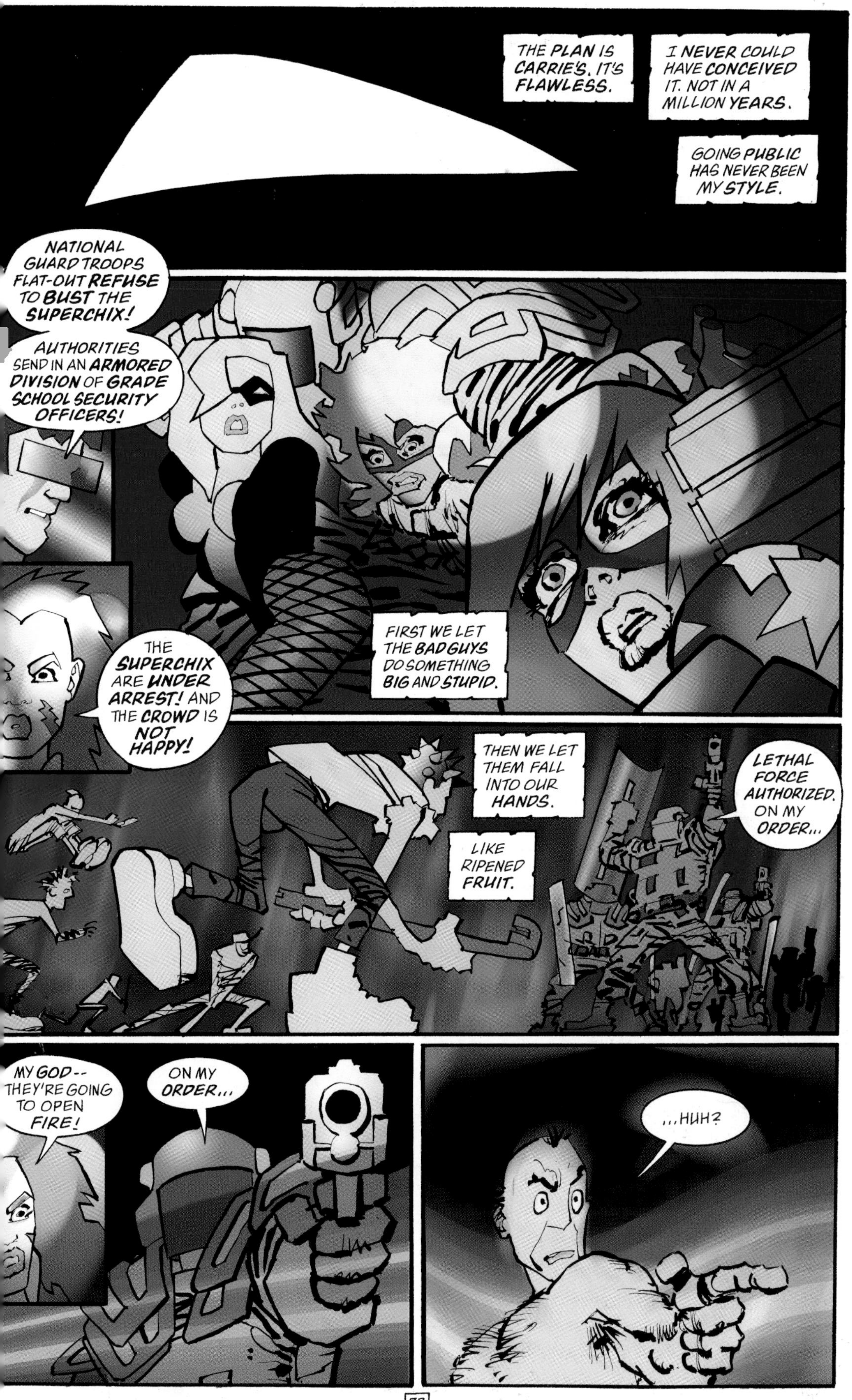
THE PLAN IS CARRIE'S. IT'S FLAWLESS.
I NEVER COULD HAVE CONCEIVED IT. NOT IN A MILLION YEARS.
GOING PUBLIC HAS NEVER BEEN MY STYLE.
NATIONAL GUARD TROOPS FLAT-OUT REFUSE TO BUST THE SUPERCHIX!
AUTHORITIES SEND IN AN ARMORED DIVISION OF GRADE SCHOOL SECURITY OFFICERS!
THE SUPERCHIX ARE UNDER ARREST! AND THE CROWD IS NOT HAPPY!
FIRST WE LET THE BAD GUYS DO SOMETHING BIG AND STUPID.
THEN WE LET THEM FALL INTO OUR HANDS.
LIKE RIPENED FRUIT.
LETHAL FORCE AUTHORIZED. ON MY ORDER...
MY GOD-- THEY'RE GOING TO OPEN FIRE!
ON MY ORDER...
...HUH?

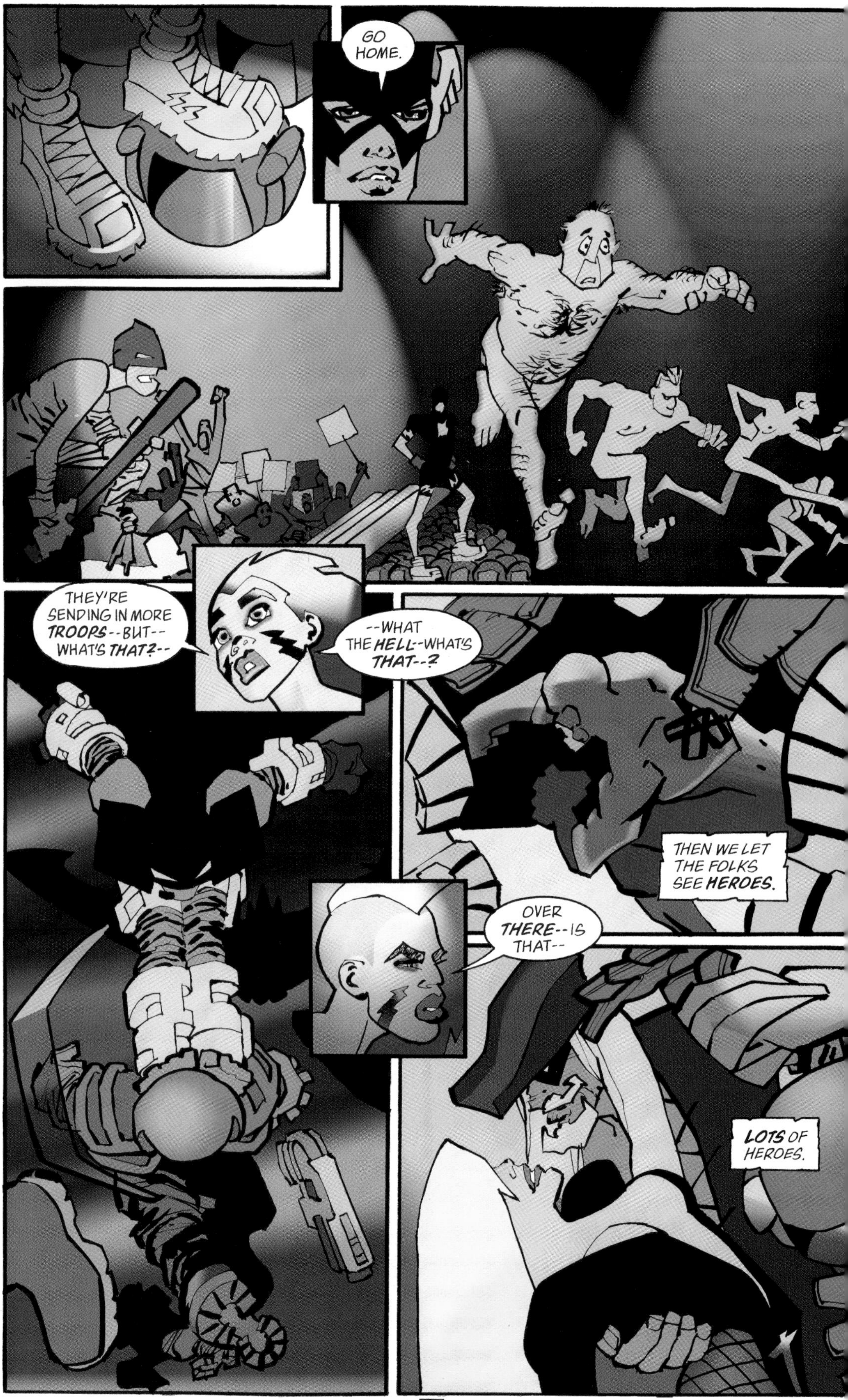
GO HOME.
THEY'RE SENDING IN MORE TROOPS--BUT--WHAT'S THAT?--
--WHAT THE HELL--WHAT'S THAT--?
THEN WE LET THE FOLKS SEE HEROES.
OVER THERE--IS THAT--
LOTS OF HEROES.

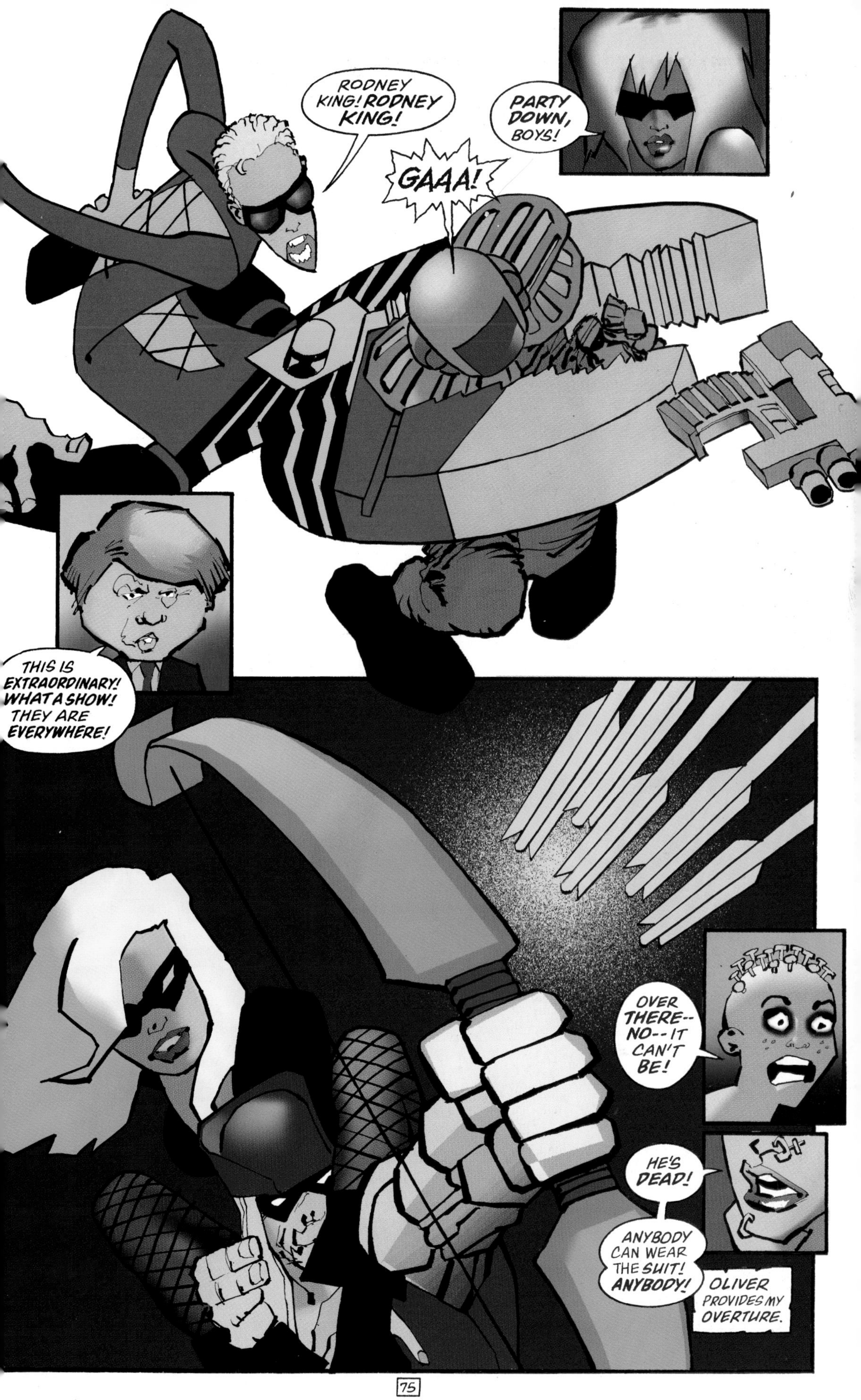

RODNEY KING! RODNEY KING!
PARTY DOWN, BOYS!
GAAA!
THIS IS EXTRAORDINARY! WHAT A SHOW! THEY ARE EVERYWHERE!
OVER THERE-- NO-- IT CAN'T BE!
HE'S DEAD!
ANYBODY CAN WEAR THE SUIT! ANYBODY!
OLIVER PROVIDES MY OVERTURE.

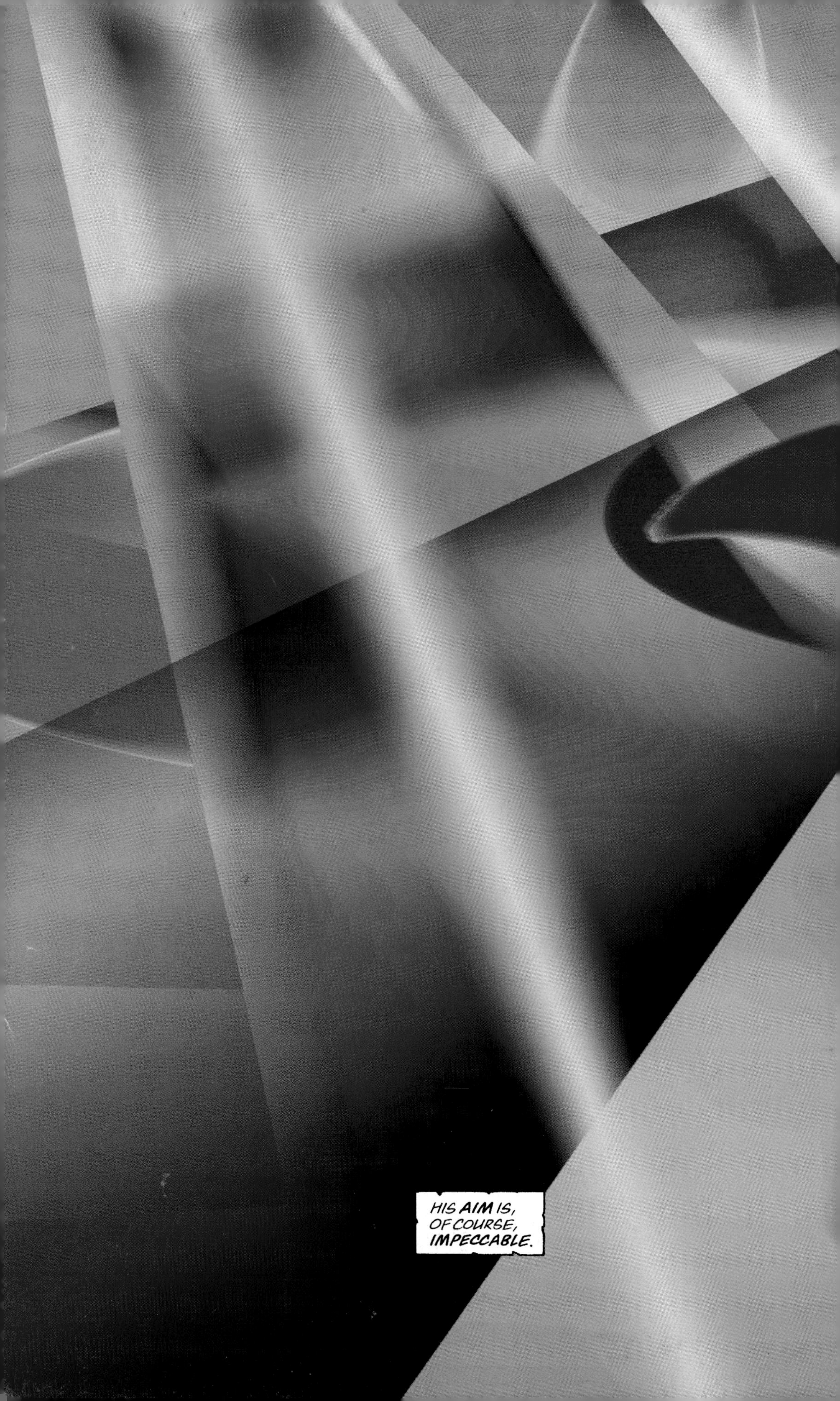
HIS AIM IS, OF COURSE, IMPECCABLE.

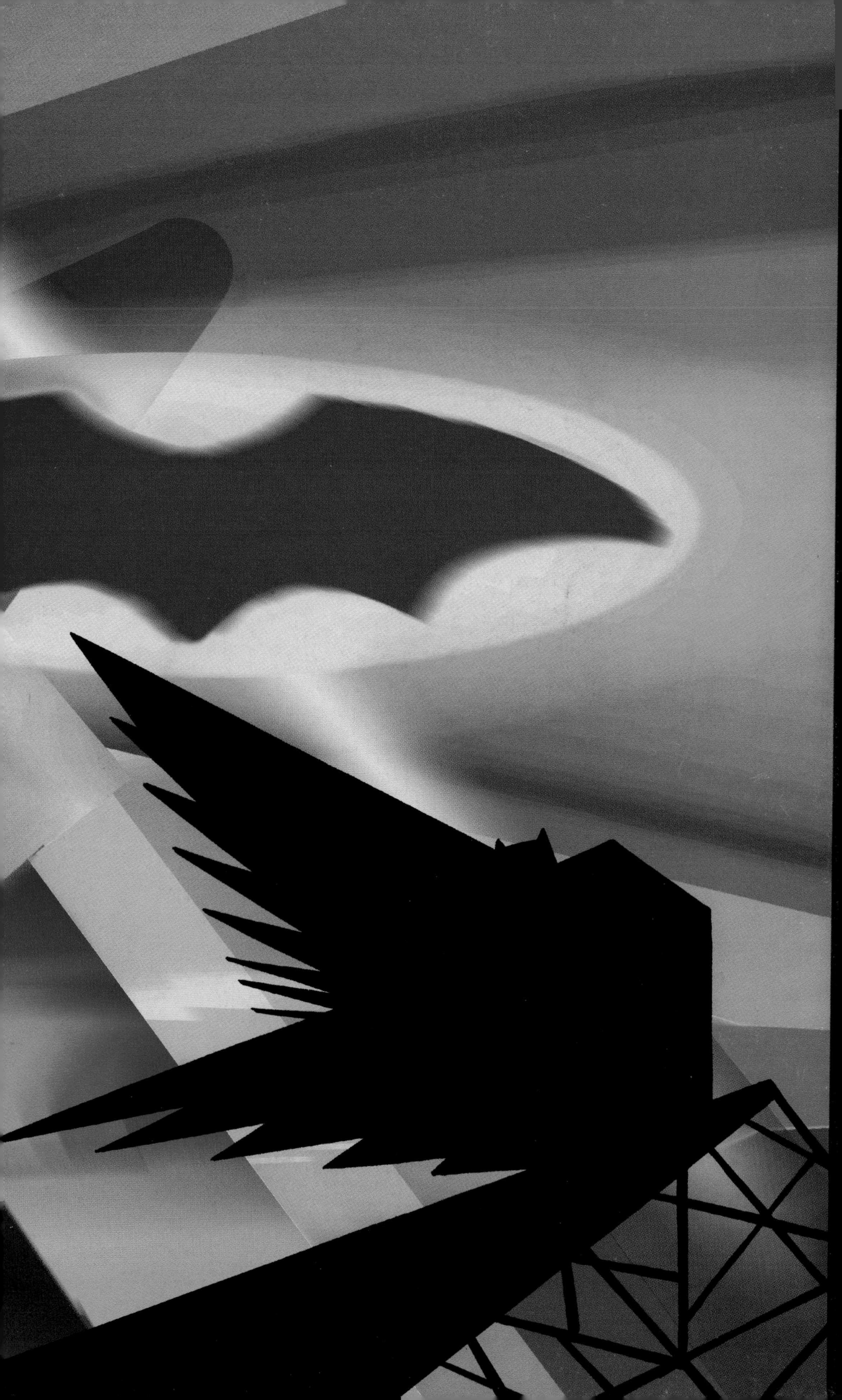

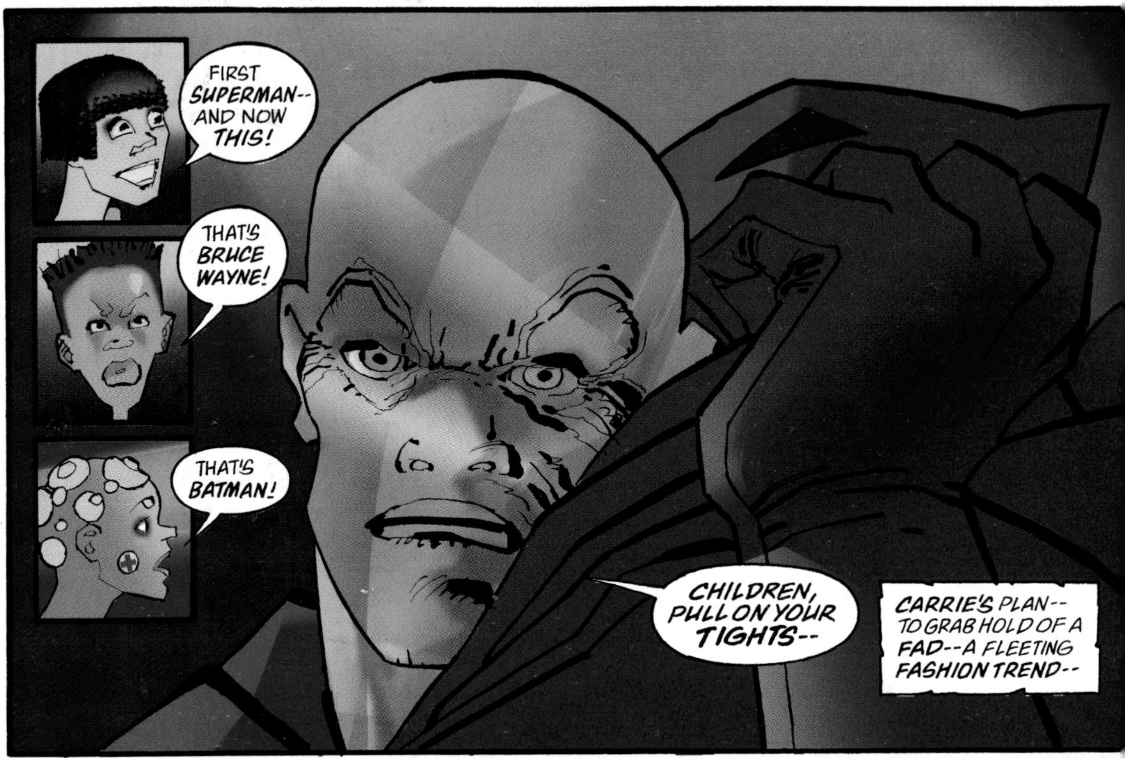
FIRST SUPERMAN--AND NOW THIS!
THAT'S BRUCE WAYNE!
THAT'S BATMAN!
CHILDREN, PULL ON YOUR TIGHTS--
CARRIE'S PLAN--TO GRAB HOLD OF A FAD--A FLEETING FASHION TREND--

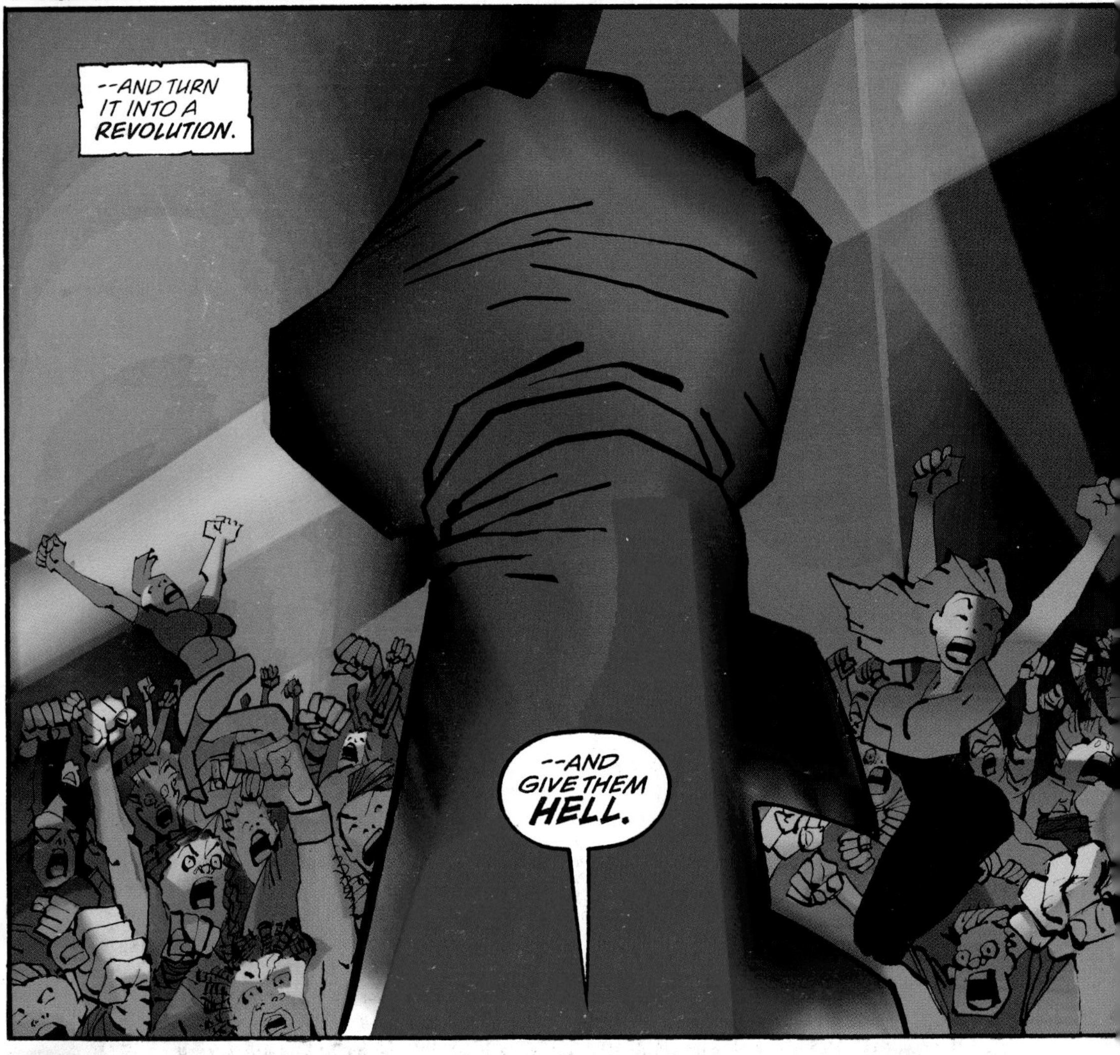
--AND TURN IT INTO A REVOLUTION.
--AND GIVE THEM HELL.